THE
MAN WHO
WOULD BE
F. SCOTT
FITZGERALD

THE
MAN WHO
WOULD BE
F. SCOTT
FITZGERALD

David Handler, 1952-

A PERFECT CRIME BOOK

DOUBLEDAY

NEW YORK   LONDON   TORONTO   SYDNEY   AUCKLAND

A PERFECT CRIME BOOK

PUBLISHED BY DOUBLEDAY
a division of Bantam Doubleday Dell Publishing Group, Inc.
666 Fifth Avenue, New York, New York 10103

DOUBLEDAY is a trademark of Doubleday, a division of
Bantam Doubleday Dell Publishing Group, Inc.

All of the characters in this book are fictitious,
and any resemblance to actual persons, living or
dead, is purely coincidental.

Book design by Tasha Hall

Library of Congress Cataloging-in-Publication Data

Handler, David, 1952–
The man who would be F. Scott Fitzgerald / by David Handler.
    p.   cm.
    "A Perfect crime book."
    I. Title.
    PS3558.A4637M3   1993
813'.54—dc20   92-30360
                                                     CIP

ISBN 0-385-46782-6

1   3   5   7   9   10   8   6   4   2

March 1993

For my friend Lee Siegel down at the plant

I want to laugh but nothing is funny. I want to cry but nothing is sad. I want to be loved but I want to be alone. The gun is cold in my hand as I pull the trigger. The pillow explodes before me, showering me with feathers. I laugh.

> —*from* BANG, *the novel*
> *by Cameron Sheffield Noyes*

No—Gatsby turned out all right at the end; it was what preyed on Gatsby, what foul dust floated in the wake of his dreams that temporarily closed out my interest in the abortive sorrows and short-winded elations of men.

> —*from* THE GREAT GATSBY,
> *by F. Scott Fitzgerald*

THE
MAN WHO
WOULD BE
F. SCOTT
FITZGERALD

Chapter One

side from the name it was the usual Soho art gallery in the usual converted cast-iron warehouse down on Spring Street and West Broadway. The door was made out of steel, and I had to buzz to get in and wait out there on the sidewalk in the rain while the surveillance camera mounted over the door checked me over to see if I was their sort of person. I'm not, but I fooled them.

Inside, the wood floor was polished, the pipes exposed, the lighting recessed. A tape of some Philip Glass nonmusic was softly nonplaying. A languid clerk wearing a tight black dress and heavy black-framed Buddy Holly glasses sat at the reception desk just inside, her nose deep into a copy of *Vanity Fair*, which is the *People* magazine of pseudointellectuals and social climbers. Me she ignored.

Like I said, it was the usual Soho art gallery—aside from the name, which was Rat's Nest.

I took off my trench coat and Borsalino and stood there politely dripping until she finally glanced up at me, then down at Lulu, my basset hound, who was wearing the hooded yellow rain slicker I'd had made for her when she got bronchitis one year. She always wears it on rainy days now. I don't want her getting breathing problems again. She snores when she has them. I know this because she likes to sleep on my head.

"I'm looking for Charleston Chu," I said.

"In there," the clerk said, one lazy hand indicating the main gallery through the doorway.

We started in.

"Sir?"

We stopped. "Yes?"

"No animals are allowed in Rat's Nest."

Lulu snuffled at me, deeply offended. I told her to let me handle it. Then I turned to the clerk and said, "We're going to pretend we didn't hear that." And we went in.

There wasn't much in there, and what was in there wasn't much. Some graffiti art left over from a couple of seasons before. A lumpy piece of statuary the size of a grand piano that looked to be from the postmodernist, neo-nonexistent school. A large white canvas that had a life-sized mannequin of a metallic-blue woman suspended from it by hooks. The prices were posted on small, discreet business cards. The lumpy statue was going for $15,000, which would have been an excellent investment if they also threw in a new Mitsubishi Galant.

Someone in the gallery sneezed. I looked down at Lulu. Lulu was looking up at me. That ruled out the only two so-called warm bodies in the room.

I approached the painted mannequin.

It was called *Blue Monday*. It had no price on it.

Its nose was running.

Lulu barked. She has a mighty big bark for someone with no legs. Also pretty definite taste in art.

"Shit!" cried the mannequin. "He won't bite me, will he?"

"He is a she," I replied. "And she won't go after any-thing larger than a baby squirrel unless challenged, in which case she'll hide under the nearest bed. May I wipe your nose for you?"

"Please. Damned tree-pollen allergy. Spoils the whole statement."

"Oh, I wouldn't go that far."

I dabbed at her blue nose with my linen handkerchief. It was a tiny snub nose, and some of the paint on it came off on the handkerchief. Her almond-shaped eyes were brown. The rest of her was quite blue. Her hair, which she wore close-cropped like a boy. Her leotard and tights. Her hands and feet, which were shackled to the canvas in a position that wasn't exactly Christ-like but wasn't that different either. She had a slim, firm body, the body of a gymnast or a dancer, which she wasn't. She was Charleston Chu, the Chinese conceptual artist who was, at age twenty-four, the new darling of New York's art scene.

"How many hours a day do you spend up there?" I asked.

"Six."

"It must get a bit uncomfortable after a while."

"I wish for it to. If I'm uncomfortable, I make you uncomfortable."

She had a girl's voice, with a trace of an accent, but she was no naive waif. This was a savvy self-promoter and entrepreneur who had climbed to the top of a rough business very fast, and on her own terms. She was her own dealer—Rat's Nest merely rented her gallery space.

"People like to sit back and judge art," she went on. "I won't allow you to. I judge you right back. Force you to have an intimate relationship with me."

"I'm willing if you are," I said gamely. "Just promise me one thing—years from now, when you talk about this, and you will, be kind."

She narrowed her eyes at me. "Do you have some kind

of problem, asshole?" she demanded coldly. She was in character now. Then again, maybe she wasn't.

"That," I replied, "may take us longer than six hours to get into. Tell me, how come there's no price tag on you?"

"I'm not for sale."

"We're all for sale. I know I am."

"What's your price?"

"A third of the action, generally. If I can find my celebrity. I had a lunch date with Cameron Noyes, and he stood me up. I was told you two . . ."

". . . Hang out together?"

"You said it. I didn't."

She smiled. Because of the blue on her face her teeth seemed unusually white, her gums a vivid pink. She had nice dimples. "We live together. Cam should be home working."

"I rang the bell. Also phoned. No answer."

"Then he must be lost in thought, or shitfaced, or out banging someone," she said mildly.

"And that's okay with you?"

"Cam Noyes is a genius," she replied. "His life is his work. To impose my will upon one is to corrupt the other. I have no right to do that. No one does. Besides, you know how writers are."

I tugged at my ear. "Yes, I suppose I do."

"Oh, I get it now—you're Stewart Hoag."

"Make it Hoagy."

"As in Carmichael?"

"As in the cheese steak."

"I'm a vegetarian," she said.

"I suppose someone has to be."

She giggled. It was an unexpectedly bubbly, delicious giggle. It reminded me of Merilee's. Almost. "Everyone calls me Charlie," she said, wiggling a shackled hand at me.

I reached up and shook the hand, and came away with more blue. "Pleased to meet you, Charlie. That's Lulu."

"She's a cutie."

Lulu turned her back on us with a disapproving grunt and faced the lumpy statue.

"I say something wrong?" asked Charlie.

"No. She's just had this thing about other women ever since my divorce. She always thinks they're coming on to me."

"Are they?"

"I seriously doubt it."

"Can't you tell?"

"A guy is always the last to know."

Her eyes gave me the once-over. I had just changed to my spring wardrobe. I wore the navy-blue blazer of soft flannel I'd had made for me in London at Strickland's, with a starched white Turnbull and Asser broadcloth shirt, plum-colored silk bow tie, vanilla gabardine trousers, and calfskin braces. On my feet were the Maxwell's brown-and-white spectator balmorals with wing tips. None of it did me any harm.

"Cam is very much looking forward to meeting you," Charlie said. "You're one of his idols."

"He has others?"

"He has few. I meant, he's excited about your new arrangement."

"There won't be any arrangement if he doesn't keep his appointments."

"Oh." She frowned, concerned. "Look, it's nothing personal, Hoagy. He's just very into chaos."

"Aren't we all."

"We were out late last night. He's probably just taking a nap. Tell you what, there's a house key in my purse at the front desk. Take it. Let yourself in."

"Kind of trusting, aren't you?"

"Am I?"

"Everything I told you could be a lie. I could be any-body. I could be trouble."

"No chance. Your eyes . . ."

"What about them?"

"They give you away."

So I rang Cam Noyes's bell again. This time I had Charlie's key in my pocket and my hat off. The rain had moved on up the coast toward New England, and it was sunny and fresh out. The green of spring across the street in the park was new and bright. Cam Noyes owned one of the Greek re-vival town houses that face right onto Gramercy Park, and that are about as prized these days as Yankee starters who can last seven innings. Only those who are both very rich and very lucky ever get to live facing the private park. Even they aren't allowed to bring their dogs in there with them. I'd have something to say about that if I were one of them, but I'm not. I've used up my money. Also my luck.

His house was white and sported an iron veranda with lacy ornamentation. He still didn't answer the doorbell. I glanced back at the curb. Parked there, as it had been ear-lier that day, was a gleaming, fully restored hot-pink 1958 Oldsmobile Super 88 convertible. The original Loveboat, the one that Olds boasted carried no less than forty-four pounds of chrome plating on it. It had to be the longest, gaudiest, most vulgar car ever made. It had to belong to Cam Noyes.

I rang one more time, and when no one answered, I used Charlie's key.

The decor wasn't what you'd call typical. Actually, it wasn't what most people would call decor. The walls, ceil-ing, and ornate molding of the ground-floor parlor had been stripped down to the bare, pitted plaster and left that way. Some tall plastic potted palms had been scattered about. In the center of the room a half dozen fifties, shell-backed metal lawn chairs in assorted pastels were grouped around an old Packard Bell black-and-white TV set. Over the marble fireplace hung a particularly awful Julian Schnabel original. It looked as if he'd dipped a dead gerbil in a can of yellow paint and hurled it against a wet canvas. The oak floor was unpolished and bare except for a twenty-foot length of Astroturf stretching toward the kitchen. Golf balls dotted it. At one end there was a putting cup with an electronic return. A putter leaned against the wall.

I called out his name. There was no answer. There was no sound at all.

Most of the kitchen was a raw, gaping wound. There was a refrigerator with some liquor bottles on it, and a utility sink, but everything else—stove, cupboards, counters—had been ripped out. The walls had been stripped down to bare, crumbling brick, the floor to the rough wood subflooring. Lulu found an open trapdoor with steep stairs down to the basement. A light was on down there, illuminating stacks of fresh lumber and Sheetrock, boxes of tile, buckets of joining compound, a new sink, copper pipe.

I called down there. No answer.

French doors led out back to the walled garden. A twelve-foot square of damp earth just outside had been cleared, leveled, and marked out with stakes and string lines. Under a wet blue tarp were piled sixty-pound bags of cement mix and pallets of bluestone. All the makings of a patio. For now the garden didn't offer much, except for a lot of dead leaves with one pink plastic flamingo standing guard over them. This Lulu carefully checked out with her large black nose before strutting back to me, snuffling victoriously.

The second-floor parlor had a higher ceiling and grander molding than the one downstairs, and tall leaded-glass windows overlooking the park. Also paint splatters everywhere. Charlie's studio. Worktables were heaped with paints, brushes, spray cans, contact cements. Huge blank canvases were stacked against one wall. Cartons were piled everywhere—cartons filled with gaily colored Fiesta ware, with empty Coke bottles, with old magazines and postcards and snapshot albums. On an easel in the middle of the studio sat a canvas to which she'd glued broken shards of the Fiesta ware as well as part of a Uneeda biscuit box. Welcome to the age of borrowing. The Museum of Modern Art and the Whitney had lined up to buy just such works of borrowed art by Charlie Chu. I'll still take Edward Hopper. He didn't borrow from anyone.

A dozen or so eight-by-ten, black-and-white photographs had been taped directly onto one of the walls. I walked over to them, broken bits of china and glass crunching under my feet. They were photos of literary wunderkind Cameron Noyes and his many hot young friends, snapped in restaurants, in clubs, at parties in expensive-looking lofts. Photos of him with Emilio Estevez and Keifer Sutherland, with Michael J. Fox, with Adam Horovitz of the Beastie Boys and Molly Ringwald and Suzanne Vega and Johnny Depp. There were no pictures of him with Charlie. She was the photographer. I found her darkroom in the bathroom off the studio.

A wide doorway opened into what had been the dining room. There was a dumbwaiter down to the kitchen below, and wiring for a chandelier in the center of the ceiling. Charlie made her heavier artistic statements in there. Hunks of iron, lengths of pipe, were heaped in a corner next to an acetylene welding torch and welder's mask. She had a heavy-duty circular table saw, a lathe, a workbench stocked with hand tools. Rough picture frames hung by the dozen from spikes in the wall. Did her own framing right here, too. Handy girl.

I called out Cam's name. There was no answer.

The third floor was somewhat more conventional.

There was fresh white paint on the walls of the short hallway. A guest bedroom in back, simply furnished. The front room was where Cameron Noyes wrote. It was an austere room, and he wasn't in it. An uncommonly lovely writing table was set before the windows. It was made of cherry in the Shaker style and rubbed until it glowed as only cherry can. On it was a yellow legal-sized pad, blank, a pencil, an oil lamp, and a genuine fifteen-inch bowie knife of the 1850s with a wrought-steel blade and brass handle and hilt. The Arkansas Toothpick—glistening, and razor sharp.

There was nothing else in the room—no books, no papers, no phone, no other furnishings.

I kept climbing.

The top floor was all master bedroom. A ceiling fan circled slowly overhead and made the curtains, which were of a gauzy material, billow. A brass bed was planted in the middle of the huge room like an island, and on that brass bed lay Cameron Noyes, naked on top of the covers. His mouth was open, his eyes closed. His head had lolled to one side in such a way that the blood from his nose had streamed down his face and onto the pillow, and dried there.

I looked down at Lulu. Lulu was looking up at me.

I sighed and crossed the room to the bed. He was breathing, slowly but evenly. There was a vial of white powder on the nightstand, next to a pocket mirror, razor blade, and length of drinking straw. Also a bottle of tequila, some wedges of lime, and two glasses—all the makings for a fine matinee horror show. I moistened a finger, dipped it into the vial, and rubbed the powder over my gums. It was coke, all right. I knew about the tingle. Also about the nosebleed. The inside of his nose was ruined from stuffing coke up it. A lot of coke.

I looked down at him. He may not have been the handsomest man I'd ever seen, but he was close. So handsome

he was almost pretty. He had wavy blond hair, a high forehead, prominent cheekbones, and a delicate, rosy mouth.
His complexion was fair and free of blemishes. The nose,
aside from the blood caked on it, was perfect. So was the
chin. His eyes were set wide apart. I wondered what color
they were. I guessed blue. It was the face of a sensitive boy.
It didn't go with the rest of him. He was a big man with
huge, sloping shoulders and powerful arms. His chest was
deep, his waist was narrow, his stomach flat and ridged
with muscle. The words *Born to Lose* were tattooed on his
left bicep. The hands were monstrous and work rough-
ened. The legs belonged on a modest-sized plow horse.
It was the body of a laborer or an outside 'linebacker, or
the young Brando. It was a body that didn't fit with the
face.

I looked down at him and wondered. Cameron Noyes
had it all. He was young, handsome, brilliant, rich, and
famous. And he was trashing it. Why? This I would have to
find out.

I heard something rolling on the bare wooden floor.
Lulu had made a small discovery under the bed and was
nosing it toward me. It was a woman's lipstick. Red. I
picked it up and put it on the nightstand next to the tequila.

Then I went downstairs to the kitchen. The refrigerator was empty except for a half-eaten sausage-and-mush-
room pizza from John's, the coal-fired pizzeria on Bleeker.
I went to work on a slice. I'd missed lunch, and there's no
greater delicacy than cold pizza, except for licorice ice
cream, and there wasn't any of that in the freezer. Just a
bottle of Polish vodka and four trays of ice cubes. These I
dumped in an empty joining-compound bucket from the
cellar. I filled the bucket with cold water from the sink,
swooshed it around, and carried it back upstairs. When I
got to the bed, I hefted it, took careful aim, and dumped
half of its contents on the naked, fully exposed groin of

Cameron Noyes. He instantly let out a lion's roar of shock and pain and sat right up, his eyes—they *were* blue—bulging from his head. I gave him the other half of the bucket in the face. Then I wiped my hands and sat down and asked myself what the hell I was doing there.

Chapter Two

You could take your pick with Cameron Sheffield
Noyes.

You could call him the brightest, most gifted
boy wonder to shine on American fiction since
F. Scott Fitzgerald lit up the Jazz Age. Or you
could call him an obnoxious, big-mouthed, young shithead.
The only thing you couldn't do was ignore him.

Not since his sophomore year at Columbia, when this
strapping young part-time male model and full-time blue
blood had submitted the manuscript for a slim first-person
novel to Tanner Marsh, who teaches creative writing there.
Marsh also edits the *New Age Fiction Quarterly*, and happens to be the single most influential literary critic in New
York. Marsh read the little manuscript, which told the story
of a shy, privileged, young Ivy Leaguer who suffers a nervous breakdown while studying for finals and runs off to an
Atlantic City hotel-casino with the middle-aged cashier at
the diner where he regularly breakfasts. There, besotted by

drugs, alcohol, and sex, he blows both of their brains out. The novel was called *Bang*. Marsh was so knocked out by it he showed it to Skitsy Held, editor in chief of the small, prestigious Murray Hill Press. She shared his enthusiasm. *Bang* was published one month before Cameron Noyes's twentieth birthday. A spectacular front-page review in the *New York Times Book Review* catapulted it, and its author, to instant celebrity. "It is as if young Scott Fitzgerald has come back to write *The Lost Weekend* while under the influence of cocaine and José Cuervo tequila," raved the *Times'* reviewer, who was none other than Tanner Marsh. "Indeed, Cameron Sheffield Noyes writes so wincingly well he must be considered the most brilliant new literary find since Stewart Hoag. One can only hope he will fare better."

Critics. One thing they never seem to understand is that everyone, no matter how gifted, can roll out of bed one morning and have just a really rotten decade.

I read the damned thing, of course. How could I not? I read all 128 pages of it, and I thought it was absolutely brilliant. Oh, I wanted to hate it. Desperately. But I couldn't. *Bang* captured the itchy ennui of the young as so few novels ever had. Cameron Noyes had a gift—for peering into the depths of his own soul and for coming back with pure gold. And he had the rarest gift of all. He had his own voice.

Lulu stayed out of my way for a whole week after I read it. I was not in a good mood.

Lonely, alienated teenagers who before might have turned to Plath or Salinger for comfort found Noyes much more to their liking. *Bang* understood them. It was dirty. It was *theirs*. It took off—and stayed near the top of the best-seller lists for thirty-six weeks, the name of Noyes crowding out more familiar ones such as Michener and King. The paperback reprint went for close to a million. The movie version, which starred Charlie Sheen and Cher, made over

$100 million, though fans of the book—not to mention the movie's first director—were put off by the studio-dictated happy ending, in which the hero has only *dreamt* the violent climax and awakens from it sobered and determined to get his degree.

Cameron Noyes wasn't the only hot young novelist in town. It seemed as if a pack of baby authors had been let loose on the literary world with their hip, sassy tales of the young, the restless, the stoned. There was Jay McInerney, author of *Bright Lights, Big City*, Bret Easton Ellis with *Less Than Zero*, Tama Janowitz with *Slaves of New York*. They were a kind of universe unto themselves, an undertalented, overpaid, over-publicized universe at that. But Cameron Noyes was not like the others. He actually knew how to write, for one thing. And he knew how to grab like no one else. He appeared in ads for an airline, a credit card, a brand of jeans, a diet cola, and the Atlantic City casino where *Bang* was filmed. *Saturday Night Live* made him a guest host. MTV sent him to Fort Lauderdale to cover spring break as its guest correspondent. *Rolling Stone* put him on its cover. So did *People*, which called him the sexiest man alive. He was seldom lonely. Not a week went by without his appearing in the gossip columns and the supermarket tabloids, squiring one famous film or rock 'n' roll beauty after another to Broadway premieres, charity bashes, celebrated murder trials. He had been with Charlie Chu, his current live-in love, for two months now. It was, they both told Barbara Walters on network TV, a "once-in-a-lifetime thing."

He made good copy. Indeed, Cameron Noyes seemed to revel in his own enfant-terrible outrageousness more than any young celebrity since John Lennon. "It's true, I brought the remote-control generation to literature," he told *Esquire*. "And they will keep on reading great books—just as long as I keep writing them." When he wasn't blasting literary sacred cows of the past ("Hemingway and Fitzgerald are officially sanctioned culture—the boredom comes built in with the product") and present ("Saul Bellow's been dead since 1961. Isn't it time someone told him?"), he was acting out his own style of commentary. He became so outraged, for instance, when real estate developer Donald Trump's book hit number one on the bestseller list that he bought up every copy in every store on Fifth Avenue—several hundred in all—carted them into Central Park and made a bonfire out of them. For that he spent a night in jail. And while that little demonstration might have displayed a certain spirited cheekiness—not to mention good taste—a number of his lately had not. He ran over a pesky paparazzo with his car one night and nearly crippled him. He punched Norman Mailer at a black-tie benefit for the New York Public Library and broke two teeth. Currently, he held the unofficial record for turning over the most tables at Elaine's while in the heat of a drunken argument: three.

He was a powder keg, a troubled young genius blessed with James Dean's looks and John McEnroe's personality. He was the perfect literary celebrity for his time, so perfect that if he hadn't come along, someone would have invented him.

In a way, someone had. The mastermind behind the meteoric rise and phenomenal marketing of Cameron Noyes was twenty-four-year-old Boyd Samuels, who had been his college roommate and was now the most notorious literary agent in the business. Boyd Samuels had made a name for himself in publishing almost as fast as his star client had—for trying to steal big-name talent from other agents, for being unprincipled, for being a liar, and most important, for being such a damned success at it. Take Cameron Noyes's much anticipated second novel. He wasn't writing it for Skitsey Held. Samuels had simply blown his nose on his client's signed contract with her, snatched Noyes away, and delivered him to a bigger, richer house willing to pay him a reported advance of a million dollars. Just exactly how Samuels had managed to pull this off—and why Skitsy Held, no cream puff, had let him—had been the subject of much speculation around town. Just as Noyes's second novel was. Word was it was on the late side. Word was his new publisher was getting edgy. Hard to blame them. A million is a lot of money for a serious novel. Especially one by an author who had only just turned twenty-three.

It was Boyd Samuels who got me mixed up with Cameron Noyes. He called me one day and invited me up for a chat. I went. I had nothing better to do.

The Boyd Samuels Agency had a suite of offices on the top floor of the Flatiron Building, the gloriously ornate skyscraper built in 1902 at the elongated triangle where Broadway meets Fifth and Twenty-third. It was about 1957 in Boyd Samuels's outer office, and it wasn't so much an outer office as it was a diner—cute and kitschy as hell, too, right down to the shiny chrome counter and swivel stools, the pink and charcoal linoleum on the floor, the neon clock and the vintage jukebox, which was playing Eddie Cochran. It seemed as if everywhere I went that season I bumped into the fifties. I suppose young people are always nostalgic for a decade they didn't have to live through.

Phones were ringing, people were bopping in and out of different office doors, snapping their fingers to the juke. None of them looked over twenty-five. Lulu and I waited at the front door until one of them, a tall, gangly, splay-footed kid with a Beaver Cleaver burrhead crew cut, hurried over to us from behind the counter. He wore a Hard Rock Cafe T-shirt, jeans, and the look of someone who was used to getting whipped. His shoulders were hunched in the anticipation of blows, his eyes set in a permanent wince.

"Stewart Hoag, isn't it?" he asked timidly, fastening his eyes to a spot on the wall about a foot over my head.

I said it was.

"I'm Todd Lesser, Boyd's assistant. H-He's on his way."

"From . . . ?"

"Home," he replied, explaining quickly, "he's running a bit late this morning. He'll be here in just a few minutes. Really. Care to wait in his office?"

"Nice decor," I commented as we crossed to a corridor of offices. "If business is ever slow, you can sell burgers."

"Business," Todd said modestly, "is never slow."

Boyd Samuels was into ugly. Ugly, kidney-shaped desk of salmon-colored plastic. Ugly art-moderne love seat of chrome and leopard skin. Ugly specimen cacti growing uninvitingly in pots in front of the window overlooking Madison Square Park. These Lulu ambled right for, sniffing delicately at them so as not to honk her large black nose on a prickle.

Todd eyed her warily. "Uh . . . she's not going to . . ."

"Just getting the lay of the land," I assured him.

One wall of the office was floor-to-ceiling shelves displaying the many best-selling books by his many best-selling clients. Framed magazine covers and best-seller lists and rave reviews crowded the walls. Standing in one corner was a life-sized, full-color cardboard display cutout of Delilah Moscowitz, the statuesque, scrumptious, and sizzingly hot young sex therapist who was blowing Dr. Ruth out of the water, so to speak. Delilah's looks, frisky wit, and bold irreverence toward such touchy subjects as fellatio, bondage, and her own rather uninhibited sex life had made her a sensation. She had a top syndicated newspaper column, a radio call-in show, a regular slot on *Good Morning America*, and now, thanks to Boyd Samuels, a surefire bestseller, *Tell Delilah*. "Good sex is all in the head," read the promo copy on her cardboard cutout. "Take home the lady who gives the best head in the business."

"Nice subtle approach," I observed.

"Our newest star," said Todd, beaming. "Her book has already hit the B. Dalton chain list. She'll be appearing on *Donahue* and *Oprah* both, and Donna Karan and Norma Kamali are still fighting over her."

"For . . . ?"

"They want her to wear their clothes on her national publicity tour. She looks fabulous in whatever she wears. The camera loves her."

"Yes, she does give a whole new meaning to the word *bookish*," I said, admiring her cutout. "I see Skitsy Held is her publisher. Interesting, considering what happened with Cameron Noyes."

Todd frowned and shook his head. "No, not at all. B-Boyd always tries to make things work out even. Coffee?"

"Please. Black."

He shambled out. I sat down on the love seat, which was as uncomfortable as it looked, and gazed over at the shelves crammed with all of the hot books by all of the hot authors. I listened to the phones ring—publishers calling with feelers, with firm offers, with promises of gold and village virgins. And I sighed inwardly. Once, the raves and magazine covers and phone calls were for me. Once, I'd swum in these swirling waters myself. And drowned in them.

Maybe you remember me. Then again, maybe you don't. It *has* been a while since I burst onto the scene as the tall, dashing author of that fabulously successful first novel, *Our Family Enterprise*. Since the *Times* called me "the first major new literary voice of the eighties." Since I married Merilee Nash, Joe Papp's newest and loveliest leading lady, and became half of New York's cutest couple. Since I had it all, and crashed. Dried up. No juices of any kind. No second novel. No Merilee. She got the eight rooms overlooking Central Park, the red 1958 Jaguar XK

150, the Tony for the Mamet play, the Oscar for the Woody Allen movie. Also a second husband, that brilliant young playwright, Zack something. She got it all. I ended up with Lulu, my drafty old fifth-floor walk-up on West Ninety-third Street, and a second, somewhat less dignified career—ghostwriter of celebrity memoirs.

I'm not terrible at it. Two No. 1 best-sellers, in fact. My background as an author of fiction certainly helps. So does the fact I myself used to be a celebrity. I know how to handle them. A lot of the lunch-pail ghosts don't. On the down side, being a pen for hire can be hazardous to my health. A ghost is there to dig up a celebrity's secrets, past and present, and there's usually someone around who wants to keep them safely buried.

Danger is not my middle name.

My juices did finally return. Not like before—they'll never be like before. But I did actually finish the second novel, *Such Sweet Sorrow*, the bittersweet story of the stormy marriage between a famous author and famous actress. Somewhat autobiographical. I felt certain it would put me back on the map. A choice paperback sale. Movie deal. Great part for Merilee Nash. Tailor-made for her, in fact.

Deep down inside, I also hoped it would help me win her back—she and Zack had split for good over his drinking and carrying on. But things didn't quite work out that way. For starters, *Such Sweet Sorrow* was not exactly a critical success. "The most embarrassing act of public self-flagellation since Richard Nixon's Checkers speech," wrote the *New York Times Book Review*. "The plot sickens." That was actually the kindest review I got. Written, incidentally, by Tanner Marsh, who, in case you haven't figured it out yet, is not one of my eight or nine million favorite people. But I can't blame the book's utter critical and commercial failure on Tanner. No one liked it. Particularly you-know-who. She called me in tears after she finished reading it to say she felt like she'd been stripped naked in the middle of Broadway, beaten to a pulp and left in the gutter, bleeding, for bums to urinate on. Her words, not mine. She also said she never wanted to speak to me again. And she hadn't.

That spring found her starring with Jeremy Irons in Broadway's hottest ticket, Mike Nichols's revival of *The Petrified Forest*. Sean Penn was bringing the house down as Duke Mantee. And Merilee was considered a shoo-in for another Tony nomination for her portrayal of Gabby Maple, the Arizona truck-stop waitress who reads François Villon and dreams of running off to France.

Me, I was facing the gloomy realization that my season in the sun had passed. I was closing in on forty and didn't have much to show for it—two small rooms, $657 in the bank, some yellowing clippings, a huge ego, and a basset hound who eats Nine Lives canned mackerel for cats and very, very strange dogs. I had no future. I was looking for one when Boyd Samuels called.

His assistant returned with a steaming *Bang* coffee mug. I thanked him. He lingered, examined the carpet. He was painfully shy. Not a positive quality in an agent, unless it can be harnessed into naked ambition.

"For what it's worth," he finally got out, "I thought *Such Sweet Sorrow* was an even better novel than *Our Family Enterprise*. I really loved it."

"That makes you and my mother—and her I'm not so sure about."

"What I mean," he added, reddening, "is I think the critics were wrong to punch you out."

"Could be. But don't forget they weren't necessarily right when they lavished praise on me before. They simply misunderstood me to my advantage." I sipped my coffee. "Todd, isn't it?"

"Why, yes," he replied, startled. He was not used to people remembering his name.

"Thank you, Todd."

"Sure thing," he said brightly.

"Been working for Boyd long?"

"Ever since he started out. We were friends in college. Well, sort of friends. What I mean is . . ."

Before he could finish explaining, Hurricane Boyd hit. The man seemed to explode into the room. He was a human exclamation mark. "Whoa, sorry about the delay, amigo!" he exclaimed as he hurled his bulging briefcase on his desk, whipped off his Ray-Bans, and stuck out his hand. "Glad to meet ya! Indeed!"

I shook it, half expecting to get an electrical shock.

Boyd Samuels was burly and bearded and over six feet tall in his ostrich-skin cowboy boots. He had thick black hair and he wore it shoulder length and didn't bother to comb it. He wore a denim shirt with the sleeves rolled up over his thick, hairy forearms, a bola-string tie of turquoise and hammered silver, and pleated khaki trousers.

"Coffee, Toddy!" he ordered as a greeting to his assistant.

"Right away, Boyd," Todd said, hurrying off.

Lulu stirred on the sofa next to me. Boyd fell to his knees and patted her. "Hey, pretty baby, what's happening?" She yawned in response. He made a face, turned back to me. "Jeez, her breath smells kind of . . ."

"She has funny eating habits."

"What's she eat—old jock straps?"

"We're going to pretend we didn't hear that."

Todd came back with the coffee. Boyd took it, dropped into his desk chair, and gave him the name of an editor he wanted on the phone at once. Todd nodded, retreated.

There was a bottle of Old Overholt rye whiskey in his desk drawer. Boyd poured a generous slug of it into his coffee, then offered me the bottle. I was starting to reach for it when a soft, low growl came from the sofa next to me. My protector. She was concerned that I was slipping back into my bad habits—I had before when things went sour. I glowered at her. She glowered right back at me, baring her teeth like Lassie trying to protect Timmy from a hissing rattler. I was definitely losing the upper hand.

Boyd put the bottle away, struck a kitchen match against the sole of his boot, and lit an unfiltered Camel with it. Then he sat back with his boots up on the desk, smoking, sipping his laced coffee. The whole routine was pretty down-home shit-kicker; especially for an optometrist's son from Cherry Hill, New Jersey. Only the eyes spoiled it. The eyes taking me in from across that desk were shrewd and alert and as piercing as twin laser beams. The man didn't blink.

Not until his phone buzzed. Then he reached for the cordless headset on the desk and put it on. It had a mouthpiece and earphones and an antenna sticking out of it. It looked like a prop left over from an old episode of *Star Trek*, the one where somebody stole Spock's brain. Boyd jumped to his feet and paced around the office as he talked, coffee in one hand, cigarette in the other.

"Yo, amigo, you sound like shit in a microwave! Gotta start living clean like me! How's the little baby? . . . That's beautiful, man. Beautiful." Boyd shifted from chummy to grave. "So, listen, I have a firm offer on the table—buck and a quarter up front." (Translation: another publisher had offered one of Boyd's clients an advance of $125,000 for their next book.) He shifted to confidential now—the man worked through the gears as fast and furious as Emerson Fittipaldi. "None of this would be happening if it was up to me. You and me, we're like family. I want you to have it. And if you'll just match their figure by the end of today, you'll get it, okay? . . . Sure, sure think it over." He said good-bye, yanked off the headset, and flung it carelessly onto the desk. Then he sat back down, chuckling to himself. "Between you and me, the cheap bastard's been all alone in the bidding since seventy-five thou. But what he doesn't know won't piss him off, right?"

"I thought that sort of thing wasn't done," I said.

"It wasn't—yesterday. But that was when publishing was about books. It's about bucks now, and anyone who says it isn't is doing a yank on your frank." He picked up a football from his credenza and gripped it by the seams. "I know, I know. A lot of editors think I'm a douchebag, and guess what—I like it that way. It means I'm doing my job. What's important to me is that my clients are happy. And believe me, they are."

He tossed me the football. It had been autographed by a drug-dependent pro quarterback whose memoir Samuels had peddled for six hundred thousand. Happy indeed.

He took me in with his nonblinking lasers. "What would you say if I told you I've convinced Cam Noyes's publisher to accept a work of nonfiction for his second book instead of a novel. Exact same money."

"I'd say," I replied, "you're almost as good an agent as you think you are."

"It's going to be a kind of portrait of his time," he went on. "His life, his friends, his scene. Charlie Chu is doing original portraits and illustrations for it. An explosive collaboration, really. Like a labor of love for the two of them. Actually, there's no existing term to describe what it is."

"I can think of one—home movie."

Boyd's nostrils quivered, but he kept right on coming. "We're talking about the top writer and top artist of this generation. There's no doubt that it'll be major." He seemed utterly sure of this. And he was. Like all topflight salesmen, he was his own best customer.

"What's happened to his second novel?" I asked.

"Too soon. Cam has to wait for his ideas to percolate—especially because everybody expects so much of him. In the meantime, he needs product out there. And some help

—pulling it together. He needs a good editor is what he needs, only there are maybe three in the whole fucking town and his isn't one of 'em. You interested in helping him out?''

"That's not my specialty. There are plenty of competent free-lance editors out there if you—"

"You're not gonna make this easy for me, are you, amigo?''

"That's not my specialty either."

He sighed, started to nibble irritably on the cuticle of his left thumb. Abruptly, he stopped himself. "Look, Cam Noyes is a cottage industry now. He has promotional commitments, personal appearance tours, speaking engagements—twenty grand a pop on the college campus tour. His time has become too valuable for him to spend it alone in a room generating material. Literary stars of his magnitude, they're stepping back from the day-to-day writing. Subcontracting it. At least the smart ones are. They're becoming like the great Renaissance artists. Those guys had a whole staff of studio artists grinding the shit out for 'em. Then they'd sign their name on it. Same thing."

"I still don't see anything here for me."

"What, you need to hear the words?"

"It would help."

"Okay. I want to hire you to ghost Cam's . . ."

"Labor of love?"

"I can't offer you any kind of coauthorship of course. But if you—"

"Not interested," I said, getting to my feet. I started for the door.

"Whoa, hold on, man! If it's the money—"

"It's not. You're talking about a book I wouldn't read. No one will. It'll sell seventy copies. The rest will be recycled into low-cost housing material."

"So make it a book people *will* read." It was a challenge.

"How?"

"If I knew, I wouldn't need you, would I?"

I hesitated. He had a point there. Besides, $657 doesn't go far these days when you have two mouths to feed. "First, I want you to tell me the part you're not telling me."

He lit a Camel and narrowed his lasers at me. "You don't beat around the bush, do you?"

"You want beating around the bush, get George Will."

He let out a short, harsh laugh. "What I'm not telling you . . . Okay, you got it."

I sat.

"I've known Cam Noyes since we were kids," he began. "I don't think of him as a client. I think of him as a brother."

"You forget, I already know how you treat family," I pointed out, indicating the headset on his desk.

"I'm trying to tell you I love this guy, okay?"

"And?"

"And . . . he's in danger of wearing out his welcome in this town. He's brought a lot of that on himself with his mouth. Genius or no genius, people are ready to bury him —no shit. And he doesn't care one bit. All he wants to do is party and chase puss. I keep telling him if he doesn't deliver some kind of class manuscript and deliver it on time, the party's gonna be over. But he won't listen to me."

"What makes you think he'd listen to me?"

"You've been there. You know the pitfalls."

"I didn't exactly step around them."

"But you understand what he's going through. He'll respond to you. You're what he needs right now. I sure ain't." He scratched his beard ruefully. "Will you talk to him?"

I shook my head. "No, thanks. I'm not in the market for a kid brother. Especially one who makes more money than I do."

"Just talk to him," Boyd pleaded. "You're gonna love the guy. I'm sure of it. Want to know why I'm so sure?"

"Not particularly."

He sat back in his chair, hands behind his head, and smiled expansively at me. "Cam Noyes is going to remind you of your favorite person in the whole world."

"And who might that be?"

"You."

Chapter Three

When he got done groaning and sputtering Cam Noyes asked me what the fuck was going on.

"What's going on," I told him, "is we had a lunch date three hours ago and you stood me up. I don't like to be stood up."

"I noticed. Sorry, I fell asleep."

"I noticed."

He sniffled and reached for a Marlboro on the nightstand. He seemed unconcerned by his nakedness. Also by the fact that he was sitting in ice water. He lit the cigarette with a silver Tiffany's lighter, pulled deeply on it, and let the smoke slowly out of his blood-caked nostrils. There was a mannered quality to the way he did it, as if he had practiced it in front of a mirror a few thousand times. When he put the lighter down, he noticed the lipstick Lulu had found. He picked it up and stared at it a moment, gripping it tight enough for his knuckles to whiten. Then he hurled it against the wall. It bounced off, rolled across the floor, and right back under the bed where it came from. Then he yawned, ran his hands through his hair, and smiled at me. It was a smile of straight white teeth, gleaming blue eyes, and long blond lashes, an unexpectedly warm and trusting smile with a hint of bashfulness underneath. It was a million-dollar smile. "Cam Noyes, Mr. Hoag," he said.

"Make it Hoagy." I shook his big callused hand.

"As in Carmichael?"

"As in the cheese steak."

"Are you from Philadelphia?"

"I am not."

"Father was," he said.

"I suppose someone has to be."

Lulu put her two front paws up on the bed and barked.

"The name is Lulu," I explained.

"Of course it is," he said pleasantly.

He hoisted her up with one arm. She made a complete circuit around the bed, snuffling happily, flopped down next to him, and immediately began to sneeze like crazy, her big floppy ears pinwheeling around almost fast enough to lift her off the bed.

He watched her curiously. "Why is she doing that?"

"She happens to be allergic to a certain perfume."

Calvin Klein's Obsession, to be exact. The bedcovers reeked of it. She had not, I recalled, sneezed when she met Charlie.

He patted her. "I had a dog when I was a boy," he said, his voice tinged now with a kind of remote, aristocratic sadness. "A cocker spaniel named Johnny. I loved Johnny more than anything. He died when I was away at camp one summer. Mother was so distressed that I'd not been able to say a proper good-bye that she saved him for me. When I got home, she took me straight to the cellar and opened the freezer door and said, 'Here's Johnny!'

And there he was, shoved in there with the Hummel skinless franks and Minute Maid frozen orange juice, teeth bared, his paws all stiff . . ." He shuddered at the memory, then looked down and realized he was petting the wet blanket. Lulu was long gone—under the bed. Not her kind of story.

"Get dressed," I said. "We'll put some food and coffee into you. Talk business."

He sniffed at his armpits. "Perhaps I ought to shower."

"Don't let me stop you."

He came downstairs a few minutes later wearing a stylishly dowdy white planter's suit, striped tie, pink oxford button-down shirt, and paint-spattered Top-Siders with no socks. His wet hair was slicked straight back. He looked scrubbed and healthy and ready for anything. He was still young enough to not show the effects of the life he was leading. It had been a long time since I was that young.

At the foot of the stairs he stopped to light a cigarette from his lighter. Again I noticed how self-conscious his gestures seemed. He posed there for me, one hand in his pants pocket, looking as if he were straight out of one of those Ralph Lauren ads, the ones where the members of an ultracivilized master-race family are lounging about their baronial country manse with their hunting dogs and their croquet mallets. There was a good reason for this—he had actually been a Lauren model before he took up writing.

"Forgot to give your key back," I said, tossing it to him. "Charlie's key, I mean."

He caught it and looked at it. "You met Charlie?"

"I did. She seems—"

"Brilliant? She is." He sighed. "She's also in love with me, the poor thing."

"Why do you say that?"

"I'm no good for her. Or for anyone. I can't love them back. You were married to Merilee Nash, weren't you?"

I nodded.

"What was it like?"

"Being married or being married to Merilee Nash?"

"Being married."

I tugged at my ear. "When it's going well, it's not the worst thing there is. When it isn't . . . it is."

"She seems like the perfect woman."

"Only because she is."

"How do you know when you're ready for it? Marriage, I mean."

"You're never ready. You just kind of feel it sneaking up on you, like the punch line to a bad joke. Not a terrible house, by the way."

"Thanks. Still no kitchen or terrace, as you can see. Charlie can't seem to get the damned contractor back for more than thirty minutes at a time, and at that only when we're not here to put our foot down. The man's uncanny. Friend of hers at *Architectural Digest* wants to do a spread when it's all done. He says it's a breakthrough in Found Minimalism."

"Play a lot of golf?" I asked, indicating the putting green. "Or is that the 'found' part?"

He went over to the putter and fingered it fondly. "One of my first loves, actually. As a boy I dreamt of being a pro. Do you play the game?"

"Some. Javelin was always more my style."

"What's your handicap?"

"An exceedingly low bullshit threshold. Yours?"

He grinned. "I don't know how to say no."

"That's not so hard. I'll teach you."

It was still sunny outside. The air was fragrant from the blossoms on the trees across the street in the park, where a black nanny was pushing a baby in a pram down one of the spotless gravel paths. An elderly couple sat on a bench together reading. They waved to the nanny as she passed. She waved back.

"Not a terrible neighborhood either," I observed.

"And steeped in a tradition of literary greatness," he agreed enthusiastically. "Henry James lived here in Gramercy Park. So did Stephen Crane, Herman Melville, Nathaniel West, S. J. Perelman . . . and now me."

Lulu stopped in her tracks and began to cough. Violently.

"What's she allergic to now?" Cam asked, frowning down at her.

"I'm afraid she got it from me."

"Got what?"

"The low bullshit threshold."

He froze, taken aback. Then he laughed and held up his hands in a gesture of surrender. "Boyd always says that if you keep telling people you're great, they'll eventually believe you. I take it you think that's bush."

"I think the work speaks for itself."

"As do I, coach." He flashed that disarming smile at me. "But it never hurts to turn up the volume a little, does it?"

We hopped into his bright-pink Loveboat. It had a white interior and plenty more chrome all over the dash. Also enough room inside to seat six with space for a skating rink left over. He lowered the top as soon as he started her up. I put down my window. Lulu planted her back paws firmly in my groin and stuck her large black nose out.

"Unassuming little set of wheels," I observed.

"Yeah, I try to keep a low profile."

He pulled away from the curb without bothering to look and almost got nailed by an onrushing cabbie, who slammed on his brakes and gave us a sample of his horn and his upraised middle finger. Cam seemed quite oblivious of him—he ignored all of the other cars on the road, as well as things like lanes, street signs, and traffic lights. He just rolled along in the giant Olds as if the road were his and his alone.

"You spoke with Boyd about the book?" he asked.

"I did," I replied as he calmly drifted through a red light at Park, cut off three oncoming cars, and made a left onto it. "He wasn't entirely specific about what your concept is."

"Haven't got one."

"That might explain it."

He pulled up a whopping two blocks away on Park and Nineteenth in front of the Cafe Iguana and killed the engine and started to get out.

"Going to leave it right here?" I asked. The car wasn't exactly double-parked—it was more like in the middle of the street.

"Too big to take inside with us," he answered simply as he headed in.

Cafe Iguana was a big, multilevel Yushie hangout colored in peach and turquoise. Its trademark was a sixteen-foot crystal iguana suspended in the air over the bar, where Rob Lowe stood by himself drinking a beer and trying to look grown-up and deep. Seeing him there reminded me just how much I missed Steve McQueen. It was nearly six o'clock so the place was practically teeming with the Young Urban Shitheads—the power-suited male variety displaying plenty of teeth and swagger, the females showing a lot of treadmill-enhanced leg and stony gazes. A few artists and models and record producers were sprinkled around for flavor. There were tables, but no one was eating yet.

Cam made straight for the bar where he exchanged low-fives and a few lusty whoops with Lowe before finding us a couple of empty stools at the end. The bartender was ready for him with two shot glasses of tequila and a wedge of lime. The man wasn't unknown here. He took a bite out of the lime and threw one of the shots down his throat. Then a bite. Then the second shot.

Then the bartender turned to me for my order, his eyes flickering slightly when he heard the soft, low growl coming from under the bar.

"Make it a bellini," I said.

He frowned, shook his head. "Don't know it."

"Three parts champagne, one part fresh peach juice. It was invented at Harry's Bar in Venice in the forties."

He nodded. "Sounds perversely good, ace, but where am I gonna get fresh peach juice?"

I dug into my trench coat. "Where do you think?" I replied, rolling two ripe peaches onto the counter. "And don't call me ace."

Cam grinned at me approvingly as the bartender retreated to make my drink. "I'm beginning to like you, coach. You have style."

"Slow down. I'm complex."

"Tell me, is Harry's Bar still there?"

"Was the last time I looked."

"That's funny," he said. "I was just out there for the Oscar parties, and we ate down at the beach one night, place called Chinois. Stupendous eats. But I don't remember seeing any Harry's."

"Italy," I said tugging at my ear. "It's in Venice, Italy. Not Venice, California."

He nodded. "That explains it. Never been to Italy. Or anywhere in Europe. Would I like it?"

"There's nothing not to like."

The bartender came back with my bellini in a tall champagne flute and with two more shots of tequila for Cam. I took a sip. It was excellent—the champagne cold and dry and enlivened by the sweetness of the peach juice.

Cam drained another shot of tequila with a bite of

lime. "Listen, when I said there was no concept for my book, I didn't mean I haven't given it a great deal of thought. I have. I just don't believe there should be one. Know what I mean?"

Before I could answer, an uncommonly leggy and lovely young blonde approached him from behind, ran her fingers through his hair, and leaned into him. "You didn't call me," she said. Then she kept on going down the bar, hips swiveling.

He gazed after her wistfully until she looked back at him over her shoulder and wiggled her fingers at him. He wiggled his back, groaning softly. "She models see-through lingerie for the catalogs. Not very high up on the food chain intellectually, but she happens to like it up the ass."

I sipped my drink. "I don't."

"Don't what?"

"Get what you mean."

"Oh, right." He lit a cigarette, dragged deeply on it. "I mean, I'm not interested in doing something that has quote-unquote form. I want this book's energy to be the energy of unvarnished chaos." He was warming up now—his voice was getting louder, his eyes brighter. Certainly the tequila wasn't hurting. "I want to surprise the reader. Ask them questions nobody's ever asked them before, like, say, do blind people *see* in their dreams? I want to have them turn the page and run smack into, say, the photographs Charlie has taken of dead bodies she's found on the streets of Manhattan." He laughed, tremendously pleased by his own brilliance. He had that special brand of cockiness that comes from never having known failure. Nobody had ever said no to Cam Noyes. Nobody had ever told him to shut up. He drained his tequila. "What do you think, coach? Don't you think it sounds stupendous?"

I glanced over at him. He was waiting for an answer. I gave him one. "I think," I replied, "that it sounds like one of the two or three biggest loads of bullshit I've heard in a very long time."

I never saw the punch coming. It caught me square on the jaw. The next thing I knew I was sitting on the floor watching that damned iguana swirl around somewhere up near the ceiling. Fireworks were going off, and somebody was ringing the bells up at St. Patrick's. And then the bartender was waving ammonia under my nose and Lulu was licking my hand. A bunch of Yushies were standing over me, murmuring. Personal-injury lawyers smelling a lawsuit, no doubt.

Cam Noyes knelt before me, his brow creased with concern. "Christ, I'm sorry." He sounded contrite.

"Kind of a short fuse you have there."

"I know," he acknowledged readily. "I've never been good at taking criticism. Ask anyone."

"That's okay. I believe you."

"Besides, you're not exactly gentle."

"You want gentle, get Sally Jessy Raphael." I sat up, rubbing my jaw.

"Care to punch me back?" he offered, quite seriously. "I deserve it."

"Not my style. But thanks."

He hoisted me up onto my feet. I was a bit wobbly, but okay. The Yushies dispersed. I got back up onto my stool. Cam started to climb back onto his. Just as his butt was about to land, I yanked it from under him. He hit the floor with a thud and a loud, surprised "Oof."

"Damn, that felt good," I exclaimed, grinning down at him.

"Is *this* your style?" he demanded crossly, glowering up at me.

"Generally."

"We even now?"

"As far as I'm concerned we are."

I helped him up. We shook hands. We ordered another

round of drinks. He drained one of his shots after they came, gazed into his empty glass, and oh-so-casually remarked, "You've had it, haven't you? Writer's block?"

My stomach muscles tightened involuntarily. They always do when I think about the void. And the fear. I glanced over at him and swallowed. I nodded.

"How do you know when you have it?" he asked, his eyes still on his empty glass.

"You know," I said softly.

He looked up at me. The twinkle was gone from his eyes. There was only a hollowness, a hurt there now. He took a deep breath, let it out slowly. "Just can't seem to start anything. Doesn't matter what it is. The novel. A short story. Even a letter. I keep thinking—hold on, don't forget who you are. Don't forget you have to be brilliant, outrageous, natural, hip . . . You have to be *Cam Noyes*." He ran his hands through his wavy blond hair. "They've set this impossibly high standard for me, you know? And they'll only be happy if I exceed it. I'm not allowed to fail. They won't let me. So I end up sitting there. And sitting there. And . . . I don't know. I feel like I'm . . ."

"Exposing yourself in public?"

"Well, yeah. Kind of."

"That's what writing is."

"I suppose it is." He shook his head. "Christ, how did you survive this?"

"I didn't. I wrecked myself and my marriage. Drove all of my friends away—except for the real ones, the ones who were there before."

"I don't have many friends like that."

"No one does."

"And then what? How did you get over it?"

"I stopped caring."

"About your work?"

"About what everybody in town was going to think of it," I replied. "Half of them don't even know what the hell they're talking about anyway. You can't write for Tanner Marsh, only for yourself, the way you did before you became the famous Cameron Sheffield Noyes. Just concentrate on the work. Forget about everything else."

He lit another cigarette. "I can't."

"I didn't say it was easy."

"This book . . . what would you do?"

"If it were up to me?"

He sniffled. "Yes."

"I think the idea of you and Charlie combining forces is dynamite. As for the content . . . I'd try to get beneath your whole gifted and tragic rebel-genius image."

"Now you're trying to provoke me again," he said coldly.

"I'm not. What makes you Cam Noyes? That's what I'd like to know—who you are. How and why you became a writer. How you made it. What it took. What it has done to you—including give you writer's block. The average reader still thinks publishing is a world of tweedy, genteel people who sit around waiting to discover great books, and that authors are shy recluses whose sole aim in life is to write those books. Your story can be the story of publishing as it really is today. Unvarnished."

He scratched his chin thoughtfully, consciously. Portrait of the artist as a young brooder. "In other words, you want dirt."

"Not necessarily," I replied, sipping my drink. "Why, what kind of dirt?"

"Did you know Tanner Marsh and Skitsy Held were once married?"

"I seem to recall it."

"When they got divorced, *he* sued *her* for alimony, and won, on the grounds she couldn't have made it in publishing without him. He gave her her start, steered a lot of important young writers her way."

"That's common knowledge."

He lowered his voice conspiratorially. "Is it common knowledge they're thieves, both of them?"

I leaned forward. "Oh?"

"That *is* what you call someone who pockets money that doesn't belong to them, isn't it?" He waited, somewhat shyly, for my response.

"It is," I told him.

"Believe me, there's deliciously sleazy stuff to tell about the way those two do business. Stuff they'd positively kill to keep quiet."

"And you're prepared to tell it?"

He nodded eagerly. "It's perfect! It's ballsy. Subversive. High profile. It's *Cam Noyes.* God, I love it! Let's do it!"

"Slow down. Boyd may not be quite so enthusiastic."

"He could care less what people think of him," Cam scoffed.

"So he said."

"As long as it makes a splash and big bucks he'll be happy. And it will. I just know it will."

"Your editor may want to—"

"All he cares about is what month I turn it in. *We* turn it in. Will you do it with me, coach? Can we do it? Please?"

Christ, he *sounded* like a kid brother—one who was begging me to take him bowling with me. "You've made up your mind just like that?" I asked.

"Just like that."

"You're a snap—I should have asked you for all of your money."

He grinned. "Then I *do* know how to say no. Is it a deal?"

I said it was. Couldn't help myself. See, the truth is I'd always wanted a kid brother.

An involuntary shudder passed through me when we shook on it. A tingle of deep, dark dread, of snakes slithering through the undergrowth. Whatever it was, Cam clearly hadn't felt it. He was whooping and pounding the bar and buying everyone in the place a round, just a big, agreeable golden retriever puppy of a kid. I half expected him to lick my face.

We drank to our success when our drinks came.

"I do have one favor to ask of you," I said.

His face darkened. "If it's about the coke . . ."

"Not at all. It's your life."

"Glad you see it that way," he said, relaxing. "What then?"

"I'd like an associate of mine named Vic Early to stay in your guest room for a while. I find he comes in very handy."

"Sure. No problem. What is he, a typist?"

"Not exactly. You'll find him easy to get along with. Just don't get him mad."

"Why, what happens?"

"You don't want to know."

I pulled in at Tony's on my way home. It's a neighborhood place on Seventy-ninth off Amsterdam that hasn't changed its menu or its decor in twenty-five years. They make their own sausages. I had mine with ravioli and a bottle of Chianti. As always, there was a little fried calamari on the side for Lulu.

While I ate, I made notes of my initial conversation with Cameron Noyes. Most of them ended in question marks, such as how much did he really have on Skitsy Held and Tanner Marsh? How would they take to his writing about it? What on earth was I getting myself into?

Merilee's Woody Allen movie came on the TV over the bar while I was putting away my cannoli and espresso. Lulu scampered in there to watch it. She never misses one of her mommy's movies. The barman let her sit up on the top of the bar so she could see better. I stayed in the dining room. I knew all of the lines—by heart.

We walked home to Ninety-third Street on Broadway. Upper Broadway was in the intensive care unit now. A solid corridor of new, thirty-story, modern Frigidaire apartment houses was taking form. My old neighborhood merchants were losing their leases daily. In their place were coming the trendy boutiques selling distressed denim jackets and twelve-dollar chocolate chip cookies, the side-walk cafes serving limp, watery arugula salads and mes-quite-grilled snapper as moist and flavorful as chalk. In their place were coming more and more Yushies, who scurried around the neighborhood after dark like cock-roaches, that new kind from Florida that the sprays won't stop.

I was losing my neighborhood. When you lose your neighborhood in New York, you lose your family, and there's no replacing it.

There was nothing in my mailbox except for another notice from the Racquet Club reminding me I'd forgotten to pay my dues.

I counted the stairs up to the fifth floor. I'd become convinced over the past few weeks that someone had added another flight when I wasn't looking. They hadn't.

My apartment was stuffy and smelled of the dried mackerel remains in Lulu's bowl. As unappetizing as her principal fare is fresh out of the can, it's even worse when it's been sitting in a warm room for twenty-four hours. I threw open the windows, scooped it into the trash, and opened a new can for her. There were no messages on my phone machine.

I undressed and brushed my teeth slowly and care-fully, using the new circular motion my dentist said just might save my gums provided I also flossed. My jaw was too sore for that. I'd floss tomorrow. I've been telling myself I'd floss tomorrow every night for the past seventeen years. My problem is I always find something better to do than standing in front of the bathroom mirror poking a piece of wet string around in my mouth.

I went to bed with a collection of Truman Capote's early short stories, which I work my way through every couple of years to remind myself what good writing is.

I had just turned out my light—and Lulu had just assumed her favorite position with a satisfied grunt—when I heard it. A dull thud on the roof above me in the darkness. Then another. And another. Footsteps . . . Lulu growled. I shushed her. The steps quickened, headed toward the big skylight over my kitchen. At the skylight they stopped. Hesitated . . . checking it out. . . . The glass was reinforced with steel mesh, but all it would take was a pair of wire cutters and a swift boot and I'd have a visitor. I swallowed, glanced at the phone on the nightstand, thought about calling the police. But that meant moving, and I couldn't seem to. . . . The footsteps retreated now. Over toward the steel roof door. That was held shut from the inside by a hook and eye. A crowbar would pop it open easily.

He had a crowbar.

It opened with a sharp crack. Now I heard the footsteps on the stairs from the roof, descending quickly . . . in the corridor outside my door. Lulu growled again. This time I put a hand over her muzzle. The steps came to a stop at my door. Silence. A rustling sound . . . something being slid under the door. . . . The footsteps retreated now. Down the steps. Rapidly. One flight. Another. And then, far below, the street door slammed shut. Gone.

I let go of Lulu and my breath. Then I turned on my light and went to the door. It was a blank white envelope, folded shut. Inside was a three-by-five card that had a warning on it: *Write this book and you'll be very sorry. Get the picture?*

The warning was written in those LetraSet press-on

letters they sell at artist supply stores. There was something else in the envelope—the ripped-up pieces of a magazine cover. I dumped them onto my bed and put them together like a jigsaw puzzle. They formed the cover of a *People* magazine from six years before. The cover story was on "The Lady Who Has It All." The face on the cover belonged to Merilee Nash.

I sat down on the bed and cursed. Yeah, I got the picture, all right. I got it just fine. Whoever it was certainly knew how to get my attention. And how to get taken seriously.

I glanced at grandfather's Rolex. It was after midnight. She'd be home from the theater now. Still wound up. I reached for the phone, stopped myself. Then I reached for it again.

It rang three times before she said hello. My heart started pounding immediately. It always does when I hear that feathery, proper, teenaged-girl's voice that belongs to her and no one else.

"Hello, Merilee," I finally got out.

Click.

I sighed, dialed again. She let it ring forever before she answered this time.

"Don't hang up, Merilee. Please. This is serious."

"Oh, no, it's Sweetness!" she cried. "What happened? Was it heartworm? A runaway sanitation truck? Oh, God, don't drag this out, Hoagy. *Please.* I can't stand it."

"Nothing like that. Lulu's fine. Obnoxious, but fine."

Merilee heaved a sigh of relief. "Merciful heavens, Mr. Hoagy. Don't ever do that to me again."

Lulu whimpered from the floor next to me. She always knows when her mommy's on the other end of the phone. Don't ask me how.

"Listen, Merilee. I seem to be in the middle of something . . ."

"Not again, Hoagy," she said wearily. "When are you going to stop this applesauce?"

"I didn't start it, believe me," I replied. "I've missed your quaint little expressions."

"Who is it this time?" she asked, sidestepping my attempt at familiarity.

"Cameron Noyes."

She gasped girlishly. "God, he's *so* gorgeous."

"Extremely well-hung, too."

"Reeeeally? How do you . . . No, don't tell me."

"You surprise me, Merilee. I wouldn't think he was your type. Kind of bratty."

"Meaning he's a pain?"

I massaged my jaw. "Meaning a lot of him is pose. I get the feeling it's almost as if he's performing a role."

"He's young," she said. "People that age are still in the process of inventing themselves. You're just not used to being around them anymore."

"Actually, his agent said he'd remind me of me."

"He *is* the new you," she said. "Gifted and handsome and full of doo-dah and vinegar."

"Ah, the me of my salad days."

"These are still our salad days, darling."

"If they are, the lettuce is wilting."

"Resent him a little?"

"Trying not to," I replied.

"And?"

"And failing," I confessed. "Charlie Chu seems like quite a girl."

"She's not a girl. She's a woman."

"Whatever she is, she's well aware he cheats on her, and seems to accept it."

"A lot of us do. We're afraid if we squawk, we'll get dumped." She was silent a second. "At least that's one thing you never did to me."

"Why, Merilee, that's the first nice thing you've said to me in—"

"I happen to be a very nice person. I'm not nearly as mean and petty and awful as you seem to think I am—in print."

"Look, we've been over that a hundred times. And that's not why I called."

"I've been speaking to Sean about us."

"Oh?"

"He's a very intelligent man," she added. "And I think he's gotten a bum rap from the press."

"Why should he be different from anyone else?"

"He said you had to do what you did, because you're an artist, and that you must write about your experiences or you won't grow from them."

"Merilee, that's precisely what I told you myself."

"I know, I know. I guess I just needed to . . . So you're in the middle of something?"

"I am. There's no reason for you to be alarmed, but they may . . . well, try to get at me through you."

"You mean you think a loon might go after me." She stated it matter-of-factly.

"I'm afraid it's possible."

"Not to worry," she said bravely. "I'm used to them. Come with the territory, I'm afraid."

"Still, I think you should be careful."

"I promised myself a long time ago I won't let them spook me. If I do, I'll become one of them myself."

"Promise me you'll be careful," I insisted.

"I'll be careful."

"Promise me and *mean* it."

"I'll be fine, Hoagy. I have a great big fierce doorman."

"Call me if you need me. It's probably nothing, but call, okay?"

"I shall. And thank you for the warning. It was very civilized of you."

We were both silent for a moment now.

"Do you ever miss us, Hoagy?" she asked, her voice softer.

I swallowed. "Only most of the time. You?"

"I miss us right now. When I've just crawled home from the theater, from all of the lights and the applause, all the energy, to this dark, still apartment. It's so quiet here. Hoagy?"

"Yes, Merilee?"

"You broke my heart, Hoagy."

Chapter Four

T ape #1 w/Cameron Noyes recorded May 6 at the Blue Mill restaurant on Commerce St. off Hudson. Arrives punctually. Seems eager, clear-eyed. Wears blue-and-white seersucker suit.)

NOYES: The decor here is bizarre, coach. Don't they know what decade this is?

HOAG: This happens to be one of my favorite restaurants.

NOYES: Is that why you made me promise not to tell any of my friends about it?

HOAG: Precisely.

NOYES: Food's not bad. I take it you get off on simple.

HOAG: It doesn't get any better than simple.

NOYES: Think so?

HOAG: You know that cherry writing table you have in your study? Its beauty is in its simplicity. But it's a deceptive simplicity. Thousands of hours of work went into it—by a craftsman who knew what he was doing and didn't take any shortcuts.

NOYES: *(silence)* I made that table.

HOAG: *You* made it?

NOYES: You sound surprised.

HOAG: No, I'm impressed. You're very gifted with wood. You know, I wondered about your hands. They aren't a writer's hands.

NOYES: Maybe I'm more of a furniture maker than I am a writer. It's the only time I feel totally at peace.

HOAG: So that's your shop next to Charlie's studio?

NOYES: Yes. I make her frames for her. Am I? Better at that?

HOAG: I don't have to tell you you're brilliant. You know that. *(pause)* But I think you're at a crossroads now. You can come back down to earth, work hard, get even better. Or you can fizzle out. Become one of those people who are simply famous for being famous, like George Plimpton or Dick Cavett.

NOYES: All I did was put some words down on paper. I have no idea why people responded the way they did. I . . . I have no idea how to repeat it. And I sure as hell don't understand where it came from.

HOAG: That's why we're here—to find out where it came from. By the way, who knows about us?

NOYES: Everyone in town, I imagine. Boyd believes in getting the word out. I told him last night about our new idea, and he loves it. I knew he would. Why do you ask?

HOAG: Just curious. Tell me about growing up. Were you an only child?

NOYES: Yes. I grew up in a typical family—no one loved anyone. I was born and raised in Farmington, Connecticut, one of those quaint, historic New England villages the tourists from Fresno go so apeshit over. I come from *Mayflower* stock on mother's side, the Knotts. There are Knotts buried all over the state. Her great-grandfather,

Samuel Knott, was a chief justice of the state of Connecticut. He helped slaves get away during the Civil War, when
Farmington was a junction of the underground railroad.
Her grandfather and father were clergymen. The family
manse passed down through several generations. Mother
grew up in it, as did I. It's a white, center-chimney colonial
smack-dab in the middle of the historic district on High
Street. The little plaque out front says it was built in 1790.
Fireplaces and family heirlooms in every room. Like growing up in a museum, really. . . . Mother was a beautiful
woman.

HOAG: She's dead?

NOYES: They're both dead. My parents died within a week
of each other when I was fourteen. . . . She was a tall,
fine-boned blonde. An only child. Jane Abbott Knott was
her maiden name. She studied at Miss Porter's School, of
course, being that it was right around the corner. And a
family tradition.

HOAG: So did Merilee.

NOYES: Did she? Mother could have become an actress
herself. She was that beautiful. But she was much too devoted to her own special brand of pretense. The Mayflower
Society. The Daughters of the American Revolution. The
local historical society. Horse and flower shows. She lived
in a permanent state of artificial grace. She insisted upon
proper speech and dress. Proper manners at the dinner
table at all times. If I pushed my food too close to the edge
of my plate, she'd sweetly say, "Danger zone, Cammy.
Danger zone." I never saw mother perspire. And I never
could imagine her taking a shit. Still, I shouldn't be un-
kind. Mother believed in me. Loved me. Father never did.
He always treated me like a stray someone had brought
into the house. I often did outrageous things just to get his
attention. I remember once, when I was perhaps five, he
promised to buy me a penknife. I've always been fond of
knives. He forgot. So to remind him I got a nail and ran it

over the length of his Mercedes. He had to repaint the entire car.

HOAG: Did you get the penknife?

NOYES: No, but I got his attention. *(laughs)* He was of beef-baron stock. His great-great-grandfather built one of the big Chicago slaughterhouses in the mid-1800s. A multimillionaire who used to go on those expeditions out onto the plains to hunt buffalo. That bowie knife I have on my writing table belonged to him. Father's grandfather married into the Main Line and settled in Philadelphia. Father was named for him—Sawyer Noyes. He and mother met when she was at Wellesley and he at Yale. He was quarterback of the football team, a handsome, fearless campus hero. Father was the sort of man for whom college was the pinnacle of his life. Everything afterward was a gradual process of slipping away into ordinariness and disappointment. Once in a great while he and I would toss a football around in the yard. One time he caught the ball and stared at it, and continued to stare at it, and then he just laid it down softly on the grass and walked inside. He was an unhappy man. Had some family money left in a trust, but not much. He used his looks and mother's connections to sell real estate. Played a lot of golf at the country club. Drank, of course. So did his older brother, Jack . . . Smilin' Jack Noyes was father's idol. Had been a race car driver and flyer in his youth. By the time I came along he was little more than a sot and a bore—twice divorced and without a proper job. Hung out a lot at the Essex Yacht Club. Uncle Jack always had yachts of one kind or another. But he was nice to me, since he had no children of his own. Once, when the two of us were out on the Sound, he told me that it was vital for a man to have a place of his own—a hideaway where he could think and be himself—and that when he died he intended to leave me his. It was a tiny fishing shack on Crescent Moon Pond in Old Lyme. Very remote. Had to row across the pond to reach it. He said no one else in the family knew of it, and that I wasn't to tell father, that it was our secret. *(pause)* I still have the damned place. It's little more than a tree house, really, and falling down at that. Town won't let me rebuild, because it's on state forest land. But I've kept it. And like Uncle Jack, I've told hardly anyone about it.

HOAG: So he's dead, too?

NOYES: Yes. *(pause)* Yes, he's dead, too.

HOAG: Something?

NOYES: *(long silence)* No, nothing.

HOAG: What sort of boy were you?

NOYES: Restless. Dissatisfied. I was a head-banger. Instead of sucking my thumb I'd bang the back of my head against my crib, sort of like a woodpecker in reverse.

HOAG: How old were you when you stopped?

NOYES: Who stopped? *(laughs)* I wasn't allowed the usual pacifier, television. Mother wouldn't have one in the house. It had, after all, been invented after the nineteenth century. So I spent a lot of time out in father's workshop in the carriage barn. That's where I learned how to work with wood. Also how to smoke cigarettes and wank off. Smiling Jack was right—every man needs his hideaway. I went to the town elementary and middle schools. I had as many friends as I wanted. I was large for my age, and could do sports well. I spent six weeks every summer at a boys' camp in the Adirondacks, learning about canoeing and shooting and taking cold showers at dawn. The rest of the summer I'd play golf at the country club, sail, cherry-bomb the neighbors' mailboxes. The usual mischief. Mine was an idyllic New England boyhood, really. Safe. Sheltered. Secure. And I felt utterly suffocated by it. It was so narrow and confining. Everyone knew everyone, and everyone was well-bred and rich and white. All of them were hiding from the real world, hiding behind their fucking antiques and good manners and garden parties. You know what I mean, don't you?

HOAG: Quite well. I grew up in a town much like that. And fled as soon as I was old enough to.

NOYES: I know you did. I was thirteen when I read your book. *Our Family Enterprise* really influenced me. Made me feel like I wasn't crazy for hating the place. Gave me the courage to cut totally loose from it the way you had. Of course, it didn't hurt that it all kind of blew up in my face, too.

HOAG: How so?

NOYES: *(silence)* I suppose I'll have to deal with this, won't I?

HOAG: Deal with what? *(silence)* Come on, Cameron. Don't hold back on me.

NOYES: Mother . . . Mother was killed in a private plane crash in the White Mountains when I was fourteen. She and one other person, the pilot. My uncle Jack. They'd run off together, Mother and Smilin' Jack. She was a cheat, you see. She'd been banging Uncle Jack for years.

HOAG: Had your father known?

NOYES: Apparently not. The letter she'd left behind for him destroyed him. He brought all of her things down from the bedroom, laid them out in the dining room, and sat down at the table with a deck of cards. Sat there and played game after game of solitaire, surrounded by her things. Sat there for days. Didn't sleep or eat or speak. I'd ask him a question and he wouldn't even hear me. A week after the funeral I came down for breakfast and he was gone. I . . . I found him in the cellar. He'd hanged himself. I just stood there staring at him. Couldn't decide whether to cut him down first or to call the police. I stood there for a long time. Finally I cut him down. He was much heavier than I thought he'd be.

HOAG: Did he leave a note?

NOYES: Yes. It said, "Don't take this the wrong way, son." Christ, I still haven't figured out what he meant by that— what was the *right* way to take it? *(pause)* It wasn't easy, losing both of them that way. I'd lived so much for their approval. Or disapproval. Now that they weren't around I found myself in total wonder at what the point of anything was. Especially with father's suicide—to be told by your own parent that life is not worth living . . . I suppose the main thing it did, besides leave me totally alone, was make me realize there is no such thing as security or trust or happiness in this world. There's only chaos. And myth. I guess I've spent the rest of my life trying to tell people that, whether they want to be told or not.

HOAG: That's an excellent insight into your work. Keep it up. You had no other relatives?

NOYES: None. No aunts or uncles. No living grandparents. The local family lawyer was appointed executor of the estate, as well as my legal guardian.

HOAG: His name?

NOYES: Why?

HOAG: Just being thorough.

NOYES: Seymour. Peter Seymour. When the dust settled, it turned out father was in terrible debt. I had to sell off the Knott manse and all of the antiques in it to pay off his creditors. I was left with a small trust—just enough to pay for my education—and Uncle Jack's shack. Otherwise I was a penniless orphan the day when I was shoved out into the cold, cruel world at age fourteen.

(end tape)

(Tape #2 w/Cameron Noyes recorded May 7 at the Blue Mill. Wears same suit as day before with torn black T-shirt, no shoes or socks. Is bleary-eyed, but punctual.)

NOYES: I ran into a friend at Live Bait last night who thought he'd seen you on a squash court at the Racquet Club yesterday, though he couldn't swear to it—he said you looked a lot older than your book-jacket photo.

HOAG: Tell him, whoever he is, that he's an asshole.

NOYES: It *was* you.

HOAG: Getting killed by a senior vice president of Kidder Peabody.

NOYES: I don't get it coach. Why are you still hanging out at that gentleman's dinosaur pit? I thought you hated those people, like I do.

HOAG: I told you I was complex.

NOYES: But how can you write the way you do and still . . . I don't understand you.

HOAG: You don't have to. I'm the one who has to understand you. I meant to ask you yesterday, do you have any old photographs of your family? Pictures of you as a child? Charlie will want to sort through them for illustration purposes.

NOYES: Not a one. I threw everything out a long time ago.

HOAG: So tell me about the cold, cruel world.

NOYES: The lawyer, Seymour, decided that a boarding school made the most sense, so he sent me off to the Deerfield Academy. Deerfield became my home for the next four years, and the people there my family. Deerfield is where I came of age, though I don't give the school much credit for that. I hated the place on sight. It's in a small village in the middle of the cornfields in western Massachusetts. Deerfield Village is like Farmington, only more so. More quaint. More into itself and its past. The whole place is a living fucking colonial museum.

HOAG: I take it you don't go in for preservation.

NOYES: I go in for destruction. On the surface, the academy was a decent enough place. Lovely campus. Superior library and laboratories and athletic facilities, second-largest planetarium in all of New England . . . But it was, for all intents and purposes, a minimum-security prison. Instead of cells we were assigned dorm rooms. Instead of prison blues we wore blue blazers and ties. We were told where to go, what to do, when to eat. Curfew was at ten. No drinking. No cars. No girls. Two proctors per corridor to keep an eye on you, and a corridor master to be your buddy. Mine was a prized dickhead named Darcy Collingwood, a middle-aged bachelor who taught algebra and wore Hush Puppies and ate Wheaties with diet raspberry soda on it. He smiled a lot. I didn't. I was used to coming and going as I pleased. Plus they really laid on that whole Eastern-elite prep-school mindset—the old-boy tradition of hearty good comradeship and spirited athletic competition. Sports do make the boy into a man. They also tire him out so he won't think about how horny he is and how there's nobody around to fuck except for the other boys. Deerfield just went coed this past year—actually joined the twentieth century. But when I was there, the nearest wool was three miles away at Stoneleigh-Burnham, and only then for purposes of organized activities like dances. It was a prison. I wanted no part of it. I would have fled, too, if it hadn't been for Boyd. As freshmen we were placed across the hall from each other in Plunkett, the oldest and ricketiest of the dormitories. I'd never met anyone like Boyd. He seemed conventional enough on the surface. Suburban middle-class background. But even then he was a visionary scam artist. Within weeks his room had become a working laboratory in the art of free enterprise. He bought and sold tests and term papers. Recruited smart kids to take the SATs for other kids at a fee, with an incentive program based on how far over 1400 they scored. When he turned sixteen, Boyd brought his car up from home and paid a local farmer to let him keep it in his barn. After curfew, he'd slip out his window, pedal his bike to the farm, drive over to Greenfield, and stock up on booze, using a forged driver's license. Then he'd bring it back and peddle it to the boys. Sold them forged driver's licenses at fifty dollars a pop, too, so they'd be able to buy it themselves on weekend leaves. He had a whole setup in his room—camera, printer, laminating machine. Probably stole all the equipment from the school. He was very resourceful.

HOAG: You sound rather proud.

NOYES: I am. Boyd and I have always shared the same vision of this world, which is that everyone in it lies, cheats, and steals to get what they want. Every single one of us. I accept that. What I don't accept is people who won't admit this about themselves. They, to me, are the liars. All that really matters to anyone is not getting caught, and Boyd never did, though one time the shit did hit the fan in a big way. A kid he sold a license to went a little *off* one night. Stole a car from the village, got a bottle, got wasted, slammed the car into a busload of kids near Springfield. Killed two of them, as well as himself. A major scandal on campus. State police said if they ever found out who sold the kid that forged license, they'd nail his ass but good. So Boyd got out of that line and into grass, hash, coke, ludes. He was the campus pharmacist our junior and senior years. Used his weekend leaves to buy quantities in Boston and Hartford. Once he even smuggled a bunch of hash back from the Bahamas when he was on vacation there over Christmas with his parents. He must have made five hundred dollars a week dealing, and he never got caught. Too smart for them. . . . I was fascinated by Boyd from the beginning. In awe of him, really. It was Boyd who got me through Deerfield, both in terms of slipping me test papers and in terms of my head. We spent a lot of hours together getting wasted and talking about life. Boyd wanted to become a rock promoter. He sort of ran things over at WDAJ, the campus radio station, until he used the word *Fuck* on the air and the dean of students wouldn't let him near the place again.

HOAG: And you? What did you want?

NOYES: I didn't know. I hadn't found myself yet. And I was different from the others. I had no future laid out for me— Ivy League education, seat on the Exchange, sturdy, well-bred wife who spoke in hushed, demure tones. Part of me was like Boyd—a rebel. Part of me desperately wanted to be accepted. The easiest way to become accepted was in sports. From the day I arrived at Deerfield I was the academy's best athlete. I was made quarterback of the varsity football team when I was still a sophomore. Everyone wanted to be my friend. I was a gung ho prince among men.

HOAG: Any resemblance to Sawyer Noyes would be strictly coincidental, of course.

NOYES: You don't miss much.

HOAG: I try not to.

NOYES: Believe me, that resemblance was short-lived. Died in the second half of the Choate game. That's when I finally got a good look at myself. We were trailing 7–0 at halftime. Not one of my better halfs. They were a big, physical team. On me before I had a chance to throw. Coach really let me have it in the locker room. Told me I was *spitting the bit*. Told me I wasn't playing like a *Deerfield* man. Made me feel like if I didn't win that game, I'd be a complete failure as a human being. And I *believed* that. I went out there wanting to win more than anything in the world. I was in the huddle calling the first play of the second half, all pumped up, when it hit me—here I was taking the same exact path as Father. Picking right up where he left off the night he threw that rope over the cellar support beam and hanged himself. That wasn't what I wanted. That was what I *hated*. I decided then and there to do something about it—I started completing passes, all right, only I completed them to the wrong men. Coach yanked me when I'd run the score up to 28–0. Screamed at me. Threw me off the team. Boyd hugged me after the game. Told me we were blood brothers. Everyone else treated me like someone with a serious psychological problem. I had, after all, repudiated everything that the school held sacred. Collingwood, my corridor master, sat me down and said to me, very sternly, "You are not a lone wolf, Noyes. You are a unit of society."

He recommended counseling. And left me alone after that. Everyone did, except for Boyd.

HOAG: Is this when you started gravitating toward writing?

NOYES: Not really. The only writing I remember doing was in a sophomore English class. The teacher asked us to do an autobiographical essay. So I told my story—unvarnished. The dickhead gave it back to me with a poor grade and a note across the top: "Life just isn't this bad, Cameron."

HOAG: And reading habits? Who were you into?

NOYES: Jim Carroll, Kerouac . . . Mmm . . . you. I skipped almost all of the required reading. Did very little on my own. Still don't read much. I'm very poorly read. I've never read a word of Hemingway, for instance.

HOAG: *(pause)* Fitzgerald?

NOYES: Fitzgerald? No. I don't think I've read anything of his either. *(silence)* Why are you looking at me like that?

HOAG: I'm just a little shocked.

NOYES: I told you—I'm not well-read.

HOAG: I know. But you're always mouthing off in interviews about the great writers, putting them down.

NOYES: Oh, that. Boyd feeds me those quotes so I'll get attention. Just a lot of publicity. You know how that goes. Actually, I think I'm better off being so ignorant. It means I haven't been influenced by anyone who came before me. My style is *mine*.

HOAG: Tell me about your summers. Where did you go? What did you do?

NOYES: Deerfield fixed me up with a job as a lifeguard at a summer camp in the Berkshires. I think the dean had a piece of the camp. Wasn't terrible, just dull. The only hard part was when the parents came up to pick up their kids. All of them had homes to go to. I had nowhere to go, except back to Deerfield.

HOAG: Did you ever go back to Farmington?

NOYES: No. Never.

HOAG: What about girls?

NOYES: What about them?

HOAG: Tall, blond lifeguards tend to fare pretty well on moonlit summer nights. I wondered if there was one shy doe in particular.

NOYES: Nobody worth talking about.

HOAG: I'd like to be the judge of that, if you don't mind.

NOYES: I *do* mind. I told you, there was nobody worth—

HOAG: Look, Cameron. If I ask you a question I ask it for a reason. That's my job. Your job is to answer me. That's how it works. Understand?

NOYES: Okay, okay. *(silence)* When I was seventeen, there was this counselor named Kirsten. She was a Dana Hall girl from Brookline. Blond. Slender. Very into horses . . .

HOAG: And . . . ?

NOYES: Why are you so sure there's an and? *(pause)* And she and I . . . she was my first, okay? I was hers, too. On a blanket by the lake with the Clash playing on my boom box. She loved me, and I—I loved her back.

HOAG: I thought you didn't go in for that.

NOYES: That was the only time. Never again. Ever.

HOAG: I see.

NOYES: We were going to go to Bennington together. Get married when we were seniors. It was for real, coach. We were in love. I really felt like I belonged to somebody. And she belonged to me . . . And then it blew up in my face— just like everything else had in my life.

HOAG: What happened?

NOYES: Her mother happened. She forbid Kirsten to see me after the summer was over. She thought I was genetically unsound—no money, no living relatives, suicide in the family. I wasn't good enough for her fucking daughter. And Kirsten . . . she did what she was told. I couldn't believe it—after all we'd meant to each other. She blew me off. Just like that. *(silence)* I never saw her again.

HOAG: Any idea what happened to her?

NOYES: None. Probably became a rich perfect bitch. Married a rich perfect bastard.

HOAG: And what happened to you?

NOYES: Boyd was planning to go to Columbia. He was very into New York. The whole idea of New York seemed, somehow, very appealing to me, too. After that thing with Kirsten, I wanted desperately to get away from those quaint historic villages with those quaint placards out front of those quaint houses. I wanted to go someplace ugly and sweaty and *real*. I wanted to meet people who had ideas and dreams and passions. I wanted to disappear. Does that make any sense?

HOAG: New York is like the Foreign Legion. People flee here for a lot of different reasons.

NOYES: What was yours?

HOAG: Mine? There was a job waiting for me in the family business. I didn't want it. I wanted to sip martinis at the Algonquin with Benchley and Parker.

NOYES: Did you?

HOAG: No, they were good and dead by the time I got here. Martinis were damned fine though. So you and Boyd both got into Columbia?

NOYES: Yes. We paid a couple of the Deerfield computer nerds to take the SATs for us. Mine did so well I actually got in on an academic scholarship. *(laughs)* I like to think that Mother would have been proud of her Cammy.

(end tape)

Chapter Five

P ub parties used to be small, dreary affairs. Three or four dozen writers, editors, and agents herded into someone's smoky, book-lined living room on West End. Wine and cheese on the dining table. Lots and lots of boring, pretentious conversation. They were never my idea of fun. Merilee used to say the only good thing about them was the chance to see so many men in the same room at the same time who looked exactly like frogs.

Pub parties are still dreary affairs, but they're no longer small. To celebrate the publication of *Tell Delilah*, Skitsy Held had rented a triple-decker cruise yacht, the *Gotham Princess*, for the entire evening. It was waiting there at Pier 63 festooned with *Tell Delilah* banners when Cam and I left his Olds in the parking lot at Twenty-third and Twelfth and made our way up the long, narrow ramp.

Two hundred glittering celebrity guests were on deck enjoying the free champagne, the late-day sun on the Hudson, and the complimentary *Tell Delilah* balloons, T-shirts, hankies, and panties. It was the usual crowd of smiling, chattering celebrities who turn out at Broadway openings and museum benefits and other such photo opportunities, people who had nothing in common with each other except that they were all celebrities, and no reason for being there except that the photographers were. Lensmen from the *Daily News* and *Post, Women's Wear Daily*, and the supermarket tabloids were busily snapping shots of Sugar Ray Leonard, of Paulina Porizkova, the Polish model with the $6 million Estée Lauder contract, of John John Kennedy and Maria Shriver and Arnold Schwarzenegger, of Ashford and Simpson, Jackie Mason, Bianca Jagger, Bill Blass, and Curtis Sliwa, founder of the Guardian Angels. Phil Esposito, the former hockey great, was there. So was City Council president Andy Stein and Ron Darling of the Mets and a former child star who had just written a scandalous book accusing Darryl Zanuck of waving his dick at her when she was nine years old. All of these people and more were there to celebrate Delilah Moscowitz's new book.

We lingered at the rail for a moment, Lulu sniffing hungrily at the air wafting up from the kitchens down below. Cam swaying slightly. He'd put away a great deal of José Cuervo that afternoon, and also taken a major toot in the Loveboat on the way over. He still wore his rumpled seersucker suit and torn black T-shirt, and no shoes or socks. I had on a glen-plaid suit of Irish linen and a straw trilby. I looked better than he did, but you'll have to take my word for it.

Skitsy Held hurried over to us almost immediately, her high heels clacking on the deck. She was a brusque, gristly little woman in her early forties with shoulder-length black hair, heavy black brows, nervous brown eyes, and the unlikeliest pair of breasts in all of publishing, if not the Empire State. They positively strained against her lavender knit dress, jutting so outrageously far forward that it was a miracle the woman didn't topple over. Those who worked for her swore that Skitsy's oversized mammeries would slowly deflate through the course of the year and that every winter she would disappear alone for a holiday—returning two weeks later tanned, rested, and uplifted.

"Well, well, you made it, young Master Noyes." She spoke in rushed, officious bursts and didn't move her mouth when she did. "Not that I ever doubted you, of course."

"Hey, sure," Cam said good-naturedly, bending forward so she could give him a maternal peck on the cheek. "Wouldn't miss it."

She gestured to a crew member. A moment later the ship lurched and began to pull away from the pier. She'd been waiting for us. She turned to me now and extended a small, bony claw. Her nails were painted red, as was her rather wide mouth. "And I know this gentleman."

"Using the term loosely," I said, taking her hand.

"We met at the Anne Beattie party, remember?" Her eyes darted over to Cameron, then back to me.

"As if I could forget," I said, trying to keep my own eyes off her breasts, and failing.

"There seems to be a bar," observed Cam, glancing across the deck.

"Yes, go have fun, dear," she said. "And *please* say hello to Delilah. She's *so* insecure."

We watched him shoulder his way through the crowd, a big disheveled blond kid at a party of sleek grown-ups.

"He can be a very bad boy," said Skitsy, shivering slightly from the breeze that had picked up as we began to chug up the Hudson. "Be firm with him. He needs that. You see, he's always felt this need to act out his view of the world."

"Which is . . . ?"

"That all people, himself included, are trash."

A white-jacketed waiter passed by with a tray of champagne. She took a glass. We both did.

"I'd like to talk to you about him for the book," I said, sipping mine. "Get your side of his story."

She raised an eyebrow, on guard now. "The rumor I hear is it's some kind of publishing exposé."

"Not really. Just his story, honestly told."

"Still, I'd be careful," she warned.

"I'm almost always careful."

"Publishing is a very small, very social business."

"Tell me something I don't already know."

She eyed me over her champagne glass. "Friends look out for each other. Lend a hand. They don't screw each other. Not without paying the consequences. Am I making myself clear?"

I tugged at my ear. "Yes. You have something to hide."

Skitsy's eyes flashed at me hotly. "I was wrong about you. You're no gentleman."

"I tried to warn you."

"So I'm in it?" she demanded. "I'm in this book?"

"Of course. You discovered him. He was your biggest star."

"He's *still* my biggest star!" she snapped angrily. "And he always will be!"

With that, Skitsky Held turned on her heel and stormed off. Well, it certainly wasn't hard to locate her little hot-button. Actually, given that Cam had so ungratefully left her for another house, it was a wonder she still spoke to him at all. Loyalty means a lot in publishing. It's rarely practiced anymore, but it's still one of the two grand delusions book people cling to. The other is that they're smarter than movie people.

Had she been the one who slid that threat under my door? True, those footsteps on my roof had sounded as if they belonged to Andre the Giant, but the sound had been magnified by the darkness and my imagination. It could have been a woman up there with that crowbar. It could have been Skitsy.

Boyd Samuels was out there in the middle of the crowded deck, his greetings hearty, his laughter forced. He had on a white linen jacket and had tied a red bandanna over his head, Hell's Angel style. I saw no sign of Delilah. I did see Boyd's burr-headed assistant, Todd Lesser, who was standing by himself at the rail, nursing a beer and ignoring the views. He wasn't watching the sun drop over the Jersey Palisades, or the lights of the Manhattan skyline beginning to twinkle in the dusk. He had eyes only for the woman photographer who was across the deck from him snapping shots of the guests. She was a trim woman, light on her feet and graceful in an oversized men's white oxford button-down shirt, faded jeans, and black penny loafers. Todd was gazing at her the way a guy looks at the one and only woman he wants, and whom he knows he can never have.

I headed over to her with Lulu and said, "Blue Monday, isn't it?"

Charlie Chu lowered her Nikon and exclaimed, "You guys made it." Her dimples were even nicer flesh-toned, especially since that flesh was the color of honey and the texture of silk. Her black hair was glossy and parted neatly on one side. She wore horn-rimmed glasses that kept sliding down her nose in a way I knew I could easily find adorable. Her mouth was like a rosebud. There was no lipstick on it. She wore no makeup or jewelry of any kind. She needed none. There was an alive, eager beauty to her, a freshness you seldom find in New York women.

"How's the tree pollen?" I asked.

"Better, thanks," she replied. "Hi, cutie," she said brightly to Lulu, who glowered up at her disapprovingly. Charlie frowned. "She still doesn't like me."

"She's peeved because there's no clam dip."

"There's shad roe downstairs on the buffet tables."

Lulu promptly waddled off in that direction.

"I waited at the house for you guys to pick me up," Charlie said gaily. "No show. Todd was nice enough to bring me."

"How chivalrous of him."

He was still over by the railing, conversing now with Boyd. Actually, Boyd was talking and Todd was nodding.

"Yes, he's very sweet," she said. "A little tongue-tied though."

"I'm sorry we stood you up. I only just found out about this little gathering. Standing up beautiful women isn't my style, believe me."

"Oh, I know," she assured me. "It's Cam's." She spotted him now across the deck, where he was gulping tequila and conversing with Sean Landeta, the punter of the New York Giants. The glow in her eyes was unmistakable: utter adoration.

"Getting any good shots?" I asked her.

She pushed her glasses up her nose. "A couple. Stuff I might be able to work off of for portraits. Skitsy. Tanner . . ."

I looked around for Tanner Marsh. I didn't see him. Possibly the illustrious critic had fallen overboard and drowned in the Hudson, untreated sewage spilling out of his mouth. There was always hope.

"And you?" she asked. "Have you and Cam been having good talks?"

"I believe so," I replied. "It's still early, of course, but so far he's been candid and cooperative. An excellent subject."

She looked up at me with a quizzical expression. "I hope he doesn't disappoint you."

"Not to worry. It wouldn't be the first time."

She cocked her head slightly to one side now. "I've decided you're going to be a positive influence on him."

I grinned at her. "I've been called many things in my time, but never that."

She giggled. It really was a delicious giggle. Then she went off to say hello to the man she loved.

I worked my way over to the bar and found myself next to Todd, who was getting a Wild Turkey for Boyd.

"He invited most of these people here," Todd volunteered. "Has me check out the gossip pages every morning to see who's in town. If they're hot, Boyd makes it a point to invite them out. Then he tips off the photographers."

"Does he have a publicist?" I asked.

"Doesn't need one. This sort of thing," Todd explained, taking in the yachtful of celebrities with a wave of his hand, "is one of the things he's best at."

Todd seemed much more expansive than he had before. He was, I realized, somewhat drunk.

"And what are you best at?" I asked him.

"Me?" The bartender returned with Boyd's whiskey. Todd reached for it, downed it somewhat defiantly, and ordered another. "Writing is what I really want to do. I've had some short stories going around for a while. Just finished a novel . . ." He trailed off, shrugged his shoulders. "I don't know. It's been years."

"Sometimes it takes years."

He gazed enviously over at McInerney, Ellis, and Janowitz—the Athos, Porthos, and Artemis of Lit Lite—who were yucking it up for Liz Smith. "Not for some people," he said softly.

"Doesn't pay to dwell on that. In the real world there's no such thing as a fairness doctrine. You said you knew Boyd in school."

"I did. Dropped out in my junior year. Some personal problems. Bummed around upstate for a while. Tended bar. Cleared brush. Worked construction. Then I found myself back in the city knocking on his door." He smiled self-deprecatingly. "And here, for better or worse, I am."

The bartender returned with another Wild Turkey. This time Todd hurried off with it.

We had reached the George Washington Bridge and turned around and started back down the river. The night air was clear and the skyline ablaze now in its fullest glory. I was standing at the rail admiring it, and marveling at how it could inspire such awe and wonder in me even when the city itself no longer could, when a young woman grabbed my arm and told me how much she'd admired the second novel. It was the guest of honor, Delilah Moscowitz, and her cardboard cutout didn't do her justice.

She was a tall, flamboyant peacock of a woman with a wild mane of frizzy red hair, creamy white skin, amused deep-blue eyes, and an upturned petulant upper lip. Her body was sculpted and sinewy, and she was showing it off. She was done up like a Place Pigalle hellcat in a lavender silk blouse unbuttoned to the navel, tight black leather miniskirt, and pink spiked heels worn without stockings. The vibes she gave off were humid enough to peel wallpaper out in Bend, Oregon.

"Glad you liked it," I said. "That makes you, my mother, and that lanky kid over next to Boyd—and him I'm not so sure about."

She swept her windblown hair back over her head. "You're very brave." She had a throaty, challenging voice. "Most men can't deal with their own impotence."

"Who says I can deal with it? I enjoyed your column in today's paper on those ten sexy summer getaways—the elevator to the top of the World Trade Center, the Maurice Villency furniture showroom, air-conditioned cabs . . ."

"I always test them myself personally," she assured me with a mischievous grin.

"I expected nothing less." I grinned back, getting the impression that Delilah Moscowitz, sex therapist, was something of a vampy, good-humored put-on.

Someone began to sneeze like crazy at our feet—Lulu,

back from trolling the buffet tables. I looked down at her, then back up at Delilah. Well, well.

"Why is she doing that?" Delilah asked.

"Your perfume—Calvin Klein's Obsession, isn't it?"

"Why, yes," she replied.

"She's terribly allergic."

Delilah pouted. "What a shame—if you and I ever have an affair, I'll have to change scents."

"It would be easier than me changing dogs."

"It'd be worth it, you'd find."

"I don't doubt that for a second."

Skitsy Held broke in on us, Cam and Charlie in tow.

"You remember Cameron, don't you, Delilah?" said Skitsy.

"Of course," Delilah said with cordial stiffness. "Nice to see you again." Most discreet. No hint that the two of them enjoyed the odd matinee together.

"Nice to see you, too," Cam agreed, grinning at her with easy, inflamed familiarity. He was a little less discreet. He was a lot less discreet. Still, neither Skitsy nor Charlie seemed to notice. Often, people won't see something right under their nose unless they're expecting to.

Boyd Samuels didn't miss it though. He stood nearby, beaming like the proud breeder of thoroughbred stablemates. I went over to him.

"Enough hi-profile celebs here to keep you busy ghosting for ten years, hey, amigo?" he said pleasantly, his laser eyes scanning the party for available talent. Agents, I noticed, inched closer to their clients when Boyd's eyes lingered on them for more than a second.

"Yes, assuming any of these people will still be celebs in ten years."

He threw back his scarf-clad head and laughed loudly. "Congrats—Cam said you two hit it off fantastically." He took a gulp of his Wild Turkey.

"Yes, and he's told me a lot about your visionary

scams," I said. I caught him unprepared with that. I know this because he airmailed his mouthful of whiskey all over my pale-yellow silk tie.

Boyd cleared his throat uneasily. "Scams?"

"Scams. You know, paying kids to take SATs. Selling forged driver's licenses. And of course, your stint as Deerfield campus pharmacist. . . ."

His eyes flickered briefly, registering what I could have sworn was relief. Why? Were there other scams Cam hadn't told me about? "This book is supposed to be about him, not me," Boyd pointed out sharply.

"It is," I assured him. "But you do appear in a featured role—The Friend. Ronald Reagan made a whole career out of it."

He nodded. "True, true, amigo. Only, you gotta protect your people. In case you haven't noticed, drugs aren't exactly a socially approved form of recreation anymore. Christ, you gotta pass a urine test before they'll even let you run a fax machine at a lot of companies nowadays."

"I thought you didn't care about what people thought of you," I countered.

"I don't," he assured me. "Only these days I deal with people like senators and Wall Street plutocrats. They think I'm a bad-ass liar, that's chill. They think I'm a crook, that's chill. They think I'm a druggie . . ."

"That's not chill?"

"Leave that part out, okay?"

"You said you wanted a quality book. A quality book doesn't tiptoe around unpleasant facts."

"Kind of a stubborn shithead, aren't you?" he said sourly.

"You noticed," I said grinning. "Look, you asked me to come up with a concept. I did. Cam told me you were crazy about it."

"Thrilled," he insisted. "I'm thrilled."

"Someone certainly isn't."

He leaned closer to me. "Meaning?"

"I've been threatened."

He let out a short, surprised laugh. "By who?"

"Evidently someone who is afraid of what Cam will say."

He mulled that over. "Could just be someone who wants to see him fall on his ass."

"Who would want that?"

He glanced over at Skitsy, who was still chatting with Cam and Charlie and Delilah. "I can think of one person right offhand." Then he scratched at his beard thoughtfully. "Know what the best way to handle this is? Liz Smith is standing right over there. Let's go tell her about it. She'll put it in tomorrow's paper, shove the slob right back under a rock. Great publicity, too."

"I'd rather keep a lid on it."

"Why?" he wondered.

"I have my reasons, okay?"

Boyd shrugged, obviously disappointed. I found myself eyeing him. He was a man who'd go to any extreme to promote a client. Had he done this? Had *he* left me that threat as a way of generating publicity?

"Oh, hey," he said, punching me playfully on the shoulder. "A good friend of yours is hanging out below. Come say hello."

Most of the second deck was a glass-enclosed dining room, where a lot of the guests were busy finding a good home for the lasagna and flank steak and assorted salads on the buffet tables.

A dozen or so senior editors sat together over the remains of their food and drink listening intently to Tanner Marsh hold forth on the subject of mysticism in modern Uruguayan literature, the master pausing only to punctuate each erudite thought with a puff on his brier pipe. You don't run into many pipe smokers anymore, and those you do run into are seldom pleasant. Tanner Marsh wasn't pleasant. He was a gross, fat little man in his late fifties, an alcoholic, and a mean one. *Spy* magazine had taken to calling him the "colorful Tanner Marsh" in snide reference to his nose, which was so red, and his teeth, which were so yellow. He wore a wrinkled, shiny tan poplin suit, a rather greasy blue knit tie, and a white shirt that he'd popped open at the belly button to give his gut some breathing room. It was cool in the dining room but he was perspiring freely, a strand of his thinning gray hair plastered to his forehead.

His piggy eyes turned to narrow slits when he saw me standing there with Boyd. "I remember you," he exclaimed in his booming, condescending voice. "You *were* Stewart Hoag."

That got a few titters from the others seated before him.

"It's true, Tanner—I was," I replied graciously, not wanting to get into a pissing contest with the man. I had matured beyond that. "And on my good days, I like to think I still am."

He drank from the gin and tonic at his elbow and puffed on his pipe. "Perhaps I am being a bit harsh, Stewart," he suggested majestically, eyeing me with amusement. He was trying to provoke me. He enjoyed these little jousts.

"Don't concern yourself," I assured him. "Everyone ought to be good at something. You're good at being a vicious scumbag."

I heard a few gasps. Ah, me, I guess I haven't matured totally.

Tanner bristled. Off came his gloves. "This man," he declared, "should no longer be allowed to own or operate a typewriting machine! His picture should be posted in every business-machine emporium on the island of Manhattan! His pencils and crayons should be confiscated! His—"

"Hey, you can't talk to my coach that way!"

Heads swiveled, my own included. Cam Noyes stood there in the glass doorway, swaying unsteadily. He was quite blitzed now. Boyd hurried over to him and tried to maneuver him back out to the upper deck. Cam brushed him aside and staggered toward Tanner.

"And why not, young Noyes?" Marsh asked his former pupil, obviously relishing this.

"He," Cam replied thickly, "is an artist. An *artist*. You are nothing. *Nothing*."

"Which is what you'll be, amigo, if you don't shut up," Boyd muttered to Cam under his breath.

"Don't tell me to shut up!" Cam snapped belligerently, his eyes never leaving Marsh. "This man . . . ," he went on, referring to me, "this man *exposes* himself in public. That's what he does. What do you do? *Nothing*. What right do you have to judge him? *None*. You sit there on your fucking throne, issuing your fucking edicts . . . And what do you know about writing? You don't understand it. Or him. Or me. You don't understand any of us!"

The dining room was filled with guests now, drawn by Cam's high-decibel harangue and by what promised to be a championship heavyweight bout—in one corner the enfant terrible of American literature, in the other the grand pooh-bah. The gossip columnists strained closer, pens poised. The photographers, Charlie included, crowded in front, cameras aimed.

It was Tanner's turn. Slowly and calmly, he lit a match and held it to his pipe. When he had it going to his satisfaction, he puffed on it until he was sitting in a cloud of blue smoke. "The critic," he lectured Cam, "serves as a guide through the vast and treacherous literary wilderness. He blazes a trail. Without him, some of the great authors in history would have never been found. You, for instance." Marsh glanced at Boyd and showed him his yellow teeth. "Young Noyes seems to have a poor memory."

"No, he doesn't Tanner," Boyd assured him effusively. "Really. Isn't that right, Cam? Huh?"

Was Samuels trying to save his prized client from making a powerful enemy or was he egging him on? I wondered, though not for long.

"Why are you sucking up to him, Boyd?" Cam demanded angrily. "You always suck up to him! All of you people do! What for? Who cares what he thinks?" Cam now stood right over Marsh, who looked up at him with cool disdain. "You haven't got the slightest fucking notion what it takes to create something, Tanner! What it *feels* like. You think you do, but you don't. Know what? I'm going to do you a favor—I'm going to show you!"

With that he grabbed the fat little man by the lapels and yanked him roughly to his feet. Marsh looked pale and frightened now, as if he'd just realized he'd gotten into something his stinging wit might not get him out of. He looked around for a rescuer but none stepped forward. Everyone on board the *Gotham Princess* was much more interested in seeing what Cam Noyes had in mind. I knew I was.

He tore the jacket, shirt, and tie right off Tanner Marsh, exposing his billowing, hairy white flesh. A lot of people gasped. It wasn't a pretty sight. Terrified now, Tanner tried to get away from him. Cam grabbed him by the belt so he couldn't.

"Don't hurt me!" wailed Tanner, wide-eyed and trembling. "Please don't hurt me! Please!"

Smiling now, Cam yanked southward very hard, ripping the waistband of Tanner's trousers and sending them plunging down to his shoes. Tanner stood there now clad only in his baggy, pee-stained boxer shorts. But not for long. Cam ripped those off him, too.

The most important literary critic in America now stood stark naked in front of two hundred of New York's biggest celebrities, most of whose jaws were down near the floor.

No one moved or made a sound, especially Tanner, who was so debased and mortified he seemed frozen there. Flashbulbs went off as the photographers, Charlie included, recorded the moment for posterity.

"There we are, Tanner," declared Cam, standing back to admire his handiwork. "Now you know what it feels like to be an author. Congratulations." With that Cam staggered over to the bar and ordered two more shots of tequila.

Tanner pulled up his ruined trousers with one hand, gathered his torn jacket and shirt around him with the other, and made his way in awkward, mincing strides for the glass door. "You shall be very sorry," he spat at Cam. To Boyd he added, "You shall *both* be."

Then he swept out of the dining room with what little was left of his dignity. Skitsy Held, his hostess and ex-wife, followed him out, horrified. The guests began to disperse, chattering excitedly.

Boyd Samuels slumped down into a chair. "Christ, not one of my clients will ever get a good review from him again." He started chewing on a thumbnail. Abruptly, he stopped. "Maybe I can get Delilah to sit on his face."

"Guess again," she informed him.

Boyd laughed. "Just a figure of speech, honeypot," he called to her. To me he grumbled, "I was told you get results, amigo. I gotta tell you—this sure isn't my idea of a solid couple of days of work from you."

Cam was over by the windows now, pulling on a cigarette and gazing out at the Statue of Liberty, which was lit up for the night. Charlie stood next to him with her hand on his arm, speaking to him softly. He seemed not to be noticing her there.

"He's rather impressionable, isn't he?" I said.

"Yeah, he's rather impressionable," Boyd muttered.

"Does he realize how much you manipulate him?"

Boyd frowned at me. "I'm not tracking you."

"You could have stopped that from happening, but you didn't. You wanted it to happen. It'll be all over town by tomorrow. Part of the Cam Noyes legend."

Boyd grinned wolfishly. "You have to admit it was righteous theater."

"He could have strangled the fat bastard with his bare hands," I pointed out. "That would have been righteous theater, too."

"He'd never do something like that," Boyd scoffed. "He's not violent."

"Don't be so sure. Dangerous things can happen when a man starts believing his own clippings."

Boyd narrowed his laser eyes at me. "Sure you're not manipulating him yourself?"

"Me? Why would I want to do that?"

"To get back at the people who made him and unmade you."

I tugged at my ear. "Interesting thought. Total bullshit, but interesting bullshit. You gave me the impression before that Skitsy would like to see him fall on his ass. Why, because he left her for another publisher?"

"That's part of it."

"What's the rest of it?"

He laughed. "Maybe some night when I'm feeling good and loaded, I'll tell you."

"And this thing with Delilah—how long has it been going on?"

He shot me a surprised look. "He told you?"

"Not exactly."

"Then how did—?"

"I have my methods."

Boyd glanced over at Cam, who was still at the window with Charlie, and then at Delilah, who was by the buffet table chatting with Frank and Kathie Lee Gifford.

"They bumped into each other in my office a few weeks ago," he said. "He was smitten on sight—like somebody hit the poor fucker over the head with a tuning fork. But it won't last. Skitsy's putting her on a national publicity tour in a couple of weeks. By the time she gets back, he'll have forgotten all about her—if I know him. And believe me, I do."

Ah, but the evening was still young, and so were we.

No literary night on the town could be complete without a stop at Elaine's, longtime Second Avenue stronghold of bookdom's heavy hitters, and the saloon where Lulu once had her very own water bowl. A few of us roared up there in the Loveboat after the *Gotham Princess* docked a little before midnight—Cam and Charlie, Boyd and Delilah, Todd and me.

John John's mommy, Jackie, was at Elaine's that night with Mike Nichols and Diane Sawyer. So were the usual gang—the Plimptons and Taleses and Vonneguts. Ed Doctorow, Joe Heller. It felt strange being back in Our Place. Elaine was a good sport about it. She made a real fuss over Lulu, who went looking for her bowl, only to come right back, confused, when she couldn't find it.

Elaine flushed with embarrassment. "Sorry, Hoagy. It's been so long since you three . . . I'll put another one down for her right away."

I asked her not to.

We were seated at a big table toward the back. Lulu lay under my chair, sniffling from Delilah's perfume. Delilah made sure she sat right next to Cam. She'd gotten a bit high from all the attention and champagne she'd been lapping up, and somewhat less discreet. She was chattering away gaily to Cam and Cam alone, touching him on the arm, her face aglow, her eyes dancing. He was nodding and smiling. His eyes never left hers. Both of them were

BE F. SCOTT FITZGERALD

oblivious of Charlie, who sat between Todd and me, not missing a thing. Dumb she wasn't. Or inhuman. Maybe she believed she had no right to control her big blond genius. But she sure as hell didn't feel it. She sat there stiffly, her eyes shining like wet stones.

I didn't like this. Not one bit.

We had just ordered our drinks when Tanner Marsh, dressed in a fresh poplin suit, walked in the door with Skitsy Held.

The place suddenly got very quiet. Everyone in Elaine's was staring at them. The evening's news had traveled fast.

Tanner got pale when he spotted us. He and Skitsy began murmuring to each other.

"This should be interesting," observed Todd quietly.

"Hey, should I invite them to join us?" wondered Boyd.

"No, no, let's wait and see what they do," exclaimed Delilah as Elaine rushed over to them.

They didn't walk out. They allowed Elaine to seat them at a table as far from us as possible, Skitsy exchanging grim hellos with the regulars as she passed by them. Slowly, the room's usual level of urbane chatter returned.

Elaine worked her way by our table. "No trouble tonight, Cameron," she pleaded, shooting a nervous look over at Tanner.

Charlie put a fresh roll of film in her camera.

I expected Tanner to retaliate. He was a critic. A critic is someone accustomed to having the last word. But I didn't expect him to retaliate in quite the way he had in mind.

When his drink came, Tanner downed it at once and struggled to his feet. Skitsy put out a hand to stop him, but the fat man shrugged it off and started toward us. Heads turned. The place got very quiet again. When he got to our table, Tanner stopped and stood over us, his eyes on Cam.

He said nothing, just stood there staring at Cam, his face an utter blank. Cam stared right back up at him.

Boyd broke the silence. "Evening, Tanner. Care to join us?"

In response, Tanner pulled a gun out of his jacket pocket, pointed it at Cameron Sheffield Noyes, and fired it.

Chapter Six

I'm quite certain Tanner would have killed his brilliant young discovery if I hadn't taken a swipe at his gun hand a split second before he fired. As it was, the bullet just took off the tip of Cam's left ear before it made a small, neat hole in the wall behind him.

Delilah screamed. Lots of people did. Others, Cam included, froze. Tanner just stood there dumbly, as if in shock. I pried the gun out of his hand and gave it to the bartender, who helped me hustle him out onto the sidewalk, where Tanner immediately threw up. Then he sat down on the curb and began to weep uncontrollably.

"Do you see?" demanded Skitsy Held, who had followed us outside. "Do you see what that boy does to people?"

"Yes," I replied. "And I see what they do to him."

"He's a cancer," she snarled. "He's terrible for publishing. Awful. And so are you for having anything to do with him."

I glanced over at the bartender, who was missing none of this, then back at Skitsy. "That's funny, I thought you said he was still your biggest star."

"You're wrong," she said, shaking her head. "It's not funny at all."

She and the bartender stayed outside with Tanner. Inside, a gynecologist who'd just written a best-selling diet book was bandaging Cam's ear. Elaine was calling the police and Cam was telling her not to.

"No harm, no foul," he said with remarkable calm, seemingly not at all fazed by his narrow brush with death. "The man simply got upset. Quite understandable. Let's just let it drop."

So Elaine put Skitsy and Tanner in a cab, and Cam bought the house a drink, and things went back to what passes for normal around there.

"Get it on film?" I asked a somewhat wide-eyed Charlie Chu as I took my seat.

"Missed it," Charlie replied, her voice quavering. Her glasses slid down her nose. She pushed them back up. "I guess I'm not very cool under fire."

"Who among us is?" I asked.

"You are, coach," Cam pointed out. "You're a genuine man of action. You surprised me."

"Not as much as I surprised myself," I said.

"I still think the dude oughta be put in jail," groused Boyd.

"Me, too," agreed Todd.

Cam shook his head. "Forget about it," he said firmly.

"But he tried to kill you, Cameron!" cried Delilah.

"That's where you're wrong," Cam said, throwing back his glass of tequila and motioning for another. "You can't kill something that's already dead."

· · ·

After a few more rounds at Elaine's we headed down to Sammy's, the boisterous Lower East Side steak house where everything comes drenched in garlic, and where things got even wiggier.

It was hot and crowded and incredibly noisy in there, even at two A.M. on a weeknight. Waiters rushed about with Fred Flintstone-sized platters of sizzling meat. Patrons took turns at the microphone singing Billy Joel songs off-key to the accompaniment of the house piano player.

We sat around a big round table laden with eggplant salad, pickles, bread, and seltzer siphons. We were one less. Todd, who had to be at work on time, had headed home. Lulu stretched out under me, grunting sourly. She hates it when I eat garlic. My own feeling is anybody who eats canned mackerel has no right to comment about somebody else's breath.

There wasn't much on the menu for Charlie the vegetarian, but she wasn't exactly a woman of appetite by this point. She just picked quietly at some eggplant salad and glowered at Cam and Delilah, neither of whom seemed to care any longer that she was there, or that anyone else was. The two of them were gazing into each other's eyes, cooing into each other's ears, giggling, touching. Maybe it was the sight of Cam's hand resting there upon Delilah's. Maybe it was simply that everyone, no matter how forgiving, reaches a boiling point. Whatever, Charlie Chu turned very human when Delilah Moscowitz got up and flounced off to the ladies' room, twitching her tail. Not that Charlie was obvious about it. She waited a moment before she dabbed at her mouth with her napkin, excused herself, and followed Delilah in there. No one thought a thing of it, including me.

All I knew is one minute everyone in Sammy's was eating and drinking and making merry, and the next minute a horrifying scream was coming from the direction of the ladies' room.

Cam frowned and looked inquiringly over at Boyd, who suddenly got very busy with his steak. Neither of them budged. Not even after the second scream. It was I who paid the call. At full speed. The ladies' room door was locked. I threw my shoulder against it and immediately regretted it. Oh, the door popped open, all right, but so did something inside my shoulder.

The two of them were on the bathroom floor. Delilah was pinned flat on her back with Charlie astride her, clutching her by the throat and brandishing a big, ugly hunk of broken beer bottle before Delilah's terrified face.

"Stay away from him, you hear?" Charlie cried. "Stay away or I'll cut you! He's mine! *Mine!*"

"Hey, Blue Monday," I said softly from the doorway, rubbing my shoulder.

"Back off!" Charlie spat at me. "This is between me and her." She turned back to Delilah, holding the glass directly against her lovely white throat now. "Say it! Say you hear me!"

"I hear you, I hear you, you crazy bitch," gasped Delilah. "He's all yours. Now get the hell off me, will you?"

Charlie relaxed her hold. I immediately grabbed her by the scruff of the neck and pulled her up onto her feet. She didn't weigh much. I tossed her glass weapon in the trash.

By this time the singular object of their affections had come reeling in, jacket rumpled, ear bandaged, blue eyes glazed, a full bottle of beer in one hand, his half-eaten steak in the other. He looked down at Delilah, whose leather miniskirt was hiked up over her hips, then over at Charlie. Then he narrowed his eyes at me, not comprehending. "So what's . . . I mean . . . ?" Before he could say more, Charlie snatched him impatiently by the arm and stormed out, dragging him along like a large, docile child.

"You'll be sorry, you crazy bitch!" Delilah yelled after her from the floor. She lay there a moment, too drained to budge, then looked down at her state of undress and raised an eyebrow at me. "Wanna climb aboard, sailor?"

"That's it, Red. Don't lose your sense of humor. You okay?"

"Just fine," she replied, giving me her hand. "It so happens I love being assaulted on filthy public-bathroom floors."

"Look on the bright side," I said, hoisting her to her feet. "You can get a column out of this—*sharp* advice on how to steal someone else's man."

"He's not someone else's," she retorted, scowling.

"I could have sworn someone else thought so."

She looked herself over in the mirror, tossed her head. "Hey, it's not my fault she can't see the signs."

"Signs?"

"He's unhappy with her. No man who is happy with someone gets as bombed as he does all of the time."

"And you think you can make him happy?"

She turned and faced me, hands on her hips. "No offense, but what business is this of yours?"

"Everything about Cam Noyes is my business now, whether I like it or not."

She thought that over. "You want the truth?"

"Generally."

"If I lose Cam Noyes, she won't have to slit my throat —I'll slit it myself." Delilah took a prescription bottle of tranks out of her purse and threw two of them down her throat. She had several such bottles in there. She had a small drugstore in there.

"Pills are somewhat neater," I countered.

"Not after they get done pumping out your stomach they aren't," she said.

"That sounds suspiciously like the voice of experience."

"Let's just say that this reporter doesn't have it as totally together as her readers think she does," Delilah confided. "And who am I to shatter their illusions." She got her brush out of her purse and went to work on her hair, glancing at me in the mirror. "What, no smart remarks?"

"Not from me. I've spent too much time in too many glass houses."

Her eyes softened. "You're a sensitive man, aren't you?"

"Yeah, I'm an utterly modern kind of guy. What kind is Cam?"

"Everything I've ever wanted—tall, blond, handsome, brilliant, tragic, a bit dangerous. Cam Noyes is the man of this fat, insecure, manic-depressive Jewish princess's dreams."

"You're not my idea of fat."

"I used to weigh a hundred and sixty-four pounds," she informed me. "I work out at a Nautilus club three hours every day to look like I do now. I live on popcorn and cranberry juice and a host of artificial chemicals. You also happen to be looking at somewhat less than half of my original nose. Christ, why am I telling you all of this?"

"I asked."

She admired the curve of her throat in the mirror and swallowed. "Charlie wouldn't really hurt me, would she?"

"Hard telling. Personally, I wouldn't test her, but I scare easy—all part of the modern-guy thing."

"God, how trashy." She started out of the bathroom, stopped, and looked around. Then she swiveled on one foot in a Tina Turner gyration and cried out, "And don't you just love it?"

The oomph kind of went out of the evening after that. I drove the happy couple home to Gramercy Park in the Loveboat. They rode beside me on the front seat. Lulu snoozed in the back. She was still sniffling, which was not a good sign. It was late. The streets were as quiet as they ever get. Very few cars, aside from the occasional cab whisking late-nighters from one club to another. No one was out walking.

We rode in silence until Charlie said to Cam in a soft, halting voice, "I got so scared when Tanner tried to . . . and then when you and she . . . I don't know what I'd do if I lost you."

"Not going to lose me," he assured her thickly. "Just being nice to her because Boyd asked me to. Strictly business. Not as if I'm planning to bang her or anything."

"Honest?" she asked, wanting desperately to buy into it.

"Honest." He put his arm around her. She cuddled into him, relieved.

"Sorry if I made you mad," she said.

"Mad is not how you made me feel."

"How did I . . . ?"

He took her hand and pressed it due south of his equator. "That's how."

She groaned and climbed into his lap, her arms around his neck. Her mouth found his. They did very little talking after that.

I kept my eyes on the road and my hands upon the wheel. My shoulder ached and I had the taste of garlic and self-loathing in my mouth. I wanted no part of this job. Cam Noyes was a liar and a cheat and a mess. His women were ouchboxes of exposed nerve endings. His best friend was a featured selection of the Reptile of the Month Club. And I was quickly turning into his silent accomplice. I wanted no part of it. What I wanted was out. But I knew I wouldn't get out. Because there was something about Cam Noyes. Maybe it was the fear and vulnerability and torment I saw beneath his golden surface. Maybe it was the kinship between us—of upbringing, of art, of boy wonderdom and the burden that went with it. Maybe it was just that he knew how to make great tables. Whatever it was, I knew I wouldn't get out. Because Cam Noyes desperately needed someone, and that someone was me.

At Eighteenth and Third, Charlie abruptly rolled off his lap and sat there glaring straight ahead, chin raised, mouth drawn tight. I glanced across her at my celebrity—he was out cold, his head back on the seat, snoring softly. All of the tequila and coke had finally caught up with him.

"Sorry," I said to her.

"Don't say another word about it," she snapped.

So I didn't.

The lights were on in the town house.

"Ah, good," I said. "Vic has arrived from Los Angeles."

"How did he get in?" Charlie wondered.

"He has a way with locks," I replied as she started to rouse Cam. "Oh, don't worry about him. Vic will take over now."

"But—"

"Trust me."

We found him in the kitchen unpacking a new microwave oven. A set of dishes, pots and pans, bags of provisions, were piled everywhere. Coffee was perking on a new hot plate. James Mason was reading *The Third Man* by Graham Greene on a cassette player. Vic Early, show biz bodyguard extraordinaire, was getting settled.

He was a balding, sandy-haired giant in slacks and a striped polo shirt. He stood six feet six and weighed 250 pounds, little of it fat. A couple of decades before he'd been a star offensive lineman for the UCLA Bruins. The Rams drafted him in the first round. He chose the Marines instead and went to Vietnam, where he took some shrapnel in the head. He has a plate in his skull. Sometimes it gives him trouble—he sees red. I know this because he once rearranged my face and rib cage. But he hasn't actually killed anyone, as far as I know, and most of the time he's extremely mild-mannered.

Lulu was delighted to see him again. The feeling was mutual. He got down on his knees to say hello and rub her ears with his big football-scarred mitts. She rolled over on her back, her tail thumping, tongue lolling out of the side of her mouth.

"Whew," said Vic, making a face. "Still eating that fish of hers, huh?"

"That she is."

"Got in a little after midnight," he informed me in his droning monotone. "Found an all-night appliance store over on Broadway and Fourteenth. That's one of the great things about New York. Picked up some things I thought we'd need. Receipts are on the fridge."

"Say hello to Charleston Chu, your hostess."

"Quite a place, miss," he observed, gently taking her tiny hand. "I assumed the guest room is for me."

"It is," said Charlie, looking up warily at the hugeness of him. "And welcome."

"Thank you. That art up there yours?"

"It is."

"Keep at it. With some training you could get somewhere. Who knows, maybe even sell some of it."

She smiled. "Thank you."

"Your illustrious host," I advised him, "is in the car."

Vic nodded grimly. "Right." Then he hitched up his slacks and lumbered out the front door.

He returned a moment later dragging Cam Noyes facedown along the floor by one ankle. When he got him into the kitchen, Vic flopped him over onto his back, coughing and gasping. He was wet and muddy head to toe, and he didn't smell too hot.

"My God!" exclaimed Charlie. "What happened to him?"

"I brought him in by way of the gutter, miss."

"The *what?*" she demanded. "Why?"

"He's a drunk," Vic replied simply. "That's where drunks belong."

Charlie crinkled her small nose. "But he smells like—"

"That unpleasant odor is dog dooty, which is what the gutter smells like—no offense, Miss Lulu. Great set of wheels, by the way."

"Wait just one second here," ordered Charlie, glaring up at him, hands on her hips, eyes hard. "Who are you? What are you? I demand an explanation."

Vic ducked his head and scuffed at the floor with a big foot.

"Vic Early," I explained, "is the world's largest nanny."

"Someone please tell me," mumbled Cam from the floor, "why I smell so overwhelmingly like shit?"

"We'll talk about it in the morning, you bum," Vic said coldly.

Cam squinted up at him. "Who're you?"

"He seems to be your new nanny," said Charlie.

"You say nanny?"

"I did," she said, pushing her glasses up her nose.

Cam giggled. "Stupendous—always wanted a nanny."

"Naturally," said Vic, his big square jaw stuck out. "Because you're a big baby."

He went down the steep stairs into the basement. By the time he came back up carrying a painter's drop cloth, Cam was out cold again. Vic rolled him up in the drop cloth, then threw all two hundred pounds of him over one shoulder as if he were a lap rug.

"You'll be wanting to use the guest room yourself to-night, miss," he told Charlie. "I'll sleep down here."

"How come?" she wondered.

"I want him to wake up tomorrow in these clothes,"

he replied. "I want him to know just what a drunken bum smells like in the morning."

She thought this over for a moment. Then her face broke into a dimply smile. "Whatever you say, Mr. Early. I'll strip the bed—no sense ruining a good quilt." She started up the stairs.

"Good thinking, miss," Vic agreed, following with Cam over his shoulder. "But you'd best step lively. I think he's about to upchuck."

Vic came down alone a few minutes later and poured us coffee. We sat in two of the shell-backed metal chairs in the living room. He fit into his like an elephant in a teacup.

"I didn't know there was a girl," he said unhappily.

"There may not be for long—it's stormy."

"She's a real doll," he observed, sipping his coffee.

"She is. And made of solid steel."

"Really? Wouldn't think so to look at her."

"No, you wouldn't," I agreed, trying to remember the last time a woman had fought for me like she had for Cam that evening. Actually, no woman ever had, unless you count the time Merilee poured that brandy alexander down the back of Sigourney Weaver's dress when she caught the two of us flirting at the *Hurly Burly* opening-night bash. But that was kidding around. Charlie wasn't kidding.

"I've always liked the Asian women," Vic said. "They have a strong sense of loyalty. Clean personal habits, too. Though I can't say much for this one's housekeeping. Place is my idea of a shambles."

"It's called Found Minimalism, I'm told."

"It's minimal, all right." He shifted gingerly in his chair, which shifted with him. "You want him totally clean?"

"As clean as possible. A few more months like this and he'll end up a casualty."

"You can count on that. How far can I go?"

"Try not to disfigure him beyond recognition. His face is his livelihood until he starts writing again. Assuming he ever does."

"He will," Vic said firmly. "I'll get him on a regular schedule starting tomorrow. Up at eight. Run him around the park a few times. Rub him down. Start him on a proper diet."

"Fine. He and I will work here in his study, ten to six. That's when I'd like you to watch Merilee. During the day is when she's most vulnerable."

"Your ex-wife?" asked Vic, frowning. "To what?"

I told him about the threat I'd received. "Probably just hot air," I admitted. "But . . ."

"Can't afford to take a chance," he agreed gravely.

"Don't crowd her. It would be better if she didn't know you were guarding her."

"Not to worry," he assured me. "She'll never know I'm there."

I got wearily to my feet and handed him an envelope. "For your first week. Glad you're here, Vic."

"This isn't coming out of your end, is it?"

"No chance. I don't like you that much."

He grinned and pocketed it without opening it. "You won't be sorry, Hoag."

"Sorry never entered my mind."

My apartment door was half open.

The lock was untouched. Instead, they'd sledgehammered a fist-sized hole clean through the plaster wall next to the door, reached in, and unlocked it from the inside. A burglary gang had worked its way through the neighborhood a few years before doing just that. The cops called them the Hole-in-the-Wall Gang. I hadn't known they were back.

I stood there on the landing and stared at the hole and

the plaster dust heaped there on the floor, my heart pounding. There were no lights on inside the apartment. I looked down at Lulu. Lulu, keen huntress, was looking up at me and sniffling and showing no interest in going in. I really was going to have to get a bigger dog, preferably a meat eater with good sinuses.

I took a deep breath and let it out slowly. Then I pushed the door open all the way and went inside.

The stereo and television were still there.

The leather-and-fur greatcoat that I got in Milan was hanging in the narrow hall closet. My silver cuff links were in their jewelry box in the bedroom.

Nothing of value had been taken. Nothing had even been touched.

Only my Olympia, my beloved late-fifties vintage manual portable, the heavy steel one that is the Mercedes 300 SL Gull Wing of typewriters, and is much, much more than that to me. It is my gallant steed. It was with me in the Périgord Valley when the first draft of *Our Family Enterprise* came. It was with me in Skye and San Miguel de Allende when nothing came. And it was with me in that little stone cottage in the Tuscan hills when I ate pasta drenched in native extra-virgin olive oil and drank Brunello di Montalcino, and *Such Sweet Sorrow* came. It had been through heaven and hell with me, and now it sat there pounded into utter submission—its body smashed, its keys crushed, its workings ruined. You can do a lot of damage to a typewriter with a sledge—even the toughest typewriter in creation. Another magazine picture of Merilee had been left in its dented roller. So had another message written in those press-on letters. *Her face is next.*

I stood there staring down at it and thinking about something someone had said earlier that evening: *This man should no longer be allowed to own or operate a typewriting machine. . . .*

It was Tanner Marsh who had said that. Tanner Marsh,

the man who'd said both Cam Noyes and Boyd Samuels would be sorry. Very sorry.

I picked up the phone and dialed Boyd Samuels and woke him up.

"Whuh . . . wha . . . ?" he mumbled.

"I'm not quitting. Put the word out." Then I hung up and went to bed.

Lulu snored on my head the whole night.

Chapter Seven

Tape #3 w/Cam Noyes recorded May 8 in his study. Sits at his writing table, one eye swollen shut, lower lip fat and oozing blood. Holds ice bag against lip. Hand shakes)

HOAG: Small shaving accident this morning, Cameron?

NOYES: That giant oaf made me get out of bed at dawn this morning and go *running* with him. Then he tried to get me to eat a large bowl of *oatmeal*. I was telling him what he could do with his *oatmeal* when suddenly his face got all red and he started rubbing his forehead real hard and breathing in these shallow gasps . . .

HOAG: I told you not to make him mad.

NOYES: Who is this crazy man, coach?

HOAG: Your bodyguard. He's here to guard your body from anyone who might do it harm—including you.

NOYES: He also threw my coke down the drain. Why would he do something so stupid? I'm just going to buy more.

HOAG: I wouldn't if I were you.

NOYES: I thought you weren't going to hassle me about the way I live.

HOAG: I'm not. He is.

NOYES: But you hired him.

HOAG: Actually, you're the one who's paying him.

NOYES: In that case, I want him out of here. He's fired.

HOAG: If you insist. But if he goes, I go.

NOYES: What?

HOAG: You heard me.

NOYES: *(silence)* What are you trying to do?

HOAG: My job, Cameron. You agreed to put yourself in my hands. This is part of the deal. See the newspapers this morning? *(sound of rustling)* Nice little item about you in Billy Norwich's column: "Observers say the association between acid-penned critic Tanner Marsh and his sizzling protégé, Cameron Sheffield Noyes, went out with a 'bang' last night at Elaine's. It seems Marsh was none too thrilled about the eye-opening experience Noyes had treated guests to earlier at the celebrity-studded pub party for Delilah Moscowitz's *Tell Delilah.*" . . . Why did you do it, Cameron? Why did you undress him like that?

NOYES: He was attacking you. You're my friend.

HOAG: That the only reason?

NOYES: What other reason would there be?

HOAG: Your reputation. Living up to it.

NOYES: Believe me, I'm not that calculating.

HOAG: Perhaps you're not. But Boyd is.

NOYES: You don't like him, do you?

HOAG: Tell me about the two of you coming to New York, about Columbia.

NOYES: I had no expectations, no plan. I was vague and rootless. Deep down inside, I'd gotten this feeling of wanting to write, this powerful feeling that I would in some way become a writer and make something beautiful and perfect out of what had happened to me. I didn't really know why I had it, or how to go about doing it, but being in a place that was *alive* seemed important to me. . . . Columbia, well, Morningside Heights is just a polite way of saying Harlem. A student got knifed on our street by a crack dealer the day we arrived. They stashed a bunch of us in a dorm over next to the river on a Hundred and fourteenth, Hudson Hall they called it. An utter hole. Walls were crumbling. My room was so small I had to close the door if I wanted to sit down at my desk. Overlooked the air shaft, which always smelled of garbage. Boyd started moving coke right away. Actually, one of his biggest customers was Todd, who lived in the suite upstairs from us. Shadowy, weird sort of kid. No friends. Used to sit alone in his room and get quietly bombed. Ended up having to leave school. Owed Boyd a lot of money.

HOAG: I guess that's what he meant by "personal problems."

NOYES: The advisers at Deerfield had warned us that college would be so hard. *(laughs)* They were dead wrong. We were stoned free—didn't have to go to class, didn't have to do the reading, didn't have some dickhead corridor master watching over us. We spent most of our time getting a real New York education. Riding the subways through Spanish Harlem at 4 A.M. Hanging out at the Mudd Club and CBGBs. Going to the Museum of Natural History on acid and watching the dinosaurs move. New York is the greatest place in the world for hanging out and collecting experiences. If you want to write, you have to come through here.

HOAG: And had you started?

NOYES: I was keeping a diary of sorts, sketches of our days and nights out that eventually formed itself into a collection of short stories. I submitted them second semester to Tanner to see if I could get into his creative writing class, which is world renowned. The man's a god on that campus. I hoped to learn at his feet. But he turned me down.

HOAG: Were you disappointed?

NOYES: Briefly, but then the modeling thing clicked for me, and that took care of any bruised feelings I might have had. I happened to be balling this black Barnard girl named Stacy who was a model with the Wilhelmina Agency. Lovely girl. She's in a soap now, plays a Rastafarian neuro-surgeon. Anyway, one time when I picked her up at her shoot, the photographer asked me if I modeled. When I said I didn't, he said I should, because I had "a very American heterosexual look." Stacy took me up to the agency with her, and they looked me over and shot some tests and signed me up. And that's how I became a model. I started going around town with my portfolio and sitting in a waiting room with two dozen guys who looked exactly like I did. I honestly can't tell you why I got picked over them, but I did. I started doing catalog work, and making righteous bucks. And then Ralph spotted me, and I became a member of his Lauren family, and what a strange, surreal trip that is. It's not just fashion to Ralph. He sees all of it—the clothes, the image, the presentation—as a story. The models are characters in that story. The photographer, Bruce Weber, would take us on location to some estate and we'd frolic about all day in Ralph's clothes before he'd ever start shooting. The idea was to capture the casual sponta-neity of family life. Or Ralph's image of family life, which is not, strictly speaking, real. I mean, that whole pseudo-English gentry thing—the models aren't those people. Buy-ing the clothes won't make anyone into those people. It's make-believe. *Ralph* is make-believe—he's really little Ralph Lifschitz of the Bronx. Fashion is a stupendous scam, coach. Maybe the ultimate scam. Boyd quickly got fascinated by it.

HOAG: Somehow that doesn't surprise me.

NOYES: Talked his way into Wilhelmina as a gofer for the summer after our freshman year—watched and listened, fetched coffee. That was his apprenticeship as an agent. He went right from it into publishing.

HOAG: Because you did?

NOYES: Because I did. . . . That was a great summer for us. He'd wangled us an illegal sublet of a great faculty apartment on Riverside. I modeled when I felt like it, wrote when I didn't. That was when I wrote *Bang*. Scribbled the entire first draft longhand in five days and nights on a coke binge. It was unvarnished stream of consciousness. I just let myself go, like cutting the ropes on a hot-air balloon. Who knows where it came from. I sure don't. When I was done, I passed out for twenty-four hours. Then I spent a couple of weeks polishing it and typing it up. The original manuscript came to a little under a hundred pages. I submitted it to Tanner in the fall, hoping once again to get into his class. This time he sent me a note summoning me up to his office. . . . He really is scary the first time you meet him—the antique rolltop desk, the framed correspondence on the wall from John Cheever and Bernard Malamud, the pipe, and the way he looks down his nose at you. I mean, the man can make you feel so incredibly insignificant without even trying.

HOAG: Oh, he's trying.

NOYES: He told me to take a seat. Then he sat down and very deliberately got his fucking pipe going and stared at me. And kept staring at me, not saying a word. Finally, he declared, in that voice of his, "Young Master Noyes, I am not impressed by your little manuscript." Just as I started shriveling in my chair he said, "I am . . . *awed.*" And with that Tanner Marsh fell to his knees before me and kissed my shoes. He really kissed them. And then he clutched me by the ankles and said, "From this day forward, I am your humble servant. Use me."

(end tape)

(Tape #4 w/Cam Noyes recorded May 10 in his study. Sips iced herbal tea, fiddles with bowie knife)

HOAG: You look well rested today.

NOYES: Couldn't help that. Vic insisted on coming to dinner with Boyd and me last night, like some kind of chaperon. I half expected him to cut my meat for me.

HOAG: He would have, if you'd asked him nice.

NOYES: At the stroke of midnight he said to me, "Let's go." I said, go where? He said, "Home." When I refused, he dragged me out of the restaurant like I was some kind of dog. I was still so wide-awake I started reading *The Great Gatsby*. I'm really enjoying it. Thanks for getting it for me.

HOAG: My pleasure.

NOYES: Fitzgerald wrote so gracefully and beautifully. I'm actually kind of surprised he's compared to me.

HOAG: He's not. You're compared to him.

NOYES: You're right. Sorry.

HOAG: Just a meaningless label, anyway. The new F. Scott Fitzgerald. The new Willie Mays. That's the only way the press knows how to deal with someone who's entirely special.

NOYES: I promised Boyd I'd talk to you about . . . Well, he's concerned over what I have to say about Tanner and Skitsy. He thinks some of it might not be so great for my image. You know, not flattering.

HOAG: Candor is always flattering.

NOYES: I know, but he said Tanner and Skitsy could just deny it anyway.

HOAG: Absolutely. I intend to give them that chance.

NOYES: You do?

HOAG: I do. A memoir that acknowledges the other side of the story is always richer and more intelligent for it.

NOYES: I see . . .

HOAG: Look, Cameron. You're an author, not a talk show host. Forget about image. That's how you got blocked up.

NOYES: I know, coach, but what would happen if I . . . if I didn't go along with you on this one?

HOAG: Same thing that would happen if you fired Vic.

NOYES: You're a hard man to please.

HOAG: It's true. Don't ever go to a movie with me.

NOYES: I don't know what to do. (*pause*) I want to please Boyd . . .

HOAG: It's not Boyd's book. It's yours.

NOYES: I know, I know. It's just that I also want *you* to respect me, and it seems I can't win either way. I lose your respect if I don't tell you what really went on . . . and I lose it if I *do*.

HOAG: As long as you tell the truth, you'll have my respect.

NOYES: You mean it?

HOAG: I mean it.

NOYES: (*silence*) Okay, coach. We'll try it your way.

HOAG: Good man. When we left off, Tanner Marsh was on his knees.

NOYES: Yes, telling me I was a genius. So I said, "You're accepting me for your class?" And he said, "Absolutely not. The last thing a talent such as yours needs is to be polluted by sitting around a table with a dozen pimply kids ranting on about their creative cores. What you need is a great editor. You need me!" He said he wanted us to work together on the manuscript. Focus it, broaden it, take out some of the self-indulgence. And then submit it to a certain publisher who he knew would share his enthusiasm—actually publish it.

HOAG: How did this make you feel?

NOYES: I was flattered, naturally.

HOAG: Not good enough. Dig deeper.

NOYES: (*silence*) As if all of it—the pain, the loneliness, the apartness—had been worth enduring. Because they had forged me. Made me into *someone*. I remember thinking I'd like to send a copy to Kirsten's mother when it came out, inscribed with the words "Fuck you." Is that better?

HOAG: Somewhat.

NOYES: Tanner worked with me every evening in his office for the next couple of weeks, talking over the manuscript page by page. He was incredibly helpful. He knew exactly where I needed to go, even though I didn't know myself. For all of his bullying and grossness, the man really does know a manuscript. The murder-suicide thing at the end was actually his idea. I'd originally left it very vague as to what happens with the gun. He convinced me I was wrong. When we finished going over it, he asked me how long it would take me to rewrite it. I told him modeling was basically how I paid my way, and between it and the occasional class I didn't think I could finish until maybe Christmas. He said that was no good, we had to strike at once because my age was such a plus. He puffed away on his pipe a minute and said, "Young Master Noyes, you've just been named a New Age writing fellow." I was *stunned*. Some of the major authors of the past twenty years had won New Age fellowships. It meant stupendous prestige. More to the point, it meant ten thousand dollars. He said he could arrange immediate residency for me at the Stony Creek Writers Colony in Vermont. He encouraged me to take a leave from school, go up there, and finish the book as soon as possible. So I did. He drove me up there. It was a lovely autumn day. The leaves were just starting to turn. An editor who happened to be visiting one of her authors up there rode along with us.

HOAG: Her name would be Skitsy Held?

NOYES: That's right. Tanner arranged it, of course. Skitsy was the editor he thought would share his enthusiasm for me.

HOAG: What did you think of her?

NOYES: She seemed hard-shell, but nice enough. The two of them spent most of the ride gossiping about people I'd never heard of. I nodded off. Of course, I had no idea then at the extent of their relationship, or how they operated.

HOAG: Let's talk about that.

NOYES: (*silence*) Tanner and Skitsy go back twenty-five years, back to when she was a blushing Barnard coed and he was an associate English professor. This was long before she had tits. Or at least the same exact pair we know today. (*laughs*) He was still married to his first wife at the time. Skitsy broke up the marriage, actually. His *New Age Fiction Quarterly* was in its infancy. When she graduated, he made her his teaching assistant and put her to work on it. She helped him start the New Age Writers Conference, which he still does for a week every summer in the Catskills. Ever go?

HOAG: Once, a few centuries ago.

NOYES: There are a number of writers' conferences now, but his was the first, and is still the biggest. The idea, as I'm sure you know, is to offer would-be writers from around the country a chance to rub shoulders with genuine New York publishers and hopefully sell them that Great American Novel they've been toiling on in their basement since 1946. He takes over a resort hotel in the Catskills for a week, and for a fee of what is now a thousand dollars, several hundred of these housewives and carpeting salesmen flock to it, manuscript in tow. He invites a dozen or so editors, literary agents, and big-name authors to come, and they do come. It's an excellent opportunity for them to promote their own books, and they usually get laid up there. There are cocktail mixers, seminars, panel discussions. Editors talk about what they look for in a manuscript. Authors say how they made it. The whole thing is a scam—not one new writer has ever been discovered at a New Age Writers Conference. But they keep flocking to it, and Tanner keeps getting rich off of it. He's really quite shrewd. By awarding fellowships to people like me, he's allowed to say the *Quarterly* is published by a nonprofit foundation. That's entirely legitimate, since the magazine never makes any money. But the conference does. Lots of it. He claims that the profits from it underwrite the fellowships. They don't. He pockets them. Keeps an entirely bogus set of books. Walks away with about fifty thousand dollars a year from the foundation, tax free.

HOAG: Which he stands to lose when this is published.

NOYES: Yes. I suppose he will.

HOAG: How do you know all of this?

NOYES: I'll get to that. Eventually, Skitsy became a very successful editor. She and Tanner married and divorced. Though the divorce was ugly, their greed still cements them together. Thanks to the *Quarterly* and to his own horn-blowing, Tanner enjoys an enviable reputation for discovering new writers. He steers a lot of them her way. It's a good deal for her because she knows he'll excerpt them in the *Quarterly*, which is the Good Housekeeping Seal of Hype for a first novel. Guarantees a review in the *New York Times*. If the *Times* review is good—and how can it not be if Tanner's writing it—then the other newspapers and the newsmagazines and the book clubs will fall into line. Then Skitsy can start taking out ads. For another ten grand she can buy her way onto the Walden's Recommended List, which gets her chain shelf-space, and from there it isn't far to the best-seller list. As a payback, she throws a nice finder's fee Tanner's way. See, Skitsy has her own little scam, and it's quite a beauty. She takes kickbacks. In the case of *Bang*, for instance, she offered $35,000. That's good money for a first novel by an unknown. I only saw $25,000 of it. Boyd had to give ten of it back to her, and she split that with Tanner. Not huge stakes, but they can be. In the case of Delilah's book, she offered Boyd $250,000 with the understanding that $50,000 came back to her. She's put away a couple of million tax free through the years that way.

HOAG: Doesn't her company get suspicious?

NOYES: Murray Hill Press is one of the last of the small independent houses, and she's the boss. As far as anyone there knows, the only thing she's guilty of is overpaying, which is no problem since her titles almost always make money. Other publishers hate her because she's inflated prices across the board to accommodate her kickback, though most of them don't really know *why* she's inflated them. The agents do. Some of them won't stand for it—the older ones in particular. She steers around them, does business with the ones who will, like Boyd, and steers clients their way. She *is* worth it. She makes authors a lot of money. And it's not like they're getting ripped off. Her company is the one that is.

HOAG: I think I understand now how Boyd pried you away from her—he threatened to tell the Internal Revenue Service, didn't he?

NOYES: No, he was much more creative than that. Boyd's an artist, coach. Want to know how he did it?

HOAG: Do tell.

NOYES: Skitsy signed me up for a second book before *Bang* came out. A smart investment on her part. She was able to get me for a modest $50,000. I was able to get an advance. Who knew the book would go through the roof? When it did, I was worth ten times what she'd paid. Naturally, Boyd was dying to get me out of it. But how? She had a signed contract. So what he did was tell her I was suffering from acute anxiety brought on by the sudden success of *Bang*, and couldn't write. He told her I felt incredibly pressured by a signed contract, that I needed to work just like I had before—on spec, no pressure. He proposed that we return the advance to her and that she tear up the contract —all of this strictly for the benefit of my delicate artist's psyche, mind you—and then when I had written a few chapters we'd submit it to her and sign a new deal on the same exact terms. Word of honor. She agreed to it. We gave her back the advance. She tore up the contract. Boyd sold my second book to another house for a million and there wasn't a thing she could do about it. Strictly legal.

HOAG: I wouldn't have expected her to fall for that.

NOYES: Let's say she was somewhat blinded by personal considerations.

HOAG: What kind of personal considerations?

NOYES: (*silence*) Skitsy Held has . . . she has this itch for young writers. And I was scratching her itch, okay?

(*end tape*)

(*Tape #5 w/Cam Noyes recorded May 12 in his study*)

HOAG: I can't believe you did this, Cameron.

NOYES: Were you really surprised?

HOAG: What, to walk into my apartment and find *your* writing table sitting here? Of course I was surprised.

NOYES: Big Vic and I took it uptown in the back of the Olds after work yesterday. He was planning to pick your lock until we discovered that giant hole in your—

HOAG: I can't accept it, Cameron.

NOYES: You said you liked it.

HOAG: I do. But you spent hundreds of hours making it. It's a work of art. It's *yours.*

NOYES: Not anymore. Besides, I can always make another. In the meantime, this old workbench will suit me fine. Your apartment is awfully dreary, coach. Why don't you get a nicer one?

HOAG: I tried once. It didn't work out. Are you sure about this?

NOYES: Positive. I want you to have it.

HOAG: Thank you, Cameron. I'll cherish it.

NOYES: Don't cherish it. Write on it.

HOAG: I'm interviewing Skitsy tonight.

NOYES: Maybe I should come with you.

HOAG: I'd rather you didn't. I'll get more out of her if I'm alone.

NOYES: Whatever you think is best, coach.

HOAG: So when did your thing with her start? At Stony Creek?

NOYES: Yes, it started then. In its own way. (*pause*) Stony Creek turned out to be the former country estate of a railroad millionaire, this huge, gothic mansion surrounded by five hundred acres of sugar maples, and dotted with a couple of dozen little cabins, one writer-in-residence to each. Dinner was a communal affair in the main hall. Breakfast and lunch were delivered to your cabin in baskets. No distractions. No TV. No radio. Nothing to do but work. Tanner headed back to New York after dinner. Skitsy stayed over for the night in the main hall. I unpacked my things, sharpened my pencils, got into bed early, anxious to get an early start the next day. I had just closed my eyes when there was a tapping at my cabin door. I opened it to discover Skitsy standing there with a flashlight and a bottle of wine. Said she couldn't sleep in a strange place and would I invite her in for a drink. So I did. She sat down on my bed and told me how anxious she was to read my manuscript, because Tanner had told her how very talented I was. Naturally, I was thrilled. She was an important editor. We worked our way through the wine, and we talked, and before long I realized her hand was on my leg. I was at Stony Creek to work, not fuck around, especially with a middle-aged woman who I wasn't particularly attracted to. I told her so. I wasn't tactful about it. She left in a huff. I tried to sleep, but I couldn't. I didn't like what had happened. I didn't like being there. At dawn I packed up and hitched a ride out of there due south on I-91, all the way down through Connecticut to New Haven, then another one east on I-95 to Old Lyme. There's a general store a few miles up Route 156 where I got provisions and some freshwater lures. Also a small marina where I rented a rowboat. I put it in Crescent Moon Pond and started rowing. I hadn't been to the shack since Smiling Jack died and it became mine. The mooring was rotted out. I had to tie the boat to a tree.

Kids had been using the place for beer parties. There were empties everywhere, windows busted out. There were a few sticks of furniture. A framed, mounted copperhead skin on the wall. Smiling Jack had found it coiled in one of his wading boots one morning. There's no electricity or running water. Just a well out back with a hand pump. I chopped some wood and made a fire in the stove. Rigged up a makeshift rod and reel and caught myself a perch for dinner. I spent three weeks there in my little shack. Probably the three happiest weeks of my life. I worked all day. Swam for miles at dusk in the cold, clear pond. Fished. Spoke to no one. Grew a beard. When my rewrites were finished, I rowed back out and caught a train for New York. Called Tanner as soon as I got home to tell him I was done, all excited. He wouldn't have been chillier. Told me he'd terminated my fellowship. When I asked him why, he said I'd violated it by running off without submitting a written application. He told me I was uncooperative and obviously not committed to my work, and then he hung up on me. I couldn't believe it. Tanner wanted nothing more to do with me. I told Boyd, and he couldn't believe it either. He said I must have done something else to warrant getting dumped. I told him about the night in the cabin with Skitsy. He looked at me like I was some kind of naive jerk. That's when I kind of realized what Tanner meant by uncooperative. I had been expected to sleep with her. It was part of the deal. A rite of literary passage, if you will, and I'd refused to pay the toll. . . . I don't know, maybe it was all of those weeks alone, but I went into a blind rage. Stormed straight downtown to her office without shaving or changing clothes. Barged right past the reception desk, locked her door behind me, threw her down on the sofa, and fucked her. There was nothing gentle or quiet about it, and she couldn't have loved it more. Took the rest of the day off. Dragged me up to her apartment, where we did a lot more deliciously nasty things to each other. The next day Tanner asked to see my revised manuscript. A week later Skitsy Held made an offer on it. I asked Boyd to act as my agent. I didn't trust anyone else. (*silence*) I suppose you think less of me now.

HOAG: What would have happened if you hadn't slept with her?

NOYES: I'll never know, will I? All I know is I wasn't going to let sex get in the way of my literary future. It just isn't that important to me. I mean, it's important, but it's not sacred or precious or anything. . . . You give people what they want, the world opens up to you.

HOAG: That's your philosophy of life?

NOYES: That's reality. I gave Skitsy what she wanted. So what if it was sick and perverted and—

HOAG: And is still going on?

NOYES: (*pause*) How did you know that?

HOAG: You just told me.

NOYES: You're awfully slippery. Would have made a damned good lawyer.

HOAG: And my parents very proud. Actually, it's that red lipstick Lulu found under your bed the day we met. Skitsy's color. Hers, wasn't it?

NOYES: You mean you've known about us all along?

HOAG: Let's say I've suspected. So that's how you know about her and Tanner's little schemes?

NOYES: Yes. Pillow talk. She tends to get blabby afterward.

HOAG: Does she know yet about you and Delilah?

NOYES: What about us?

HOAG: Don't kid a kidder.

NOYES: No, I don't think she does.

HOAG: What would happen to their editorial relationship if she found out?

NOYES: It wouldn't be enhanced. Skitsy is definitely the jealous type, and vindictive as hell.

HOAG: Delilah knows about you and her?

NOYES: Yes.

HOAG: She must like to play with fire.

NOYES: She does. She believes danger heightens the intensity of the female orgasm.

HOAG: Does it?

NOYES: (*laughs*) It certainly doesn't reduce it in her case.

HOAG: Why don't you break it off with Skitsy?

NOYES: What makes you think I want to?

HOAG: Something about the words "sick," "perverted" . . .

NOYES: I happen to be into that. The fact is I'm total scum. Don't ever introduce me to your sister.

HOAG: Haven't got one.

NOYES: Good.

HOAG: I repeat, why are you still seeing Skitsy? (*no response*) Does she have something on you?

NOYES: Like what?

HOAG: You tell me. Why does she own you?

NOYES: She doesn't own me.

HOAG: Bullshit. What is it? Tell me!

NOYES: There's nothing to tell!

HOAG: There *is!* You're holding out on me—I can see it in your eyes. What is it? (*no response*) Damn it, Cameron! I *won't* collaborate on a whitewash, you hear me!

NOYES: (*silence*) I hear you.

HOAG: Then decide what you want. And let me know. Until you do, we have nothing more to say to each other.

NOYES: But coach—!

(*end tape*)

Chapter Eight

Tanner Marsh was naked again, this time on the canvas Charlie was working on in her studio when I came down the stairs from Cam's study. Tanner look frightened and vulnerable in the painting, like a turtle with his shell yanked off. He had no penis. She had given him a Bic pen there instead.

She worked intently in the late-day sun, often substituting her fingers for a brush. She had on an old, white, paint-splattered shirt, gym shorts, and clogs. There was yellow paint all over her nose from pushing her glasses up with her painted fingers.

"He'll look terrific hanging next to you at Rat's Nest," I observed.

She smiled wearily. "Thanks."

"Here." I took out my linen handkerchief and began to wipe the paint off her nose. "I'm afraid you're making better progress than we are."

Charlie's brow furrowed with concern. "Trouble?"

"The worst kind. He's hiding something from me."

Lulu stretched out between us. Charlie kicked off a clog and rubbed Lulu's ears with her toes.

"Don't take it personally," she said. "He hides things from everyone."

"Even you?"

"Especially me. He *is* getting it on with that redheaded bitch, isn't he?"

I left that one alone. I wasn't going to lie for him.

"I'm leaving him," she announced quietly.

"Sorry to hear that. You want to be the one to tell Barbara Walters or shall I do it?"

"I'll finish these portraits. I won't allow this to jeopardize our project. But I'll finish them elsewhere."

"That's very professional of you," I said. "I don't know if I'd feel the same way in your shoes. In fact, I'm sure I wouldn't."

"I don't blame him," she explained. "He can't change the way he is. He's just making me too crazy. I don't like myself when I'm that crazy." She closed her eyes and shook her head. "God, what I've been through with him. You know one night I found him naked out there in the park, three in the morning, on his hands and knees, face bleeding, babbling incoherently, 'Dead inside. All of us are dead inside.' I had to drag him inside, patch him up, put him to bed. I won't anymore. I won't bring him home so he can go to another woman's bed. I'm not his mother." Her eyes searched my face. "Am I?"

"No, you're not."

"I just don't know what I'll do with myself," she said, her eyes locking onto mine now. "Alone, I mean."

"Oh, I wouldn't worry about that," I assured her.

With that, Lulu got up and went over to the stairs and sat with her back to us.

Charlie watched her and swallowed. "No?"

"No. I'd say you'll be alone for about as long as you feel like it, and no longer."

She reddened, "Are you . . . offering your services?"

"If I were, I'd have to go stand at the end of a long line."

"You could get right up to the front of it if you wanted to," she offered matter-of-factly.

I tugged at my ear. There was no idle flirting with this one. There was only the real thing. "You wouldn't want another writer. We reserve our best qualities for our lead characters. There's not much left over for real life."

"Oh." Disappointed, she pushed her glasses up her nose and got paint all over it again.

I sighed and dabbed at it again with my handkerchief. "What am I going to do with you?"

"You could hold me," she said, her eyes filling with tears.

I put my arms around her. She buried her face in my shirt and sobbed, shuddering violently. I held on to her. I liked holding on to her. When she was done, she held her face up to me, her cheeks wet. She wanted me to kiss her. I wanted me to kiss her, right on that little bud of a mouth. But I didn't. For me, there was still the matter of Merilee. There was also Lulu glowering at me threateningly from the stairs.

"Sorry," Charlie said, taking my handkerchief and wiping her eyes with it.

"No reason to be."

"Could we maybe have a drink sometime? Talk?"

"I'd like that," I replied. "I'll even teach you how to flirt."

"What for?" she wondered, frowning.

"For fun. Beats the hell out of dirty bathroom floors."

She offered me my handkerchief back. It was soaked with paint.

"Keep it," I insisted. "A gentleman always carries two."

Downstairs, Vic was running a vacuum in the parlor. He had on a chef's apron and his Sony Walkman, on which he was listening to Ian Carmichael read *Jeeves in the Offing* by P. G. Wodehouse. A pot of his chili bubbled on the hot plate in the kitchen.

When he saw me, he turned off the vacuum and the tape. "She got to the theater safe and sound, Hoag," he reported, pulling a small spiral notepad out of his apron pocket. "Let's see . . . had a visitor at her place from noon until two. Fellow named Ulf Johansson, former member of the Swedish Olympic bobsled team."

"Oh?"

"Now a personal fitness instructor. A lot of the Broadway stars use him."

"Oh."

Vic chuckled. It wasn't a pretty sound. "Still stuck on her, aren't you?"

"I'll ask the questions," I growled.

"At two she went out to the Fairway Market on Broadway to buy nectarines and skim milk," he droned. "Then she stopped at a newsstand for the current issue of *People* magazine. Also at the cleaners and the liquor store, where she bought two bottles of champagne. Dom Pérignon. Then she returned home. Didn't go out again until she left for the theater." He closed the notepad and put it away.

"Still no hostile contact from anyone?"

"None. Of course, I'm not tapping her phone. I can, if you want me to."

"Let's hold off on that. No reason to invade her privacy. At least not yet."

He went into the kitchen to stir his chili. I followed.

"How do you think our boy wonder is doing?" I asked.

"The man has a definite substance-abuse problem, Hoag. I've got him on two-a-day workouts and a good diet.

I'm letting him have two beers at dinner. We've had some episodes, but nothing I can't handle. I may be able to turn around the abuse problem. He's young. His bad habits aren't that deeply ingrained. Discipline and structure will do him a world of good. But . . ." Vic ran a big hand over the lower half of his face. "I get the feeling he may have a deeper problem. He's angry. Self-destructive."

"I've noticed."

"If that's the case, he'll need professional help to get him in touch with it."

"Any idea what it might be?"

"None." Vic tasted his chili, hesitated a moment, added more chili powder. "You?"

"No, but I sure would like to find out."

I walked uptown to Skitsy's apartment. The air was soft and warm. The tulips were blooming in the window boxes, and the spindly little sidewalk trees were beginning to leaf out. Lulu waddled along beside me wheezing slightly. Her sniffles seemed to be moving down into her chest now. A rottweiler. That's what I needed. Name of Butch.

A celebrity's story can keep changing right before a ghost's eyes. That's what was happening to me with Cam Noyes. His had turned faintly sleazy on me, and so had he. I can't say I was disappointed—you have to be expecting something of people to be disappointed by them. I was more puzzled. I couldn't figure him out. He could be an open, sensitive, and very appealing kid capable of fierce loyalty and tremendous generosity. He could also be a total louse, a cynical scam artist who thought nothing of hurting the people who cared about him, or dropping his pants for the ones who could help him. So which Cam was the real Cam? Who was he? What did he believe in? Why was he trying to destroy himself? Why was he still seeing Skitsy? What was he hiding? Questions. I had lots of them. That's the most frustrating part of writing a memoir. Whenever you dig close to a person's core, you begin to face a lot of questions like these and damned few answers. There aren't many when you're trying to figure out what makes another human being tick.

I was anxious to talk to Skitsy. Tanner, too, only he wasn't in for my calls and wouldn't return them.

Skitsy Held lived in the seven-figures district—the penthouse apartment of a fine prewar doorman building on Riverside and Seventy-second. The lady did okay on her fattened editor's salary. She did more than okay.

A bright green awning stretched from the building's front door to the curb, where polished brass posts anchored it to the sidewalk. I was just a few steps from the door when suddenly the awning tore sharply over my head and something exploded on the pavement next to me.

Something that had been a woman.

Skitsy Held had been anxious to talk to me, too. So anxious she didn't wait for the elevator.

They'd thrown a tarp over her, but it didn't hide the stream of blood down to the curb, or the high-heeled shoe lying twenty feet away. Two uniformed cops stood grim watch over the body. Several more had gone upstairs. Their blue-and-whites were nosed up to the curb, along with an ambulance. Passersby were clumped around the front of the building, gawking, talking. In another ten minutes someone would be selling hot dogs and sodas.

A walkie-talkie crackled next to me. One of the uniformed cops, a beefy young Irishman with red hair and a baby face, spoke into it. Then listened. Then looked at me. "You're the friend?"

"We had a business appointment."

"Go on up. Penthouse D."

The front door to her apartment was open. An Italian

racing bike was parked in the doorway. I slid past it into the living room, which was done up like a Pennsylvania farmhouse. Antique grandfather clock. Spinning wheel. Quilts on the walls. Oil portraits of dead Pilgrims. A pair of glass doors led out onto the terrace, where there was white wicker furniture and potted plants, and where two uniforms were talking to a short, stocky street kid who was chewing gum with his mouth open. He had on the uniform of a bike messenger—yellow tank top, electric-blue spandex shorts, wristbands, bicycle shoes and gloves.

All three of them looked up at the sight of Lulu and me in the terrace doorway.

It was the kid who said, "Yo, help ya, dude?"

I glanced uncertainly over at one of the uniforms, who nodded encouragingly at me. I turned back to the kid. His hands were on his hips now, his chin thrust somewhat defiantly up in the air.

"They sent me up from downstairs," I said to him. "I had an appointment with Miss Held."

"Oh, right." He came over to me. He was deeply tanned and had a lot of thick black hair and an earring and those soft brown eyes that some women get jelly knees over. I doubt he was more than five feet six, but his biceps and pecs rippled hugely and his thighs bulged in his racing shorts. He stuck out a gloved hand and said, "It's Very."

"It's very what?" I said, frowning.

"Very, *Very*. Romaine Very. Detective Lieutenant. It's my name, dude."

We shook. He had a small, powerful hand and an air of great intensity about him. His head kept nodding rhythmically, as if he heard his own rock 'n' roll beat.

"And you're, like, who?" he asked.

"Stewart Hoag. Make it Hoagy."

"As in Carmichael?"

"As in the cheese steak."

"Whatever." He popped his gum, glanced down at

Lulu, back up at me. "Know any reason why Miss Held did herself in?"

"She jumped?"

"What it looks like," he replied, nodding.

"Not offhand I don't."

"Any idea who her next of kin might be?"

"You might try Tanner Marsh. He's in the English department up at Columbia. They used to be married."

Very's eyes shot over to one of the uniforms, who went immediately inside to use the phone.

"Did she leave a note?" I asked.

He shook his head. "We're still looking."

"And no one was up here with her?"

"Doorman says she came home maybe three-quarters of an hour before it happened. Nobody else came or went. Neighbors didn't hear or see a thing. Not that they would—pretty private." He narrowed his eyes at me. "Why, you know something I don't know?"

"Possibly. It depends on what subject we're discussing."

He sighed, exasperated. "You got some reason to believe somebody was up here in the apartment with her?"

"No."

"Stay with me." He headed across the terrace over to the railing.

I stayed with him. The view of Riverside Park and the Hudson wasn't terrible. The sun was getting low now over the Jersey Palisades.

"Was riding my bike down there in the park on my supper break when I heard the commotion," Very explained. "Came on over."

"Hence the outfit?"

"Yeah. Hence the outfit."

"Sound like quite a zealous guy."

He laughed. "That's me. Zealous. Okay, check it out

. . . we make it she went over right about . . . here." He positioned himself at the railing. "No sign of a struggle. No fresh scratches in the paint on the railing, which would also tend to rule out any kind of accidental fall. Reads jump to me all the way."

I stood next to him and looked down over the railing. Twenty-three floors below, Skitsy Held was being loaded into the ambulance. One of the cops was dispersing the crowd on the sidewalk, another was directing traffic.

"Understand she was in publishing," Very said.

I said she was and gave him the name of her company.

"You a publisher, too?"

I tugged at my ear. "I'm a writer."

"Oh, yeah?" he said, nodding. "What kind?"

"Lately I've been ghosting memoirs."

"No shit," he said, impressed. "You do *Vanna Speaks?*"

"She shouldn't have."

"We oughta talk sometime, you and me. I got a million stories I could put in a book. Real-life stories about cases I been on. We oughta talk sometime."

"Now wouldn't be a good time."

"Whatever." He grinned at me, started back inside, stopped. "Stay with me."

I stayed with him. The living room opened into a den, where there were shelves of books and a glass case holding a collection of antique dolls, all of them staring at us.

"Spook the shit outta me," Very said, staring back at them. "If any of 'em says 'Where's mommy?' I'm outta here."

There was one dirty cup in the kitchen sink. Half a pot of coffee in the glass Melitta on the stove. Cold. Otherwise the kitchen was clean, the counter bare. Down the hallway was her bathroom. Very turned on the light. Pink was the dominant color statement. She had used the shower when she got home. It was still damp and fragrant in there. The towel draped over the rod was wet.

He poked open her laundry hamper with a finger. It was empty inside. He closed it and made a face. "Whew, I'd *swear* it smells like fish in here. Is it me?"

"No, it's Lulu." She stood between us in the small bathroom, panting and wheezing. "Isn't it a little odd for somebody to take a shower just before they commit suicide, Lieutenant?"

"Yo, if the lady *had* her act together, dude," he replied, one knee quaking impatiently, "she *wouldn't* a jumped, would she?"

I let him have that one.

Then I let him have my address and phone number and got the hell out of there.

I ordered a boilermaker at the Dublin House bar. Lulu showed me her teeth. I showed her mine. I look meaner. I ordered another.

The liquor didn't help. It didn't make the sight—or the sound—of Skitsy Held hitting the pavement any less vivid. Or troubling.

Romaine Very wasn't wrong. It all pointed the way he said it did. Skitsy came home from a hard day of wrestling with authors and agents—enough to drive anyone to suicide. She showered. She strolled out onto her terrace. She did her finest Greg Louganis impersonation. It could have happened that way, only I didn't believe it. The timing was much too convenient. I had been on my way up to talk to her. About her crooked business dealings. About what she had on Cam Noyes. Somebody had shut her up. Somebody had pushed her. The woman hadn't weighed more than a hundred pounds. Tanner Marsh could have done it easily. A good-sized man like Boyd Samuels easier still. There'd be no sign of a struggle, not if he acted quickly and decisively enough. She'd have no time to dig her nails into his arms, or to scream or to . . .

Maybe I was letting my imagination get the best of me. The doorman had said no one went in or out after Skitsy got home. Maybe Very was right.

I got change for a dollar from the bartender and called Cam's house from the pay phone. Vic answered. I told him he'd better put our boy on.

Vic hesitated, cleared his throat. "You didn't get my message?"

My stomach muscles tightened involuntarily. "What message?"

"I left it on your machine."

"What happened, Vic?"

"Cam gave me the slip, Hoag. Took his car and split."

"When?"

"Couldn't tell you exactly. I went up to his study maybe half an hour ago to let him know me and Charlie were going to sit down for chili. I made it vegetarian style, so she could eat it, too, you know? And he was gone. Don't know how he got past me."

"There's the iron veranda outside the studio windows," I suggested. "He might have gone out that way when Charlie was downstairs with you. Jumped down to the sidewalk."

"Could be. I sure feel lousy, Hoag. Like I let you down."

"Don't worry about it, Vic."

"Is there anything I can do?"

"Stay by the phone. I'll call you back." I sat there staring at the phone for a moment, wondering if it was as bad as it looked. Wondering if I was working for a murderer. I dialed Boyd's office. It was past seven but most agents work late hours. Todd Lesser answered.

"It's Stewart Hoag, Todd. Is he around?"

"Sorry, Hoagy. He's at the Algonquin wooing a prospective client. Big one. Anything I can help you with?"

"If you know Delilah's address and phone number, you can."

"How interesting," he said, amused. "I had a feeling you two would be—"

"Business, friend. Strictly business."

"Sure, sure."

He gave me the information. She lived in the Village, on West Twelfth. I thanked him. Then I asked him if he'd heard the news yet about Skitsy.

"Don't tell me she's finally forming her own company."

"Not exactly. She jumped off of her terrace a little while ago. She's dead."

Todd gasped. "Christ, Boyd will be . . . Hey, I'd better get a hold of him right away. Bye."

I got Delilah's phone machine. I hung up on it without leaving a message at the sound of the beep. Now you know —I'm that kind of person. I called Vic back and asked him to run down there to see if she and Cam were around. I told him I'd check back with him in thirty minutes.

I thought about heading down to the Racquet Club. My shoulder still ached. A rub wouldn't be the worst thing. But there wasn't anyone there I felt like talking to just now. Or listening to. Instead, I had a cab drop me at Cafe Un Deux Trois, a big, noisy Parisian bistro on the edge of the theater district. I had a Pernod and water at the bar. Then I tried Vic.

"She lives in a real nice brownstone," he droned. "Looks just like the building Kate and Allie lived in. She has the top floor. She didn't answer. Mail's still in the box. No sign of Cam's car. I checked the garages in a four-block—"

"If he were there, it would be parked right out front."

"He's not there. Nobody is. I persuaded her front door to open—just to make sure. You know she has a trapeze in her bedroom?"

"Good work, Vic. How's Charlie holding up?"

"She's in her studio, working with a vengeance."

"Give her some chili. Keep her cool, I'll check in later."

"You're seeing Merilee home?"

"As it were."

I took a table and split some mussels vinaigrette with Lulu. There was a jar of brightly colored crayons at my elbow. The tablecloth was of white paper. I wrote *SSH + MGN* on it in blue, then drew a big red heart around it, and an arrow through that. The middle *S* stands for Stafford. My mother's maiden name. Don't ask me to tell you what the *G* stands for. Merilee's middle name is a deep, dark secret. She hates it. She'd kill me if I told you. It's Gilbert.

After the mussels I tucked away steak frites and a bottle of Côtes du Rhône, and finished off with mousse au chocolat and an espresso. By the time I got over to the Martin Beck, the doors were opening and *The Petrified Forest* audience was starting to spill out. I stationed myself across the street a couple of buildings down and waited like I'd been waiting every night. Several dozen fans crowded around the stage door, along with the autograph hounds and the paparazzi, all of them hoping to catch a glimpse of Sean. And maybe an incident.

The bit players and character actors filtered out first, unrecognized. Then Jeremy Irons, who smiled and signed some autographs before he headed on down the block with his hands in his pockets, alone. Then no one came out for a while. Then Sean did, behind aviator sunglasses. A large male companion was alongside him to ward off the autograph hounds, many of whom yelled and screamed and pushed toward the young star. Sean and friend didn't stop to exchange pleasantries. They hurried off down the block. Flashbulbs popped as the photographers pursued him— taunting him, shouting obscene things about Madonna after him, hoping to get a rise out of him. And a photo they could sell. They were out of luck that night.

The sidewalk got quiet after that, except for the dozen or so faithfuls waiting for Merilee. Her fans are always polite, for some reason. My eyes scanned them. None looked menacing. Or familiar. No prominent New York literary figures, for instance. No one was lurking in the shadows or in a parked car. No one was watching for her. Just me. I waited.

The old guy who worked the stage door hailed a cab for her, as he did every night. When it pulled up, she came striding out, her big Il Bisonte bag slung over one shoulder. Lulu moaned softly. I shushed her. She was casually dressed—sweatshirt, shorts, and moccasins. Of course, this being Merilee, the sweatshirt was cashmere, the shorts pleated lambsuede, and the moccasins alligator. She stopped to sign autographs and exchange gracious pleasantries. Then she climbed in the cab and it started its way down the block in the slow crosstown traffic, Merilee chatting away with the driver. She loves cabbies, provided they don't ride the horn or spit out the window.

I hailed one and hopped in. Mine was a Russian immigrant who spoke just enough English to understand I wanted him to follow her. He did.

We stayed right on her tail until she pulled up in front of our old place on Central Park West. I had my driver wait a few car lengths back as she paid and crossed the street and went inside. She and her doorman had a brief chat, then she gathered up some packages waiting there for her and headed for the elevator. We waited. As soon as I saw the lights go on in the windows overlooking the park, I had him take me home.

Another notice from the Racquet Club was waiting for

me in my mailbox. This was a discreet, handwritten one from the club secretary, who wondered if perhaps I was intending to relocate abroad and wished to let my membership lapse. If not, might he bring the matter of my dues balance to my attention?

Why was it I hadn't paid them yet? Or felt like going near there lately? A "gentleman's dinosaur pit," Cam had called it. He had told me how much he wanted my respect. Did I want his, too?

Had he killed Skitsy? Where was he?

My phone started ringing as soon as I opened the door. Vic with some answers, I hoped. I lunged for it.

"It h-hurts, Mr. Hoagy . . . Oh, God . . . !"

"Merilee!"

"I need you, Hoagy," she cried, voice choking with sobs. "I n-need you. Oh, God, it hurts . . ."

"Don't move, Merilee! I'll be right there!"

"Hurry, darling. Hurry . . ."

I hung up and dashed out the door, Lulu scampering on my heel.

Chapter Nine

L ulu started whooping in the elevator. As soon as the doors slid open, she went skittering down the tile corridor and hurled her body, paws first, at her mommy's door. The thud brought Merilee.

"Merilee, what—?"

Sobbing, she threw herself in my arms before I could say another word. I held on to her and smelled her smell, which is Crabtree & Evelyn avocado-oil soap.

"What did they do?" I demanded. "Tell me!"

She wiped her eyes and her nose with my linen handkerchief. They were going fast that day. "They . . . they . . ."

"They *what?*"

"N-Nominated me," she finally got out. "Today, for *Petrified Forest*. For a Tony. Oh, the *pain*."

I breathed for the first time since I'd answered my phone. "Jesus Christ, Merilee . . ."

Lulu was circling around her and moaning for some attention. Merilee knelt and stroked her and cooed at her. Then she stood and we gazed at each other, and I got lost in her green eyes. Merilee Nash isn't conventionally pretty. Her nose and chin are too patrician, her forehead is too high. Plus she's no delicate flower. She has broad, sloping shoulders, a muscular back, and powerful legs. Standing there in her size-10 bare feet, she was just under six feet. Right now her eyes were all puffy from crying and her cheeks flushed. Her waist-length golden hair was tied into a loose bun atop her head. She had on a silk target-dot dressing gown that was identical to my own. In fact, it was my own until she stole it and I had to buy another one. Holding on to my clothes had been tough for me when we were together—she always looked better in them than I did. Under the gown she wore a pair of Brooks Brothers white pima-cotton pj's. Men's pj's, because she insists they're better made. She sews the fly shut.

"Merilee, how could you do this to me?"

She bit her lower lip. "You said to call if I needed you, darling. I did. Need you. And you *came.* It means so much to me that you—"

"Merilee, there've been two threats on your life. My apartment has been attacked by a sledgehammer. My celebrity's onetime editor has jumped off the terrace of her penthouse, or been pushed—that's presently up in the air, so to speak. I don't mean to be unsympathetic, but getting nominated for your second Tony Award simply does not qualify as—"

She put a finger over my lips. "You'll wake the neighbors."

She dragged me inside and closed the door behind us. "I'm sorry, darling. Truly. I simply didn't . . . Merciful heavens, you must have thought I got . . . that I was . . ."

"Yes, I did."

"Poor Hoagy. I feel dreadful now. How can I make it up to you?"

"Depends on how far you're willing to go," I replied, grinning.

"How would a swift kick in the tush be?" she wondered sweetly.

"More action than I've had in over a year."

"That," she declared, "makes two of us."

She had redone the place in mission oak, but not just any mission oak—signed Gustav Stickley Craftsman originals, each piece spare and elegant and flawlessly proportioned. There was an umbrella stand and mouth-watering tall-case clock in the marble-floored entry hall. In the dining room she had a hexagonal dining table with six matching V-backed chairs around it and a massive sideboard with exposed tenons and pins. The living room, with its floor-to-ceiling windows overlooking Central Park, was most impressive of all. Here she had made a seating area out of two Morris armchairs and a matching settee of oak and leather. A copy of the poetry of François Villon lay open on the settee. The coffee table was heaped with fat mailing pouches full of new plays and film scripts that producers and agents wanted her to read. Part of the game. If she showed any interest, the money people would.

I sat in one of the Morris chairs, which was as comfortable as it was beautiful. Merilee curled up on the settee, where Lulu promptly joined her, head in her lap, tail thumping. Me she had forgotten about.

"Congratulations, Merilee. About the nomination. It's wonderful news."

"Thank you, darling," she said softly. "But it's not wonderful. It's dreadful. It means I have to go through the uncertainty and self-doubt all over again, just like when I got nominated before."

"But Merilee, you *won* before."

"That didn't make the waiting any easier." She sighed. "I know I should feel happy, but I don't. I feel empty. I feel as if I have nothing meaningful to show for all the work I've done. I feel as if I don't have a life." She gazed across the coffee table at me. "Do you ever feel that way?"

"Only most of the time. I take it you're not seeing anyone these days."

She stiffened. "I hate that," she snapped. "Why is it if a man is depressed, it's a weighty existential crisis, and if a woman is, she's just not getting serviced regularly enough?"

"That's not what I meant," I said. "I've missed your quaint little expressions."

"Hmpht." She leaned over to pat Lulu, and frowned when she heard her wheezing. Concerned, she felt her nose. "It's warm and dry. Is she getting sick again?"

"I hope not."

"Did you give her a decongestant?"

"I did not."

Merilee shook her head. "And you call yourself a parent." She got up and hurried off to the kitchen. Lulu watched her.

"Just for that," I advised Lulu, "you get steak for dinner tomorrow."

I reached for the phone on the plant stand next to me and called Vic. There was still no sign of Cam. Damn.

When Merilee came back, she had half of a Sudafed buried in a blob of cream cheese on her fingertip. She'd also brought a chilled bottle of Dom Pérignon and two glasses. "I don't know—maybe we should celebrate the cursed thing," she said grumpily.

"What an excellent idea."

I popped the cork and poured while Lulu daintily licked the cream cheese off Merilee's finger. When she found the pill, she resisted, until Merilee massaged her throat and spoke a lot of baby talk to her. She likes it when Merilee talks that way to her. Me it makes fwow up.

"To you," I toasted, holding my glass up. "And to Gabby Maple."

"To us, and to long ago." She drained half of her glass and made a discreet hiccuping noise. Among her many gifts Merilee owns the world's most elegant belch. "Are *you*, darling? Seeing anyone, I mean."

"I think I could fall into Charlie Chu pretty easily if I wanted to."

Up went one eyebrow. "And do you?"

"She's an interesting woman."

"She's not a woman. She's a girl." Merilee emptied her glass and held it out for me. I refilled it. "As for me, they'll never, ever be suspending me from any canvas—not unless its fortified with steel mesh and anchor-bolted to the wall. Gracious, look at the roles they're offering me . . ." She snatched a pile of manuscripts off the coffee table and opened one. " 'Approaching middle age.' " She dropped it unceremoniously on the wood floor with a *thwack*, opened another. " 'A handsome, sturdily built, *mature* woman.' " *Thwack.* " 'Spinster.' " *Thwack.* She slumped back against the sofa. "Lord, I'm turning into Betty Bacall!"

"You've never looked lovelier, Merilee," I assured her, sipping my bubbly. "And you know it."

"A gal only knows it if her guy tells her." She sighed. "And I haven't got one. I've been trying the substantial, noncreative type lately. A banker. A dermatologist. Both of them hearty, well-adjusted, content . . ."

"And?"

"They just don't seem to understand me." She gazed at me over her glass. "You look tired, darling."

"Shoulder is bothering me."

"Old javelin injury?"

"New bathroom-door injury."

"Shall I rub it for you?"

"No, that won't be . . . would you?"

She knelt next to me on the floor and began to work her strong fingers into my shoulder. It made me think of when she was in the Sondheim musical. Her legs would cramp up on her in the night, twitch and thump in the bed. I'd rub them for her, then rub the rest of her, then . . .

"Feel good?" she asked softly.

"Better than good."

From the settee, Lulu watched us drowsily. The decongestant was taking effect.

"And how is Cam?"

"Among the missing right now. In more ways than one. I wish I could figure him out."

"He's gotten under your skin, hasn't he?"

"What makes you say that?"

"It has been known to happen."

"Any hint of trouble at this end?" I asked her.

"None," she assured me. "I told you—there's nothing to worry about." She wrapped her arms around my calves and rested her chin on my knee. "Will you take me, darling? To the Tony Awards, I mean."

"Be glad to. Does this mean you've decided to forgive me?"

She gave me her up-from-under look, the one that drove Bill Hurt to madness in the Cain remake. She surprised a lot of people in that movie. She didn't surprise me. "It means I can never pass up a chance to see you in black."

We got lost in each other's eyes for a second.

Abruptly, she went back to work on my shoulder. "I have no idea what I'll wear."

"Talk it over with Cher—I'm sure she'll have some excellent ideas." I cleared my throat. "Perhaps I don't need to say this, Merilee . . ."

"Perhaps you do," she said coolly.

"I never wanted any of this to happen. This rift between us."

"I think . . . I think what hurt me the most was the way you characterized me. Indecisive. Flighty."

"I didn't."

"You *did*."

"Well, you're not."

"I keep wondering what you'll write about me next. Gracious, this very conversation we're having right now could end up in some book of yours someday."

I tugged at my ear. "It could."

Lulu was asleep now on the settee.

"Know what I was thinking about tonight, darling, when I was sitting here all alone? How much I feel like retiring from the business. Getting a country place, raising some . . . now this will surprise you . . ."

"Midget human life-forms?"

"Herbs. I'd give anything to just play in the mud all day and never do another sit-up. If someone wants me to come back in a cameo role as, say, the aircraft carrier USS *Chester Nimitz,* fine. Otherwise, I'm perfectly content to hang it up. Buy every spade and cultivator in the Smith and Hawken catalog. Plant bulbs from White Flower Farm, and feed the birds and watch *The Victory Garden* and wear flannel-lined jeans and rubber boots."

"And what would you do with your mink?"

"It gets cold at night there, too. Why, think I'm full of baked beans?"

"I think you need a vacation. Why don't you take a few weeks off?"

"Actually, I was thinking of going to—"

"France?"

"Why, yes. How did you know?"

"Call it a wild guess," I said, glancing over at the volume of Villon on the sofa next to Lulu.

"Oh, I see. It's because Gabby wants to in the play, and you think I take on the characteristics of whomever I'm playing."

"It has been known to happen." The only part of this equation I didn't care for is that Gabby Maple falls for a doomed gentleman writer who is shot dead at the end of the third act by Duke Mantee and buried in the Petrified Forest with the other fossils.

She sat back on her haunches and drank some more champagne. "I can't go to France. France belongs to you."

"To me?"

"To us. You took me there on our honeymoon, when things were so lovely, and I-I can't go anywhere we went together. I made the mistake of going into Elaine's once last year, and Lulu's water bowl was gone and I started to weep." Her green eyes filled up. "Oh, horseradish, I was hoping you'd cheer me up. I suppose no one can." Half-heartedly, she pulled a pile of unopened mailing pouches off the coffee table and began to sort through them there on the floor.

I poured out the last of the champagne and held up the bottle. "Shall I open its friend?"

"Please do." She frowned. "How did you know there was a friend?"

"Masculine intuition."

I found the champagne on the top shelf of the fridge right next to Merilee's most secret, junky passion—Velveeta. I returned with the bottle, sat back down, and began working the cork out as she tore into a fat pouch, pulled out the squat, square box inside, and tossed the envelope away.

I had a delayed reaction. I was busy fiddling with the champagne, and preoccupied with thoughts of Cam Noyes. I must have stared at that discarded pouch for five full seconds before I noticed the press-on letters that spelled out her name and address. And recognized them. And reacted.

I dove for Merilee just as she pulled the lid off the box. I heard a sharp metallic snap as I dove. A glass jar shot out of the box as I landed atop her. It just missed her—splashed its liquid contents all over the floor and the Persian rug and my back. Almost at once the varnish on the floor began to bubble, the rug to smolder and stink. Something hot nibbled at my back. I jumped to my feet and whipped off my silk hounds-tooth sports jacket, which already had several holes eaten in it, and then my shirt, which had just started to go.

Then I fell back on my knees, gasping with relief. I was the only one. Lulu, bless her, was still asleep on the settee. And Merilee seemed more bewildered than frightened.

"What is all of this, Mr. Hoagy?" she wondered as she reached for the jar.

"Don't touch that!" I cried. "It's sulfuric acid. Battery acid."

"But what—?"

"It was meant to hit you in the face when you opened the box."

Her fingers shot involuntarily to her face. She got very wide-eyed and pale. It was sinking in now. "W-What would it have done . . . ?"

"Put an end to your movie career for real," I said. "Unless they needed someone to play Freddy's sister in a new *Nightmare on Elm Street.*"

"And if it had gotten in my eyes?"

I left that one alone.

"Omigod!" She threw herself in my arms, shaking uncontrollably.

"It's okay," I said, hugging her tightly. "It's okay now."

When she had calmed down a little, I gingerly examined the box. The jar had been set inside it on a catapult held in place with a retaining wire. Pulling the top off the box had triggered the catapult, which in turn had snapped back the jar's spring-loaded lid. A simple, monstrous jack-in-the-box. Also untraceable—you can buy battery acid from any hardware supply house.

"I-I don't understand it, Hoagy," she said. "What sort of person would *do* something so . . . so . . . ?"

"Somebody who is really sick," I told her, fingering the envelope it had come in. "How did you get this?"

"It was downstairs waiting for me when I came home tonight."

"Call the doorman, would you? Ask him if he remembers who delivered it."

She went to the house phone by the front door. Lulu finally stirred from her slumber.

"Lassie," I pointed out sternly, "would have barked out a warning. Dragged the pouch off into Central Park with her bare teeth. She *wouldn't* have snoozed through the whole damned thing."

Lulu yawned in response. And went back to sleep with a peaceful grunt.

Merilee returned a moment later. "Ned said he noticed it there earlier this evening after he'd been hailing a cab for a tenant. He didn't see who left it."

"Too bad. Mind if I borrow one of my old shirts back?"

"Not at all, darling. I'll get it for you as soon as I call the police." She picked up the phone, started to dial it.

"Don't do that, Merilee," I said quietly.

She stopped. "Why not?"

"I have my reasons."

"Hoagy, I've been attacked!"

"Don't call the police."

"But you said yourself someone may have been murdered tonight. You said your apartment was trashed. You said—"

"It may be Cam."

"What do you mean it may be Cam?"

"I mean he's a big strong kid, and he's good with his hands and he's violent."

"I see." She bit her lip fretfully. "You don't trust him?"

"I don't know. All I know is he's hiding something from me, and that it may have cost Skitsy Held her life. Only, say it *is* Cam. Why would he go to so much trouble to scare me off of this project—threaten me, try to disfigure you? All he has to do is fire me. I don't get it. I don't know what's going on. Until I do, I owe him the benefit of the doubt. Friends . . ." I trailed off, swallowing.

"Friends what, Hoagy?"

"Friends don't call the police on one another."

She stared at the phone in her hand, then slowly put it down. "Okay, Hoagy. If it means that much to you."

"Thank you."

"Hoagy?"

"Yes, Merilee?"

"Why do you keep getting caught in the middle of such messes?"

"Just lucky, I guess."

Somebody was sleeping in my chair.

My new, easy-opening front door was ajar, my reading lamp was on, and Detective Lt. Romaine Very, the rock 'n' roll cop, was slumped there, snoring. A copy of my second novel lay open in his lap. Another critic. He had changed into a Rangers sweatshirt, jeans, and Pony high-tops. His bike was propped against my bookcase. Lulu sniffed at it, and at him, disagreeably.

"Good and comfy, Lieutenant?" I asked him, my voice raised.

He jumped and sat up blinking, immediately alert. "Yo, saw the hole in the wall, dude. Thought somebody broke in. So I came in to check it out. Waited around for ya."

"Why didn't you just put on my jammies and hop into bed?"

"Sorry, dude. It's this ulcer I got. Used to drink ten, fifteen cups of coffee a day to keep going. Doc won't let me drink any now, so I keep sort of, like, drifting off." He got to his feet, popped a piece of gum in his mouth, and began to pace around my apartment, chomping. "Place is a real dive, y'know?"

"Thanks. It's nice of you to say so."

"What's with the hole?"

"Had a break-in a few days ago. Haven't gotten around to getting it fixed yet." And what was the point? It wasn't as if fixing it would keep out anyone who really wanted in. Besides, I'd always wanted cross-ventilation.

He stopped pacing, started nodding to his personal rock 'n' roll beat. "You report it?"

I shook my head. "Nothing was taken. Must have gotten scared off or something." I put down some fresh mackerel for Lulu, then found some Bass ale in the fridge and offered him one.

"Naw, I'm off beer, too. Also chocolate and anything spicy, which means no pizza, no souvlaki, no hot dogs, no pastrami, no moo shoo pork, no whatever tastes good. Christ, you ever taste that herbal fucking tea?"

I opened an ale and drank some of it. "Kind of young for an ulcer, aren't you?"

"Doc says I have an intensity problem," he replied. "Too much of it."

"Not exactly a calm line of work either," I suggested.

"You got that right, dude."

I glanced at grandfather's Rolex. "I don't mean to be inhospitable, Lieutenant, but it's three A.M. and I'd like to get to bed. Did you want something?"

He flopped back down in my easy chair. "I got a bunch of calls tonight from the press about Miss Held. Seems she was a pretty important lady."

"In certain circles."

"You said ya had some kind of appointment with her."

"I did."

"What about?" he asked.

"Is that important?" I asked.

He popped his gum and narrowed his eyes at me. "Maybe you oughta just tell me, huh?"

"Tell you what?" I shoved aside the newspapers and magazines piled on the love seat and sat down. "Skitsy Held and I were business acquaintances. I had nothing to do with her jumping."

"Who said she jumped?"

"You did." I drank some more of my ale. "Why, have you found something that's changed your mind?"

He shrugged. "Her dirty laundry."

"What about it?"

"There wasn't any. Doorman says she came home in a yellow dress. She died less than an hour later in a blue one. We know she took a shower. But her laundry hamper was empty. No yellow dress. No stockings. No soiled undies. We turned the place upside down. Closets, dressers, everywhere. So, like, where'd the shit go?"

I tugged at my ear. "Laundry room?"

"We checked there."

"Dry cleaners?"

"She used the Empire Cleaners on Broadway. I called the dude at home. He remembered her right away. She was a regular customer for years. He said she hadn't been in for at least a week, and none of his people picked anything of hers up tonight. I also talked to her doctor. He said she had no history of depression or other mental illness, and wasn't seeing a therapist. Not that that necessarily means anything. People can fall off the shelf like that . . ." He snapped his fingers. "But still . . ."

"You think maybe she was pushed?"

"I'm thinking there's something a little bizarre going on. Maybe it's nothing, but sometimes nothing turns into, y'know . . ."

"Something?"

He nodded. "Man, I could tell you stories—"

"Now wouldn't be a good time." I sipped my ale. "To answer your question, I was there to talk to her about my next novel. I was hoping to get her interested enough in it to sign it up."

"What's it about, your new novel?"

"A man and woman who can't stay together but who can't stay apart. I'm hoping it reads better than it lives."

"Why'd you go to her place to talk? Why didn't you meet her in her office during business hours?"

"Common practice. Editors have most of their creative conversations over meals or drinks."

"Sure you weren't involved with her?"

"I told you—I was a business acquaintance."

"Right, right." Very yawned and scratched his stomach. "Got wind of a little scuffle recently at Elaine's," he said casually. "According to an eyewitness, you and Miss Held had some angry words on the curb outside."

"A few," I acknowledged. "You're a busy guy, aren't you, Lieutenant?"

"I liked you better when you called me zealous."

"I liked you better before you started making accusations. I was on the sidewalk in front of Skitsy's building when she hit the pavement. I couldn't have pushed her off her terrace and then made it down to the street before she did. The elevator isn't that fast, and I didn't happen to have my cape with me. I didn't kill her."

"Didn't say you did, dude," he said soothingly. "Just trying to figure out what's going on. Stay with me."

"I'm with you, I'm with you."

"Where were you immediately before you got to her place?"

"Walking."

"Anybody see you?"

"Half of Manhattan."

"I mean, anybody recognize you?"

I sighed inwardly. Maybe they would have in the old days, when it was my picture that was plastered all over the newspapers. Not anymore. "No one."

He nodded. "Hear you're ghosting Cam Noyes's memoirs."

"I am."

"Why didn't you tell me that before?"

"You didn't ask me."

He stuck his chin out challengingly. "You jerking my chain?"

"I am not."

"Dickhead lived in my dorm when he was a freshman."

"You went to Columbia?"

"You sound surprised, dude. Think I'm some kind of Ricky Retardo?"

"Not at all. What did you major in?"

"Romance languages. Did me beaucoup good, too." He belched. "I hear Miss Held was his first editor."

"She was."

"I don't suppose your meeting with her tonight had anything to do with him."

"It did not."

"Just a coincidence?"

"That's right, Lieutenant. Publishing is a small community. Cam and I happened to be at a party she threw recently for another of her writers. She and I got to talking about my new novel. She suggested we get together."

He gave his gum a workout. "Got an answer for every-thing, haven't you dude?"

I left that one alone.

"What else aren't you telling me?" he demanded, scowling at me now.

"Nothing I can think of."

He shook his head. "I'm not supersatisfied."

"Who among us is?"

He stood up and went over to his bike, still shaking his head. "I ran a check on you, y'know? You got no record, but I still keep getting the feeling you been down this par-ticular road before. Why is that?"

I shrugged. "I couldn't say, Lieutenant. Possibly it's the tire tracks across my back."

Romaine Very stood there facing me a minute, his hands on his hips, one knee quaking, chin stuck out. He looked as if he wanted to punch me or say something real nasty. He didn't do either of those things. He just said, "Whatever," in a voice filled with quiet menace. And stormed out the door with his bike, gum popping furiously.

Chapter Ten

Lulu woke up coughing, her chest rumbling like the aged Morgan Plus-4 I drove in college, the one I couldn't find a replacement muffler for. I fixed her a spoonful of lemon and honey—her old bronchitis nostrum—and after she licked it clean, the two of us took a nice, hot shower together. Lulu hates showering with me. I'm not too crazy about it myself. She slips and slides around, and moans and keeps trying to jump out—all this plus the steamy, enveloping stench of fish breath. It's kind of like bathing with an otter. But she needed the steam for her congestion, and after I warned her it was this or a trip to a vet for a s-h-o-t, she stayed put, withstanding the indignity of hot water beating down upon her head with heroic stoicism.

She seemed to be breathing a little easier when I dried her off. I assured her she was a brave little girl and gave her an anchovy.

Skitsy made the front page of all three morning papers. The *Times* used a file photo of her standing at a cocktail party with her great discovery, Cam Noyes. The *Post* had a picture of her tarp-covered body on the bloody sidewalk in front of her building. If you looked real carefully, you could see me standing there in the background, looking tall and dapper and somewhat nauseous.

I read the stories as I cabbed down to Gramercy Park. They played her death as an apparent suicide. None of the suspicions that Lt. Romaine Very had raised in my apartment were included—no mention of her missing clothes, no hint that he felt somebody may have pushed her. He was being careful until he had something more to go on. After all, there were some important people involved here. There was her ex-husband, noted critic and scholar Tanner Marsh, who was quoted as calling her "the most brilliant editor since Maxwell Perkins." There was that prominent literary agent and gent Boyd Samuels, who called her "a colleague and a friend and a great lady." There was Cam Noyes, who was not available for comment.

Where was he?

Vic was pulling a fresh-baked cranberry bread out of the toaster-oven when I got there. "I checked Delilah's place this morning at seven," he reported. "Again at eight. No sign of either of them. Her mail's still in the box. She never came home last night." He reached into his apron and produced a white envelope. "When I got back, this was under the door. For you."

My heartbeat quickened at the sight of the press-on letters spelling out my name on the outside of the envelope. I ripped it open. Inside it said: *Go to Farmington*. Nothing more. I stared at it, wondering what it meant. Wondering who'd left it.

"Charlie's upstairs packing, Hoag," Vic droned as he poured us coffee. "She sat down here all night waiting for him to come home. He's a real bastard, you know that?"

I couldn't disagree with him, so I didn't.

Vic had moved a white wrought-iron table and a couple of the pastel garden chairs out onto the still-unfinished patio. We took the cranberry bread and our coffee out there and sat in the warm sun.

"Still no sign of that darned contractor," Vic said. "Charlie keeps calling him and calling him. I'm half tempted to go out to Brooklyn and throttle the guy."

"He'll show up when he feels like it and not a moment sooner," I explained. "All a part of the joy of renovating."

I was just starting to fill him in on Very's visit and Merilee's brush with battery acid when Cam Noyes walked in the front door.

Chapter Eleven

T ape #6 w/Cam Noyes recorded May 13 in his garden. Appearance is disheveled, eyes bloodshot. Vic brings him coffee, disappears inside, glowering)

NOYES: Big Vic doesn't seem particularly happy to see me.

HOAG: He's disappointed in you—you broke training. Also wounded his professional pride somewhat. Where were you last night, Cameron? (no response) You have heard about Skitsy, haven't you?

NOYES: Saw it in this morning's paper. Couldn't . . . can't believe she did this to me.

HOAG: Did what to you?

NOYES: First mother, then father, now Skitsy. . . . Anybody who matters to me bails out on me. I just . . . I can't handle it anymore, you know? I mean, why does this keep *happening* to me?

HOAG: For what it's worth, Cameron, Skitsy didn't do anything to you. Someone did it to her—she was murdered.

NOYES: But the newspapers said—

HOAG: Forget what the newspapers said.

NOYES: W-Who . . . ?

HOAG: Offhand, I'd have to consider you the top suspect right now.

NOYES: *Me?*

HOAG: I've done my best to shield you from the police, but I can't shield you for much longer.

NOYES: Damned decent of you, coach, but there's no need for you to get involved.

HOAG: Goddamn it, I *am* involved! Don't pull this shit on me! Where were you last night?!

NOYES: You don't actually think *I* killed her, do you?

HOAG: I think you refused to tell me yesterday what Skitsy had on you. I think before I could ask her, someone made sure she couldn't tell me. I think you can draw your own conclusion.

NOYES: (*silence*) I went somewhere with Delilah, okay?

HOAG: Where?

NOYES: She gets off on sleaze. It's her thing, you know? We drove out to this adults-only motel in Ozone Park she wanted to go to, the Galaxy. It's got porn movies on the TV and round water beds and mirrors on the ceiling and complimentary champagne that tastes like carbonated monkey piss. We fucked all night, okay? She has that early-morning gig on *Good Morning America*. Before dawn we drove back and I dropped her at the studio. Then I stopped at an all-night diner on Eleventh Avenue and had steak and eggs and bought the newspapers. That's when I found out about Skitsy. I called Boyd right off. He's totally blown out. (*pause*) I've just been walking and thinking for the past couple of hours. I cried a little. She was kind of a second mother to me, you know?

HOAG: Let's not get too oedipal.

NOYES: Okay, maybe we had a sick relationship. But it was a relationship. I haven't had many.

HOAG: She was killed a little before seven last night. Where were you?

NOYES: On our way to the motel. We got there at about a quarter to eight.

HOAG: Stop anywhere on the way?

NOYES: For hamburgers at a White Castle on Ridgewood Avenue.

HOAG: Kind of an all-around classy evening.

NOYES: Coach, I have no idea what happened to Skitsy, or why it happened. That's the truth. I may be scum, but I'm not a killer. Christ, no. Where's Charlie?

HOAG: Upstairs packing.

NOYES: Good. I'm glad she's over me.

HOAG: I wouldn't say she's over you, but she is leaving you.

NOYES: Any idea for where?

HOAG: She can stay at my place for now, if she wishes.

NOYES: Well, well.

HOAG: It's not like that. I won't be around. Going away for a couple of days on personal business. Strictly an above-board offer.

NOYES: It needn't be. On my account, I mean.

HOAG: Duly noted. Why would you want Skitsy dead?

NOYES: I wouldn't. I didn't.

HOAG: Cameron, if I'm going to stick my neck out for you I have to know the whole story. I'll ask you again— What did Skitsy have on you?

NOYES: I already told you, you needn't stick—

HOAG: What was it, goddamnit!

NOYES: Stop yelling at me!

HOAG: I'll stop yelling when you start answering! Why didn't you break it off with Skitsy?! Tell me!

NOYES: (*long silence*) That's what I've been thinking about all morning, actually. Telling you. It's . . . It's been slowly killing me inside. The horror if it. The guilt. Wanting to get it off my chest. I-I can't stand it anymore. I really can't. And now that she's dead . . . Shit, I didn't kill her. You have to believe me. Do you? (*no response*) She can't tell on me anymore. Can't hurt me. That's a tremendous . . . it's a *relief.* My secret is safe now. I'm safe. Except for you, damn it. You think I'm some kind of liar or killer, and I can't handle that. I want you to know the truth, coach. I'm going to tell you the truth. But only if you promise to leave it out of the book. This is just between you and me. It's personal, understand?

HOAG: Off the record?

NOYES: Yes, off the record.

HOAG: Go ahead.

NOYES: (*silence*) Do you remember how I told you that Boyd peddled fake driver's licenses at Deerfield?

HOAG: Yes.

NOYES: And that he had to shut down when some kid got loaded and smashed into a busload of kids and—

HOAG: Killed two of them and himself. Yes, yes. Go on.

NOYES: I lied to you about that. He wasn't killed. Didn't get a scratch on him, in fact. Got away clean. None of the survivors saw him. It was early morning, and dark, and he had bailed out of that stolen car a good fifty feet before it slammed into the bus. He chickened out. No guts. He was attempting suicide, you see, and was simply too fucked up to realize that the other people would . . . that the bus would explode when the car hit it. That he would sit there in the ditch hearing their screams. That two of them would die. That he . . . that *I* killed them.

HOAG: Let's try it from the beginning, shall we?

NOYES: Very well . . . Boyd had gone home for the week-end—his mother was ill. He left me some acid. Saturday night I dropped it and went to this dance we had with Stoneleigh-Burnham, thinking it would be a trip. It wasn't. All of those smug, status-conscious people. All of that role playing. Pissed me off. Made me feel caged, like I just had to get out of the place, you know? So I split. Trolled the village for a car with its keys in it. I didn't find one, but as I was walking past the Inn, a guy in a BMW pulled up there to drop some people off. He went inside with them to say good-night, and left his engine running. People do that up there in the winter, to keep the heater going. I just hopped in and took off. Got on I-91 and pointed it south toward Springfield—away. Got it up over a hundred, flying, tripping my brains out. Felt like I was living in some kind of arcade game. I bought a bottle of Jack Daniel's somewhere and stretched out in a farmer's field, just lay there in the snow and drank it and stared up at the stars and the moon. I lay there for hours, wondering if I was doomed like Mother and Father had been. Wondering if life was as awful as it appeared to be. Lying there, I realized that I had no control over my life. Not any of it. That it was simply going to unfold before me, and then it would be over. And that the only real, meaningful control I could ever have was to choose when and how I would die. I felt tremendous *power* at this realization. *Calm.*

HOAG: Your character in *Bang* felt that calm. You wrote so well about it I felt you must have contemplated suicide at some point.

NOYES: I did more than contemplate it. I got back in the Beemer toward dawn and looked around for how to do it. I was *sure* it was the right thing to do. . . . I saw that bus sitting there at the intersection. And I said to myself, there it is. Perfect. Just go right into it. Go for it. I didn't know it was full of kids on their way to a ski outing. I didn't know anything. I was still tripping. The bottle was empty . . . I went for it. Picked up speed. Made straight for it. Got closer. Closer still. And then, suddenly, this *force* took over me, this force that yanked me out of the car. I landed in the ditch. I heard the crash, the explosion. Saw the flames. The flames were . . . beautiful. I didn't do the decent thing. I didn't help those kids. I heard them screaming, but I didn't

help them. I ran. For miles and miles, until I was near the
highway. A trucker gave me a ride north toward Deerfield.
I was back in my room early enough Sunday morning that
no one even noticed I'd been gone. As the acid wore off
that day, I started to pull out of my suicidal depression.
And began to realize the enormity, the sheer *horror*, of
what I'd done. I'd killed two people! . . . I told Boyd
when he came back. I had to tell someone. He shrugged it
off. Told me I was lucky to be alive, and a free man, and
that I should just forget about it. I couldn't. I thought about
turning myself in, of course. But I realized how meaningless that would be, because there was nothing that prison
could do to me that would rival the torment I would have
to live with—that I *have* lived with ever since. It wouldn't
wipe out the screams I hear in my dreams. . . . From time
to time, I've thought again about suicide. But the clarity,
the *calm*, have never returned. That was a onetime thing.
So I suppose you could say I'm doing myself in slowly. I
drink, I snort, I do whatever. To forget. But I don't forget.
Not a day goes by when I don't think about it. It's my black
pit. Some days, I'm hanging on by my fingertips, trying not
to get sucked down into it. Other days, I'm sitting on the
edge, dangling my feet into it. I can never, ever walk away
from it. It's always there between me and other people,
particularly women, who are always so anxious to peer
inside of me. . . . One night, when Skitsy and I were
drunk and fucked out, I told her about it. She's the only
woman I've ever told. This was before *Bang* came out, and
she kept wanting to hear all about how wild I was. I guess I
was just trying to impress her, I don't know. After the book
came out, I started getting bored with her. I'm used to
seeing a lot of women, none of them for very long. When I
told her I didn't think it was going to work out between us
any longer, she said, "Fine. Go off and lay anyone you
want. But you're mine twice a week or I call the law on

you." She would have, too. She was that tough. So I've been her boy every since. Stuck with her. That's the truth, coach. The whole, ugly truth.

HOAG: I see. Tell me, why didn't she hold this over you when you broke your contract with her?

NOYES: That was something between her and Boyd. That was business. This was personal. She . . . she loved me. I never loved her back, but I didn't kill her. I *swear* to you I didn't . . . (*silence*) Say something. *Please.*

HOAG: You won't like it.

NOYES: You think that I should turn myself in, don't you? Take my medicine. Am I right?

HOAG: That isn't what I was going to say, though I think a good case could be made for it. You said it yourself—you're killing yourself slowly. You're still young and strong, but soon you won't be. The process will speed up quite dramatically, and that will be the end of you. And what a waste it will be.

NOYES: What *were* you going to say?

HOAG: That aside from the death of your parents, this is the major event of your life. It tells me who you are. Tells me about the pain and intensity of *Bang*. Tells me about the anger inside you. About why you can't write, or have a serious relationship with a woman, or face responsibility. . . . I was going to say, Cameron, that *this* is our book.

NOYES: No, you promised me! You said it didn't have to—

HOAG: Listen to me, Cameron. I can't make you do anything you don't want to do. It's your book. I'm only here to advise you. My advice is this—let this book be your confessional. Come clean. You'll never be able to get on with your life and your work until you do. Confront this thing on paper—openly and honestly. And then face the music. At least this way you've got some control of the situation. Your story will be on the record, complete and accurate.

NOYES: My career will be ruined.

HOAG: And what career is that? A bunch of endorsements? It's your *work* that matters, not some wine-cooler commercial. It's being able to live with yourself.

NOYES: I don't know, coach. I just don't know.

HOAG: I won't pressure you. It's your decision. And your life—you'll have to pay the consequences. Talk to a good lawyer. Talk to Boyd.

NOYES: I know what he'll say—that you're crazy.

HOAG: Don't bet on that. If you do this, you'll get major attention. Maybe even your second *People* cover.

NOYES: Third.

HOAG: My mistake. Sorry.

NOYES: No problem. Could happen to anyone.

HOAG: Think about it, Cameron. Will you do that?

NOYES: (*silence*) I'll do that.

(end tape)

Chapter Twelve

I left for Connecticut that night.

I wasn't alone. I talked Merilee into coming alone. She needed to get away from her acid-splashed apartment for a couple of days, and I needed to keep an eye on her. It also meant I could drive the red Jaguar XK 150 drophead convertible we'd bought when we were together; and which she got to keep. It's a rare beauty, every inch of it factory original—the engine, transmission, black top, sixty-spoke wire wheels, tan leather interior, polished hardwood dash. The damned car only has 31,000 miles on it. Its previous owner had been an elderly East Hampton cereal heiress who'd only driven it to the beauty parlor and the Maidstone. I'd missed how it handled and purred. I'd missed Merilee's riding next to me with the wind in her golden hair.

We left after her curtain with the top down and Lulu in her lap. Merilee wore a baseball jacket and cap of matching suede, a white linen camp shirt, faded blue jeans, and her Converse Chuck Taylor red high-tops. Lulu had her custom-knitted Fair Isle vest on against the night air, and one of Merilee's white silk aviator scarves wrapped around her throat.

"What do you think he'll decide to do?" Merilee asked me when I told her about my breakthrough with Cam.

"Tell all. Take his punishment. Not that it's entirely fair. He'll be judged for the rest of his life over something that he did on a drugged-out suicidal binge when he was sixteen years old. That's tough."

"Not as tough as it was on the children who were on that bus," she pointed out.

"I know that."

"He's not above the law just because he's gifted."

"I know that, too."

"And if he decides *not* to confess?" she asked. "What will you do—turn him in?"

"I don't know," I admitted.

"He's made you into something of an accomplice, hasn't he?"

"I'm afraid I did that to myself."

"Do you think he pushed that Skitsy Held woman?"

"No, I don't." I believed Cam. I wanted to believe him. Still, part of me wasn't so sure—the part that had asked Vic to check out his sleazy-motel story. The part that was making for Farmington without telling him. What I would find there? What was I even looking for? I had no idea. But I had to go.

The late-night traffic on I-95 was light through the commuter towns—Greenwich, Stamford, Fairfield. After New Haven it was nonexistent. I let the Jag out to eighty. It seemed happiest at that speed. Lightning began to crackle in the sky when we were outside Guilford, and a light rain began to fall. I stopped and put the top up. It was pouring by the time we pulled off the highway at Old Lyme, the wind gusting sheets of rain before our headlights as we eased slowly through the snug, slumbering little historic village at the mouth of the Connecticut River. The Bee and Thistle Inn there was saving two rooms for us. Old Lyme isn't exactly next door to Farmington, but the Bee and Thistle holds a special attachment for us—it's where we stayed on our first weekend together. Besides, I never claimed we were practical. Just cute.

The inn has been there since 1756. A stand of maple trees shields it from the road, and a broad circular driveway leads to its front door. Inside, a fire blazed in the parlor fireplace. We were greeted like family and shown directly to our rooms. There are eleven of them in all, each furnished in antiques. Ours were across the hall from each other on the third floor. Merilee's had a canopied bed. I unpacked and put down mackerel and water for Lulu, then escorted Merilee back down to the parlor. The kitchen had been closed for hours, but they dug us up some leftover cold sliced duck and crabmeat ravioli, and heated some scones. We devoured it in front of the fire with a bottle of Sancerre while the rain beat down outside and Lulu dozed on the floor. Our hosts served us Irish coffee before they went to bed. We stayed up awhile, sipping it and gazing into the flames.

"I'm glad I let you talk me into this, darling," Merilee said, sighing contentedly.

I glanced over at her. Her face was aglow in the firelight, her hair shimmering. "So am I, Merilee."

"Do you remember what you said to me that first night here?" she asked me softly, her green eyes fixed on the flames.

"Yes. You said, 'Did you ever dream you'd one day find yourself drinking champagne in a bathtub with a glamorous, award-winning actress?' And I said, 'Yes, the very first time I laid eyes on you.' "

She smiled. "That's when I knew I was a goner."

"That's not what you told me later on that night, under the canopy," I pointed out, grinning.

"*Mister* Hoagy, not in front of the child."

Lulu ignored us. She was out. We sipped our Irish coffees.

"Darling?"

"Yes, Merilee?"

"Do you remember everything we said?"

"I'm afraid so. Elephants and writers never forget."

"Who was it that said that?"

I yawned. "I forget."

Upstairs, we lingered in the hall for an awkward, silent moment before Merilee said good-night in a hoarse whisper, darted inside, and closed her door.

I went to bed with Truman Capote, who was my second choice. The storm picked up even more. Lightning lit up the night sky. Thunder rattled the windows. The wind howled. Lulu didn't like it. She jumped down from the bed and scratched at the door, whimpering. She wanted her mommy. I told her to shut up. She wouldn't. I told her to come back to bed. She wouldn't. I got out of bed and put on my dressing gown. The light was still on underneath Merilee's door. I tiptoed across the hall and tapped on it.

"Yes . . . ?" she demanded, instantly suspicious.

I turned the knob. She'd locked the door. "Why, Merilee, don't you trust me?"

"I see I had good reason not to, mister."

"Lulu wants to sleep with you."

"Oh, that's *low* Hoagy. So, so low. Using a puppy as your Trojan horse. And a sniffly little one at that."

"I'm perfectly serious—she wants her mommy."

Lulu thudded against the door and whimpered.

"Oh, Sweetness!" Merilee cried. "Gracious, why didn't you *say* so, you son of a sea cook."

"I did."

I heard her bedsprings creak and her bare feet on the floor. She opened the door. She was wearing her red flannel nightshirt and a pair of round, oversized tortoiseshell glasses. Those were new.

"I've missed your quaint little expressions," I said.

"Hmpht."

Lulu scampered straight for the bed, where Kazan's memoir lay open on the pillow, and barked. Merilee shushed her and hoisted her up.

"So what's with the new look?" I asked, referring to the specs. "Getting in character to play Annie Sullivan?"

She'd forgotten she had them on. Aghast, she whipped them off and hid them behind her back. "They just get a little tired sometimes," she explained, blushing furiously. "My eyes, I mean. Lately. When I'm reading."

"Uh-huh."

"Oh, *beans,* I hate them!"

"You look cute in them, kind of like a sexy owl."

She softened. "Do I really?" she asked me girlishly.

"Trust me."

Lulu curled up, tail thumping happily. Merilee went over and said some baby talk to her. To me she said, "I haven't had Sweetness with me in ages. I always sleep better when I do."

"She's all yours." I started back to my own room. "Oh, if she starts snoring again in the night, just throw her in the shower for a while."

Merilee's eyes widened. "Just throw her in the *what?*"

"Sleep tight, four eyes."

The rain blew away during the night. It was the sun slanting into my room that woke me. I threw open my window and inhaled. The country air was fresh and clean, and fragrant from the pink and white blossoms on the apple trees. Beyond the thick green lawn, the Lieutenant River sparkled in the morning light.

A plump, giggly teenaged girl brought me fresh-squeezed orange juice, a basket of warm blueberry muffins, and a pot of coffee. I had it in bed while I pored over the transcripts of my tapes with Cam, in particular the material on Farmington—the town where he was born and raised, and where he buried his parents. The town he couldn't get out of fast enough.

I was interrupted by a tapping at my door, followed by a woof. And Merilee calling out, "We want our daddy."

"This is *low*, Merilee. So, so low."

"*Mister* Hoagy. Open this door at once."

"It's open."

Lulu scampered in first, snuffling happily, paws and belly soaked. She went right for her mackerel bowl, paying me not the slightest attention. Chomping followed.

Merilee had on a white cotton fisherman's knit turtleneck, gray flannels, and her oiled English ankle boots. Her cheeks were ruddy, her eyes agleam. "It is *glorious* out," she exclaimed. "*We* have been out walking. *We* have devoured flapjacks and sausages. *You*, mister, are a slug-a-bed. A sloth. A potato."

"Am not. I've been working."

"Sweetness didn't snore one teeny bit last night. And her nose is cold again. I think she's *aww* better."

"That's a relief." Her face was still in her bowl. Not so much as a good-morning. "Shall I drop you in East Haddam?"

Some friends of Merilee's were rehearsing a summer production of *Guys and Dolls* at the Goodspeed Opera House.

"Think I'll stick around here awhile," she replied. "I feel like going horseback riding. I can get a lift up there later. May I keep Sweetness for the day?"

"Feel free. She doesn't even know I'm alive."

"Don't be churlish, darling. She's mine too, you know."

"Hmpht."

It took me forty-five minutes to get to Farmington, with its streets of carefully preserved center-chimney colonial houses, its graceful old oaks and maples, its sense of gentility and grace—everything that Cam Noyes despised.

I made my way up Main Street past Miss Porter's and turned onto Mountain Street. High Street, where Cam had lived, ran into Mountain. I tooled along it slowly. Workmen were out battling back against winter. Carpenters were rebuilding rotted front porches. Roofers were reshingling. Tree surgeons were operating. There were a few newer homes set back behind great lawns, but most were old and close to the street. White, with black shutters and little historic plaques, some dating them back to the 1600s. I wondered which had been his. A number of them matched his description of the old Knott house, but none said Knott, at least not that I could make out from the car—several were discreetly hidden behind hedges of hemlock and clumps of lilac.

High ran a half mile or so before it ended at Farmington Avenue. I took this to the outskirts of town where there was a modern complex of antiseptic concrete buildings. The library was directly across from town hall. Its doors whooshed open by themselves.

I was hoping to hook up with the family lawyer, Peter Seymour. I'd had no luck reaching him from New York—information had no listing for him in Farmington or any of the surrounding towns, including Hartford. It had been several years since he'd handled the Noyes estate. Could be he'd retired to Hobe Sound, or died. But if he was still practicing, he was probably still somewhere in Connecticut. Lawyers tend not to leave a state after they've passed its bar exam.

I worked my way through every Connecticut phone book they had there, and they had them all. It's not a very big state. No Peter Seymour, attorney-at-law, anywhere.

The town clerk's office was over in the town hall basement. Small-town lawyers are in and out of the clerk's office filing property deeds and estate records. I figured someone there would know what had happened to him.

The town clerk was a tall, erect woman with blue hair and Marilyn Quayle teeth. She'd never heard of any Peter Seymour, but she'd only been on the job six months. She suggested I contact the local bar association. I did, from a pay phone out in the corridor. They advised me there was no such member of the local bar. I asked them to look back in their records a few years. They did. No attorney named Peter Seymour had practiced law in Farmington in the past twenty years.

Frustrated, I went back across to the library. Again, the doors whooshed.

One entire room upstairs, the Farmington Room, was devoted exclusively to local history—from the town's original settlement back in 1639 right up to the present. There were glassed-in bookcases, framed oil portraits, maps. Quite dignified, all of it. I parked myself in there. I wanted to read up on Cam's fine old family—on his mother, Jane Abbott Knott, on her father and grandfather, both clergymen, on her great-grandfather, Judge Samuel Knott, a chief justice of the state of Connecticut. Maybe it wasn't so fine. Maybe there was something Cam hadn't told me about his Yankee bloodlines. Maybe that was why I'd been sent here.

A local scholar had compiled a nine-volume history of the town, which contained an exhaustive site-by-site account of each home in the historic district—its architectural history, the sequence of its ownership, family trees of those owners, births, marriages, careers, deaths. Nice light reading. The volumes were organized by street name and house number, not by family name, since those changed so many times through the years. I didn't know the house number of Cam's home on High Street, but the Baker and Tilden 1869 Atlas of the Inner Village was included to show me how High Street had looked then. There had been a hotel on the westside corner of High and Farmington, the William Whitman. Four residences had existed on the west side of High, belonging to Hurlburt, Gallager, Manion, and Westcott. The Congregational parsonage was at the other end of the block at Mountain. Across from it was the E. L. Hart Boarding School for Boys, and homes belonging to Whitman, Miles, Badwell, Cahill, and Porter. No Knott residence. Apparently, it had been under a different name then—a Knott daughter who had married. So I plowed through the history of each of those historic homes on High Street. Followed the family trees of all of those families, read of their prosperity, their sickness, their joy, their sorrow. The Revolution. The Civil War. The First World War. The Second. There was enough there to make for a James Michener novel. Certainly the prose was just as turgid. I read and I read. I read until my eyes were bleary and my temples throbbed.

I read until I was quite certain that no home on High Street in Farmington had ever belonged to or ever been associated with the Knott family.

I kept searching. I looked through book after book about the founding and development of Farmington, its prominent citizens past and present. I examined indexes and maps. I stayed in that damned room four hours, and here is what I learned: There had been no local clerics named Knott. There had been no chief justice of the Connecticut Supreme Court named Samuel Knott. There had been no family in the entire history of the village of Farmington named Knott. Period.

Dazed and confused, I reeled back over to town hall and down the steps. It was a discreet town. The town clerk wouldn't let me look at the birth records. Insisted they were confidential. I suggested they were public record. Public record or not, I couldn't see them. I asked if there were any vital records I *could* see.

Deaths.

Through the vault door I went. Into the chilly fireproof records room . . . Noyes, Sawyer, who had hung himself in the cellar of the old house on High Street . . . *Don't take this the wrong way, Son* . . . Noyes, Jane Knott, who had flown off to have dirty fun with Smilin' Jack and crashed in the White Mountains.

There was no record of either death.

I went outside and got in the Jaguar and sat there. Now I knew why the note had told me to come to Farmington.

Cameron Sheffield Noyes didn't exist.

Merilee and Lulu were still out when I got back to the Bee and Thistle. I went straight up to my room and stretched out on my bed. I wanted to get off my feet—the sands under them were shifting too rapidly.

Who was Cam Noyes? Why had he made up his life story? Had anything he'd told me been true? Who had sent me here? What did this have to do with Skitsy's murder?

I phoned down to the bar for a mug of Double Diamond dark English draft. Then I called Cam. Vic answered.

"How is he?" I asked.

"Pretty well, Hoag," Vic replied in his droning monotone. "We did five miles this morning. Attended Miss Held's funeral. I'll put him on. He's been anxious to—"

"Coach!" cried Cam, wrenching the phone away from

him. "Coach, I want to do it. I want to tell the truth. All the way, just like you said."

"Glad to hear it, Cameron," I said quietly.

"You were right," he went on, sounding boyish and up. "As long as I hide from what I did that night, I'll never be able to get on with my life and work. I've got to come clean."

"That you do. And what does Boyd say about this?"

"Haven't told him. I'm the one who's in charge of my life, not him. Some cop came by today after Skitsy's funeral."

"Was he short and muscular?"

"Very."

"That's him."

"Huh?"

"What did he want?"

"To know how well I knew Skitsy. Where I was when she died."

"Did you tell him?"

"No."

"Why not?"

"I just didn't feel like it."

I sipped my ale. "I'll be back tomorrow afternoon, Cameron. We have lots to talk about."

"Where are you, anyway?"

"Connecticut," I replied, waiting for his reaction.

"What are you doing out there?" he asked, trying not to sound uneasy. He failed.

I wanted to say who the fuck are you? Why have you been lying to me? I wanted to say that friends don't do that to each other. I stopped myself. I wanted more facts first. I hoped I'd get them in the morning. "Working some things out with my ex-wife," I answered.

"Ah, good," he said cheerfully. "Coach?"

"Yes, Cameron?"

"Are you proud of me?"

"Proud doesn't begin to describe it."

I hung up and called my apartment. Charlie Chu answered.

"Oh, hi," she said warmly. "I was just doing some sketches, and they're going great. It's really helping my head being here, Hoagy. I appreciate it."

"No problem."

"I love your skylight. If you ever decide to move, let me know. It's a darling place."

"That's one word for it." I pictured her there, sitting by the phone with her glasses sliding down her nose. I liked picturing her there. "Any messages?"

"Very."

"Very what?"

"He called a little while ago. Lieutenant Very. He seems real nice. We talked about his ulcer for a while."

"And . . . ?"

"I told him he should eat a lot of rice."

"No, what did he want?"

"For you to call him." She gave me his number. Then she lowered her voice. "I . . . I've been thinking about you, Hoagy. I mean, being surrounded by your things and sleeping in your bed and everything. I feel like I'm getting a special guided tour of you."

I left that one alone.

"I like what I see, Hoagy. A lot."

"Careful, or you'll turn my head."

"What do you think I'm trying to do?" she said. Then she giggled and hung up.

Romaine Very was mad at me.

"What the fuck ya doing in Connecticut, dude?" he demanded harshly when I got through to him.

I could hear the din of the precinct house in the background. "Working. Why?"

"I like everybody at arm's length, that's why."

"I had no idea, Lieutenant. I still have a book to turn in, you see."

"Ya shoulda said something to me about it."

"I apologize. I had no idea I'd be hurting your feelings."

"You're not hurting my—"

"I understand you phoned."

"Yeah, I phoned," he replied, popping his gum. "Your honeypot sounds supernice."

"She's not my—"

"A lot of ladies, they find out you're a cop, they talk to you like you're some sack of shit. Not her. Said she's an artist. Doesn't Cam Noyes live with an artist, too?"

"What was it you wanted, Lieutenant?"

"We found Miss Held's dress this morning. The yellow one."

"Where was it?"

"Stuffed in a trash bin three blocks away with her bra and panties. That makes it official—it's now a murder investigation. Thought you'd wanna know."

"Thank you. That wasn't very smart, was it? Ditching the clothes nearby like that."

"No, it wasn't," he acknowledged. "They were wet."

"It rained last night," I pointed out.

"I know, but they were inside a plastic bag and the trash bin had a lid on it. None of the other trash around it was wet. Lab's checking 'em over. We'll see. Coroner's office thinks she died from the fall, period. They didn't find nothing to indicate a struggle. No scratches or finger marks, nothing under her nails. You got anything for me?"

"Me?"

"Thought maybe you was tracking something down out there."

"Nothing to do with this, Lieutenant."

"I don't know about you, dude," he grumbled. "I really don't. I mean, my head hears ya but my stomach don't." He burped. "And my stomach's usually right. When you coming back?"

"Tomorrow."

"See that ya do," he ordered. "Connecticut. I went there once."

"Oh?"

"Didn't like it. Stay with me, dude."

Merilee still wasn't back yet. It was nearly seven. I didn't know whether to be concerned or not. I decided not to be. I'd been careful not to tell anyone where we were staying.

I had another glass of draft outside on a bench by the river. The sun was setting over the tidal marshes. I watched it, and found my thoughts straying to someone fresh and cute and talented. Someone Chinese.

When the sun fell, I went inside. Miss Nash had returned. I made a dinner reservation and went upstairs. Her shower was running. Lulu was waiting for me in my room, incredibly happy to see me. Of course—it was dinnertime. I put down her mackerel, had a quick shower, and stropped grandfather's pearl-handled straight-edge razor. After years of going through packages of disposable razors, I'd decided there was already enough plastic waste in the world. I now make less of it, and the shave isn't terrible— as long as the blade is sharp and my hand is reasonably steady. I dressed in my double-breasted white Italian linen suit, a lavender broadcloth shirt, and a woven yellow silk tie. After I'd doused myself with Floris, I headed downstairs, where I was shown to a candlelit table on the dining porch.

Merilee joined me a few moments later. I could tell the

second she entered the dining room—heads everywhere turning at the sight of her—that something was very wrong. She looked beautiful enough. Her hair was up, and she had on a high-throated Victorian silk blouse, a cameo brooch, paisley skirt, and her Tanino Crisci shoes. When she sat, her cheeks glowed in the candlelight. But her back was stiff and she was chewing on her lower lip. Her eyes carefully avoided mine.

I ordered dry martinis with extra olives, and asked her if everything was okay. She said everything was absolutely, totally fine. I let it go. I learned long ago that I couldn't dig anything out of Merilee. She spills only when she's good and ready to spill. So we ate our baby lamp chops and new potatoes and pecan pie in sphinxlike silence. As soon as we were done, she said she was very tired and went directly up to her room. Lulu joined her. I had a large calvados before I headed up, too. When I got to my door, I could hear Merilee weeping behind hers. I tapped lightly on it. She told me to please go away. I went away.

Her time to spill was three A.M. That's when she and Lulu came in my room and got on my bed, and she said, "I bought a Land-Rover today."

"A Land-Rover?" I yawned and rubbed my eyes. The moonlight was slanting through the window and across the foot of the bed. She looked lovely in it as she sat there in her red flannel nightshirt, hands folded neatly in her lap.

"A dear, battered old one. It looks like something out of a Stewart Granger movie. Super for hauling things and it runs like a—"

"Hauling what things, Merilee?"

Her forehead creased. It does that when she's trying not to cry. "I-I bought an eighteen-acre farm today."

"You did what?"

"In Hadlyme. The house was built in 1736." Her words tumbled out quickly now. "It has nine rooms. Exposed beams. Wide-oak floors. Seven fireplaces. The one in the dining room has a baking oven. There's a three-story carriage barn and a duck pond and an apple orchard and the dearest, sweetest little chapel with stained-glass windows and . . ." She came up for air. "I took one look and said I'm home."

"But when did you—?"

"I got to talking this afternoon with the folks at Goodspeed about how much theater there is around here now—them, the Ivoryton Playhouse, the National Theater for the Deaf in Chester . . . and I started thinking how nice it would be to be involved in something so decent and non-Hollywood. I could teach, direct a little. And I've always adored this area. So I drove around with a local realtor and she showed me this place and I bought it. I was afraid to say anything about it at dinner because I knew you'd tell me how impulsive and impractical I am."

"I wouldn't."

"You would. You'd get all male on me. Want to go out and survey the place yourself, strut around with your hands on your hips and—"

"I don't strut around with my—"

"And cluck at every little—"

"I don't cluck."

"And try to talk me out of it. You can't. I'm going through with it. I got a good price, and before I did a thing I checked it out first with my lawyer and my agent and my manager and my accountant and my psychic, and they all told me to go ahead." She sighed. "It's *time*, darling. To settle down, and live, and not worry anymore about meaningless things like Tony Awards." Her eyes found mine in the moonlight. "I thought the chapel would be lovely for you—in case you ever wanted to come up and . . ."

"Pray?"

"Write, you ninny. It's wonderfully quiet, and has a wood stove, and you could stay as long as you like."

"Thank you, Merilee. That's very kind."

She took my hands. "Please tell me I'm not a fool."

"You know you're not. It sounds . . . well, it sounds fantastic. Truly."

We sat there holding hands a moment on my bed.

"I have something to tell you, too," I said. "It's about Charlie."

Merilee dropped my hands. "Charlie?"

"I may start seeing her."

Merilee frowned. "I thought she was living with—"

"Moved out on him. She's staying at my place while I'm gone."

"And when you get back?"

"I don't know," I admitted. "All I know is she's the first woman I've felt something for in a long, long time. Present company excepted, of course."

"I see," she said very quietly.

"Do you have a problem with it?"

"Of course not, darling."

"Would you tell me if you did?"

"Of course not, darling." She stretched out across the bed with her head on my feet. "Oh, God, are we through?"

"Our divorce pretty much meant that, didn't it?"

"In name only."

"I thought one *married* in name only."

"I mean truly through." She gazed at me, her eyes shimmering pools. "In our hearts through."

"Do you want us to be?"

"I don't think I could stand it, darling," she confessed. "I hated it when we weren't speaking. There were so many times I reached for the phone. So many times I wanted you."

"Me, too, Merilee."

"But I also don't think I could stand *us* again, either. You have this way of making me feel like an awkward thirteen-year-old girl again, all vulnerable and misty-eyed. I'm sorry, true love just isn't for me anymore, darling. It hurts too much."

"Not if you let yourself go."

She shook her head. "I'm no longer that young or that foolish."

"Sure you are. We both are."

She smiled. "Cam Noyes has been good for you, hasn't he?"

"I seriously doubt that."

She looked over at the window dreamily. "When I was looking at the farm today, the very first thing I thought of was how . . . how nice it would be if only . . ."

"If only what, Merilee?"

She shuddered. "Nothing. Just turning into a sentimental fool, I guess."

Then she said good-night and went back across the hall to her own room.

I was already up and dressed when the plump, giggly teenager tapped on my door at dawn with my muffins and coffee. As soon as I'd eaten, I took off in the Jaguar with Lulu.

I drove north along the Connecticut River on Route 156, through marshland and forest, past the old Yankee dairy farms with their colonial farmhouses and lush green pasturage dotted with cows. There was early-morning fog, but it was lifting. I found the small marina at Hamburg Cove and rented a rowboat. It fit nose-down in the Jag with the top down and Lulu in my lap. Sort of. The state forest turnoff wasn't far. It was a dirt road, heavily rutted and still muddy from the rain. I took it slowly. After a mile or so it dead-ended at Crescent Moon Pond, which wasn't what

I'd call a pond. It was a good half mile across to the dense forest on the other side. I saw no shack there. No one was out fishing.

I got the boat into the water and Lulu into her life vest. She's the only dog I've ever met who can't swim—she sinks to the bottom like a boulder. Then I pushed off and started rowing. It was very quiet out there aside from the birds and the sound of the water lapping gently against the boat. Lulu sat stiffly in the bow, weight back on her butt, front paws splayed awkwardly before her. Her large black nose quivered at the unfamiliar smells.

It wasn't until I got halfway across that I realized how Crescent Moon Pond got its name—it had a severe crook in its middle. I hadn't been looking at the other side at all, merely the bend. As I rounded it, the other side now came into view. And so did the shack, set back in the trees.

The mooring was rotted out, the footpath up to it over-grown. The wooden steps to the front porch were wobbly. So was the porch. The front door swung open and shut in the breeze off the pond. I heard something scurrying around inside. This time Lulu took charge—tore headlong into the shack, snarling ferociously. She flushed out an entire family of field mice. Then came strutting back to me, immensely pleased with herself.

"Good work, Lulu."

Inside there was a black cast-iron wood stove, scarred pine table and chairs, an empty oil lantern, a few kitchen rudiments, piles of empty beer cans. Cigarette butts had been ground into the bare wooden floor. The tiny bedroom off the main room had a stained, mildewed mattress in it, and a pine dresser. Out back I could see a well with a hand pump, and an outhouse.

I had seen enough already, but when I went back into the main room and noticed what was hanging on the wall over the table I was convinced: It was the framed, mounted snakeskin. The one Smilin' Jack had found in one of his wading boots.

It was just as Cam had described it to me.

The shack was real.

Old Lyme's town hall was a stately old white building down Lyme Street from the Bee and Thistle. It being Saturday, they were open until noon. Locals were lined up at the front desk for their summer beach permits.

The town clerk here was round and white-haired, and a lot jollier than the one in Farmington. She told me all property deeds were recorded and filed by index number. To find out the index number you looked it up in the index book under the deed holder's name. Not surprisingly, I found no deed holder named Cameron Sheffield Noyes. I asked the clerk what to do if I knew where the property was but not who owned it. She sent me to the assessor's office to find out who'd been paying taxes on it.

The town assessor was a gruff, impatient old Yankee with two hearing aids and a white crew cut that he'd no doubt had since before they staged a comeback. I had barely begun to describe the shack at Crescent Moon Pond when he cut me off, pulled a surveyor's map book down off a shelf, and began searching through it, licking his thumb as he went. When he found what he wanted, he dove into his files, harrumphed, and presented me with a name: Ferris Rush, Jr., c/o the Boyd Samuels Agency in New York, New York.

Hello, Ferris. Wish I could say I was pleased to meet you.

Back in the clerk's office I tried the name Ferris Rush, Jr., in the index book. This time I got a number, and a look at the deed. Ferris Rush, Jr., of New York City had taken title to the shack on Crescent Moon Pond a little less than two years before, when he turned twenty-one. The property had been held in trust for him for the previous eight years by Ina Duke Rush of Port Arthur, Texas, received from the estate of John Rush of Essex, Connecticut, for no financial consideration.

I still didn't have a lot of the answers. But now I did know something I hadn't known throughout this whole damned collaboration.

I knew what questions to ask.

Chapter Thirteen

Charlie had brought in my mail. Bills. Yushie gadget catalogues. And another, even sterner, handwritten note from the secretary of the Racquet Club. I was really going to have to do something about that.

The bed was neatly made. Her clothes were folded in a wicker, rope-handled trunk that she'd stashed in the closet. An extra toothbrush and a tube of Tom's organic toothpaste were in the bathroom. A gauzy nightshirt hung from the hook on the back of the door.

A most unobtrusive little roommate. Hardly knew she was there, aside from the cloying smell of oil paint in the air. And from the kitchen. An easel stood in the middle of it on a drop cloth, directly under the skylight. Her paints and brushes were crowded onto the counter, along with spray cans and cements and rough charcoal sketches. Boxes of broken crockery and old bottles and magazines were piled up against one wall, her portfolios stacked against them.

This invasion of her turf made Lulu uneasy. She nosed warily amongst the stuff, tail between her legs, as if she expected to encounter a cache of Mexican jumping beans.

Another nude was in progress on Charlie's easel—this one a study of a young man. Her style was primitive. So was her subject. He was heavily muscled and exuded a raw, crude power. From the neck down, that is. She'd pasted the head of the Gerber's baby on his shoulders.

It was Cam Noyes, or Ferris Rush, or whatever the hell you wanted to call him. I had a few choice names in mind myself. So, evidently, did she.

She'd left me a note by the phone, her handwriting square and careful. *H — I'll be hanging around Rat's Nest till six. Call me when you get back. We'll go to lunch on my break at two. Hope I haven't messed up your kitchen too much. I've missed you — C*

I was really going to have to do something about that, too.

I glanced at grandfather's Rolex. It was just past one. I called Rat's Nest and left word with the clerk at the desk that I'd be there at two. Then I showered and dressed and called Vic.

"He's taking his nap now, Hoag," he reported. "We did our five miles and our errands and now he's out cold. That contractor actually showed up while we were out. Put some dry wall up in the kitchen, then split. Nervy bastard was in and out before I could give him a piece of my mind."

"They have an uncanny instinct for that," I said. "They flit from job to job all day long, keeping as many as four customers unhappy at once."

"I checked out that adult motel Cam said he went to the night of Miss Held's death. He was there, all right, he and Miss Moscowitz. From eight until four the next morning. I found two White Castles on Ridgewood Avenue they might have stopped at on their way out, when Miss Held was pushed. Nobody remembered them at either place. That's not a good sign. They're both recognizable celebrities.''

"That car of his doesn't exactly whisper, either."

"She was with us last night—Miss Moscowitz," said Vic. "She's some kind of handful. A little strident for my own personal taste, but—"

"She stay the entire night?"

"She'd already left for the studio when I got up at six," he replied. "I figured it was okay, her staying here. She's encouraging him to stay off the coke. And better they're here together under this roof than out who knows where."

"I agree."

"He's starting to make some progress, Hoag. The last couple of days he's had a real sparkle in his eyes. He's practially a new man."

"I'll say he is."

"Excuse me?"

"I think we should keep up our guard on Merilee."

"I'll leave right now, stay with her until tonight's curtain. Can you get down here and take over Cam?"

"There's a lunch date I'd like to keep first, unless . . ."

"No, no, go ahead," Vic insisted. "He's fast asleep. She didn't let him get much rest last night, believe me. He'll be fine here by himself for an hour or two. And of more use to you afterward. Enjoy your meal, Hoag."

I caught a cab downtown.

Charlie was up there on her canvas waiting for me, blue from head to toe. Blue Monday. All except for the red stain where the bowie knife had been plunged into her stomach right up to its brass hilt.

Two blue-and-whites and some unmarked sedans were parked out front. The steel door was wide open with a yellow police cordon across it. A uniformed cop stood guard. Gawkers crowded the sidewalk.

At the reception desk a plainclothesman was inter-viewing the clerk with the Buddy Holly glasses. She was shaking her head and sobbing.

A half dozen cops were fanned around Blue Monday, staring, murmuring grimly to each other. They could have been admirers at an exhibition, except for the one who was dusting the handle of the knife for fingerprints.

I stood there staring, too. At the blood. At the eyes that didn't move or blink. My chest felt heavy. I was thinking about that extra toothbrush in my bathroom and those neatly folded clothes in the wicker trunk. I was thinking about what might have happened that was never going to happen now. Not ever.

I stood there staring at the bowie knife. His bowie knife.

Lulu shifted restlessly at my feet.

One of the cops was watching me. It was Romaine Very. His bike was leaning against the lumpy fifteen-thou-sand-dollar statue. They hadn't sold it yet, for some reason. He motioned for me to step outside with him, I took one more look at Charlie. Then I did.

"Yo, like, how come you keep showing up at murder scenes, dude?" he demanded, gum popping, one knee quaking. "I mean, it's getting a little *funny.*"

"It's getting hysterical."

He belched and made a face. "I hate looking at dead chicks. Especially pretty ones."

"Can you tell me what happened?"

He looked up at me, head nodding rhythmically, eyes narrow slits. He took his time. Finally he shrugged, yanked a pad out of the back pocket of his jeans, and opened it. "The clerk, one Rita Gersh of Great Neck, Long Island, stepped out for a break at two. Went to hit the cash ma-chine at her bank, get herself a sandwich and coffee. Miss

Chu, the victim, usually went out for the sandwiches, on account she liked to get out and stretch her legs, y'know? But today she was expecting someone for lunch."

"That was me. We had a date."

"I know. Miss Gersh said you called. I was kinda hoping you'd volunteer it—fact is, we was just about to come looking for you, dude."

"I didn't do it."

"Maybe not," he conceded, working his gum with a hard tightening of his jaws. "But you look real good for it."

"Please tell me the rest."

"Before she left, Miss Gersh helped Miss Chu down so she could use the powder room before her date arrived. Before *you* arrived. Miss Gersh hung a sign on the door saying she'd be back in ten minutes. She left the door unlocked. Whoever did it worked fast. He was most likely watching the door for his chance. When he saw Miss Gersh split, he took it. Stuck her with a vintage bowie. The genuine article. Don't appear to be any prints on it. It was wiped clean. No sign of forced entry at the front door. Someone knocked and Miss Chu let him in."

"So it was someone she knew?"

"Pretty much had to be. Miss Gersh says she wouldn't have let any customers in."

"Did the surveillance camera record anything?"

He shook his head. "No tape in it. It's just a monitor."

The local TV news crews were showing up now, crowding the front door, barraging the cop there with questions. We stepped farther away from them.

"How did she get back up on the canvas?" I asked Very.

"Her killer put her up there."

"Before or after he stabbed her?"

"After. We found blood in the middle of the room. We're assuming it's hers. Gotta check it."

"Why did he do that—put her back up?"

He shrugged. "Make some kind of statement, maybe. Who the hell knows?"

"You'd have to be pretty strong to lift up a body like that, wouldn't you?"

"About as strong as you'd have to be to toss Skitsy Held off of her terrace."

"You think it's the same person?"

"Don't know, dude. I did get the lab test results on those clothes of hers we found."

"And?"

"They had Wisk on 'em."

"Wisk?"

"It's a liquid detergent. Y'know, ring around the collar?"

"I know what Wisk is, Lieutenant. What does it mean?"

He shifted uncomfortably there on the sidewalk. "It means her killer was downstairs in the laundry room doing a load of wash while we was there. It means the fucker left *after* we did."

"You didn't check the laundry room at the time?"

"We had no reason to," he replied sharply. "It read suicide, remember?"

"But how did he get in?"

"We don't know," he snapped, nostrils flaring. "We blew it, okay! That what you wanna hear? You happy?"

"Not particularly."

He shoved the notepad back into his jeans, softened. "She was the one I talked to on the phone at your apartment, wasn't she?"

"She was."

"Seemed real nice."

"She was."

"Lived with Cam Noyes, didn't she?"

"Until recently."

He nodded away. "How'd you figure in that?"

"I didn't. I let her use my place while I was away. That's all."

"So she dumped him?" he asked, smelling a motive.

"He's been seeing someone else."

"That'd be Delilah Moscowitz, huh?"

"Why, yes. How did you—?"

"I staked out his house last night for the helluv it. She stayed over. Noyes wouldn't by any chance own a bowie knife, would he?"

I hesitated. It didn't make any sense. He'd *wanted* Charlie to leave him. Or so he'd said. *Had* he killed her? Killed them both? How much more did I owe him? How much farther out on the limb was I prepared to go for this man who'd done nothing but lie to me?

Very was staring up at me, eyes narrowed. "A bowie knife?" he repeated.

"I wouldn't know," I finally replied.

"I see," he said doubtfully, popping his gum. "Been doing some more checking on you, dude. Your other ghosting gigs."

"Learn anything interesting?"

"Yeah. People have this way of dying around you."

"You noticed."

"Of course I noticed. I'm a detective. Noticing things is my business. You got something against me?"

"Absolutely not, Lieutenant."

"Then how come you're not being straight with me? You haven't been straight with me from the start."

I left that one alone.

Very shook his head. "I oughta take you in. I really oughta. Only you're a paddle. You'll do me more good out here, stirring up the water. I'm putting you on a tight leash, understand? If I feel like yanking, I yank. Hard."

"Thanks for the warning, Lieutenant. Anything else?"

He belched. "Yeah, don't leave town again."

"I wouldn't think of it."

I looked around for Lulu. I didn't see her. I found her inside with the cops. They were ignoring her. They shouldn't have been. She was sneezing.

The Loveboat wasn't out front, and he wasn't in the house. His clothes had been cleared out of his closet. His suitcases were gone.

He was gone.

I sat down on his bed, took a deep breath, and let it out slowly. I had no choice now. I had to believe it. The man I'd been working with these past weeks was a murderer.

I reached for the phone on the nightstand to call Very and tell him. But I couldn't make myself dial the phone.

I had to find him myself first. Had to ask him who he really was. Had to ask him why. Only then could I turn him in. Step away. Lick my wounds. I never said I was smart. In fact, when it comes to getting involved with my celebrity subjects, I definitely am not.

The contractor had shown up again. The new kitchen sink was in now. Out back, the bluestone patio had finally been laid in its bed of cement. It came out real nice.

Too bad there wasn't anybody living there anymore to appreciate it.

When all else failed me there was still Bobby Short. I took in his midnight show at the Hotel Carlyle. It's what I do when I can't see life's bright side no matter how damned hard I look for it. There's just something about the way Bobby has with Cole Porter, about the sharp brine of the caviar and the tart cold of the champagne that cures what ails me. Usually. Not tonight. Tonight I kept thinking about how he shouldn't have done it. Any of it. Tonight I kept thinking about how big a jerk I was. I should take out an ad: *This friend for hire. Give him a table and he'll follow you anywhere.* Tonight I kept thinking about Charlie, and the way her glasses slid down her nose.

Bobby was playing "I Get a Kick Out of You" when there was a rustle next to me, and the scent of avocado oil. It was Merilee, in a shimmering white strapless dress. Her hair was brushed out long and golden and she had on one of her old trademark white silk headbands. She slid into the banquette across from me.

"What are you doing here?" I asked as Lulu whooped and licked her fingers.

The waiter brought her a glass and poured her some champagne. She heaped some caviar on a wedge of toast, ate half of it, and fed Lulu the rest, almost losing a finger in the process. Lulu has mighty expensive taste for someone who eats canned mackerel.

"I'm taking in the rest of this show and this caviar with you, darling," she said, sipping her champagne. "Then I'm taking you to the Cat Club on East Thirteenth, where they have a dance floor and a seventeen-piece swing band that's as loud and hot as they come. If you're still on your feet after that, and if you're good to me, I'll take you down to Ratner's and buy you a large plate of lox and onions and eggs before I deposit you at your door." She poured herself some more champagne. "But first I'd switch to single malt if I were you. I understand the barman has a fine old Glenmorangie."

"Merilee . . . ?"

"Yes, darling?"

I got lost in her green eyes for a moment. "You're not the worst person I've ever known."

She smiled and took my hand. "That's positively the second-nicest thing you've ever said to me, Hoagy."

"What's the nicest?"

" 'I felt that one all the way down to my toenails.' "

"Why, Merilee, you're getting awfully frisky in your gentler years."

"It's true, I am. Isn't it odd?"

I got the waiter over and ordered a double Glenmorangie. I downed it in one gulp when it came, and ordered another.

Lulu didn't growl at me.

Chapter Fourteen

*T*ape #1 w/Delilah Moscowitz recorded May 16 in
her apartment on Twelfth St. Decor is modern, expensive, impersonal. Wears black sleeveless jump-
suit, sweat socks, no makeup. Hair is tied in a
tight ponytail

MOSCOWITZ: You look like you were out all night drinking.
HOAG: Only because I was, Red.
MOSCOWITZ: I didn't sleep a wink either, thinking about
Cam. The police were here asking me all sorts of questions,
like they think I know where he went or something.
HOAG: Was it Very?
MOSCOWITZ: Very what?
HOAG: Lt. Romaine Very.
MOSCOWITZ: Is he gorgeous? (*no response*) Has an ulcer?
HOAG: Yes.
MOSCOWITZ: It was Very. They know it was Cam's knife

now. They dug up a *Rolling Stone* photo of him cleaning his fingernails with it. Same markings and everything. Can I get you more cranberry juice?

HOAG: This will be fine.

MOSCOWITZ: Sorry I don't keep anything else in the house. I'm a compulsive eater—whatever's here I go through. Where's your little dog?

HOAG: My ex-wife gets her on Sundays.

MOSCOWITZ: Just like child custody. How cute.

HOAG: Do you?

MOSCOWITZ: Do I what?

HOAG: Know where Cam went.

MOSCOWITZ: How would I know?

HOAG: Look, I'm not the police. I'm on his side. If you want to help him, tell me what you know. Have you heard from him?

MOSCOWITZ: No, damn it. All I know is he's gone and they're after him and . . . promise you won't tell the police this?

HOAG: We don't pool information.

MOSCOWITZ: I'm pissed as hell that he didn't take me with him.

HOAG: You'd have gone?

MOSCOWITZ: Are you shitting me, jack? The man I love is a hunted desperado. He's *front page news.*

HOAG: He's a murderer.

MOSCOWITZ: I don't care. I'd give anything to be on the run with him.

HOAG: Just like Bonnie and Clyde?

MOSCOWITZ: Better. My parents wouldn't shit bricks over Bonnie and Clyde.

HOAG: I guess you got to know him pretty well.

MOSCOWITZ: I guess.

HOAG: Did he ever talk to you about his childhood?

MOSCOWITZ: Never. He's peculiar that way. Most men I've known like to unload after they unload. Not him.

HOAG: Does the name Ferris Rush mean anything to you?

MOSCOWITZ: Ferris Rush? Is that a man or a woman?

HOAG: A man.

MOSCOWITZ: No. Never heard it before. Look, I don't mean to rush you, but I have to finish packing.

HOAG: Going out on tour, I understand.

MOSCOWITZ: Yes, I'm doing the Carson show on Tuesday. Local L.A. TV and radio. Then San Francisco. Then I work my way back across the country. Twenty-one cities in eighteen days. A major grind.

HOAG: Any chance you're meeting up with Cam somewhere along the line?

MOSCOWITZ: Only if he gets hold of me and says come.

HOAG: And you will?

MOSCOWITZ: I will.

HOAG: Even if it hurts your career?

MOSCOWITZ: I couldn't care less about my career.

HOAG: He told me the two of you went to Ozone Park the night Skitsy was killed. Got to the Galaxy Motel at about eight. That part checks out. What doesn't is where he was an hour earlier when she was thrown off her terrace.

MOSCOWITZ: We were eating at a White Castle.

HOAG: So he said.

MOSCOWITZ: It's the truth.

HOAG: You're claiming he didn't kill Skitsy?

MOSCOWITZ: Look, maybe he killed Charlie. It sure looks like he did. But he was with me when Skitsy died. I swear it.

HOAG: I see. You know, it's funny how alibis work. You're his for the time of her death. But you can also turn that equation around—he's *yours*.

MOSCOWITZ: What's that supposed to mean? .

HOAG: Pretty strong, aren't you?

MOSCOWITZ: My coach at the club said I bench press more weight than half the men he has.

HOAG: You'd do anything for Cam, wouldn't you?

MOSCOWITZ: Yes, I would.

HOAG: Would you kill for him?

MOSCOWITZ: (*silence*) I didn't throw Skitsy off of that terrace.

HOAG: Were you happy with her as your editor?

MOSCOWITZ: Of course.

HOAG: No creative differences?

MOSCOWITZ: Skitsy Held put this reporter on the best-seller list. That has a way of smoothing over all sorts of creative differences—not that I'm saying we had any.

HOAG: You would have if she'd found out about you and Cam.

MOSCOWITZ: That's true.

HOAG: Had she?

MOSCOWITZ: Not that I know of.

HOAG: What did Cam tell you about the two of them?

MOSCOWITZ: Very little, except that she liked to be tied up.

HOAG: Nothing about why he continued to see her?

MOSCOWITZ: I guess he liked doing the tieing. I wasn't thrilled about her, but I didn't consider her any sort of rival. It was Charlie who was his main squeeze. You already know how she and I got along.

HOAG: I guess you were pretty happy when Charlie gave up on him.

MOSCOWITZ: Sure I was.

HOAG: Any idea how Skitsy felt about her?

MOSCOWITZ: Cam said she never found her particularly threatening.

HOAG: You she would have found?

MOSCOWITZ: Me she'd have freaked over. But what's the point in going on about it? It never happened.

HOAG: Just thinking out loud. It's kind of interesting how the three of you were all involved with the same man, and how the two of them are dead, and you're not.

MOSCOWITZ: You don't actually think *I* did away with them, do you?

HOAG: I think you were at Rat's Nest yesterday. I think you were there right around the time Charlie was murdered.
MOSCOWITZ: I-I wasn't. I've never even been near the place.
HOAG: Don't kid a kidder, Red.
MOSCOWITZ: What makes you so sure I was there?
HOAG: I have my methods.
MOSCOWITZ: (*silence*) Do the police know?
HOAG: Not from me they don't.
MOSCOWITZ: All right . . . Cam trusted you. I'll trust you. (*pause*) I went to see her.
HOAG: What for?
MOSCOWITZ: So there'd be no hard feelings. She and Cam still had to work together on their book, and I wanted it to go well. I did it for his sake.
HOAG: It had nothing to do with her threatening to cut you if she ever caught you near him again?
MOSCOWITZ: She didn't scare me.
HOAG: How did your visit go?
MOSCOWITZ: Shockingly well, though I must admit it was a little weird having this serious conversation with a blue mannequin. I told her how sorry I was it had happened, and how I'd never meant to hurt her. She said she understood and that she was fine. That she'd already met someone else who she really liked. She thanked me for coming by, and apologized for what happened in Sammy's. And then I left.
HOAG: What time?
MOSCOWITZ: I don't remember exactly. I got there about one. She was alive when I left. The clerk saw me go. Ask her. Go ahead.
HOAG: That's for the police to do. Not my concern.
MOSCOWITZ: What *is* your concern?
HOAG: Cam Noyes.
MOSCOWITZ: Why?
HOAG: I work for him.
MOSCOWITZ: That's all?

HOAG: He's a friend. He's in trouble.

MOSCOWITZ: I think I'd like to have you as a friend myself.

HOAG: We wouldn't stay friends for long.

MOSCOWITZ: Meaning we'd become enemies or meaning we'd become lovers?

HOAG: One of the above.

MOSCOWITZ: Agreed. . . . Charlie didn't seem at all upset when I left. I really don't know what happened between them to set him off. I guess she made him mad about something and he lost control.

HOAG: I don't buy that. He took the knife there with him from home.

MOSCOWITZ: So?

HOAG: So that's what they call premeditation—he went there planning to kill Charlie. What I can't figure out is why.

(end tape)

(Tape #1 w/Boyd Samuels recorded May 17 in his office in the Flatiron Building)

SAMUELS: This place has been a frigging madhouse. Cops, reporters, TV. Everybody wants to know where he is. How the fuck should I know? He's gone. Wigged out, the poor fucker—don't say it. I know you warned me. And I didn't listen to you, and I feel like shit about it, okay? *(pause)* Think he did in Skitsy, too?

HOAG: So it would appear.

SAMUELS: Man, when he breaks it off with a chick he makes it permanent, huh?

HOAG: Possibly he did it to keep her from talking to me about how he'd hit that busload of kids. That makes some sense. But then he went ahead and told me about it himself the next morning. That doesn't.

SAMUELS: You know about the bus?

HOAG: I encouraged him to put it in the book.

SAMUELS: You *what?*

HOAG: He couldn't stand holding it in anymore. He was prepared to go to jail for it if he had to.

SAMUELS: Why the fuck didn't he mention any of this to me?

HOAG: Doubtless because he thought you'd talk him out of it. I don't suppose *you* did Skitsy in. To protect him, I mean.

SAMUELS: Me? (*laughs*) I'm an agent, amigo. The telephone is my bayonet. I'd swear the law was following me though. Maybe I'm just being paranoid.

HOAG: You're not.

SAMUELS: You, too?

HOAG: Yes.

SAMUELS: Well, they can forget it. I'm not making it easy for them to catch him. They're getting zilch from me.

HOAG: Meaning you know something?

SAMUELS: (*silence*) Turn off that recorder a second.

HOAG: (*rustling noise*) Okay, it's off.

SAMUELS: Okay . . . We have heard from him.

HOAG: Where is he? What did he say?

SAMUELS: Todd talked to him. I was talking to Ovitz on the coast. By the time I got off the line, he'd split. He was at a gas station somewhere in Mount Vernon.

HOAG: What's he doing there?

SAMUELS: How should I know? He's on the run. He called to say he was sorry to bring all of this down on me. And on you, too. He mentioned you.

HOAG: He's doing himself no good. He should turn himself in.

SAMUELS: You and I know that, amigo. But it's his life. His decision. I'm not turning him in. They keep asking me if I know where his financial records are, since they turned up zilch at the house. I told them no. I didn't tell them that everything—tax records, bank statements—is kept right here. Let 'em search the place. Nail me for obstructing justice. I don't care. I owe him that much.

HOAG: Mind if I turn the recorder back on now?

SAMUELS: Sure, Go ahead.

HOAG: (*rustling noise*) I want to talk about Ferris Rush.

SAMUELS: (*silence*) Shit. You know about that, too, huh?

HOAG: I know very little about anything. All I know is that Cam Noyes doesn't exist. Nor does his family tree.

SAMUELS: Okay . . . Ferris Rush is his real name. I guess you figured out that much already. The two of us made up the name Cameron Sheffield Noyes in college when he started modeling. We thought it suited his look better. Give him the right sort of image, you know? And gradually, he's sort of invented a past to go with the name.

HOAG: All of it?

SAMUELS: The Farmington part, for sure.

HOAG: That explains why he doesn't have any family photographs.

SAMUELS: My favorite part is the bit about the father hanging himself. That weird suicide note and everything. He's a born storyteller.

HOAG: He certainly is. And to think he told me he was suffering from writer's block. Hell, he and I have been writing his second novel all along, haven't we?

SAMUELS: Hey, look, it's not such a big deal. He's no different than a million other performers with stage names and made-up backgrounds, is he?

HOAG: I suppose not. Only, I don't do windows or heavy cleaning or bogus memoirs.

SAMUELS: I know. That's why we didn't take you into our confidence. We knew you wouldn't do it, and we wanted you. No hard feelings, huh?

HOAG: What did you guys think, that I wouldn't check any of his stories out? That I'd accept it all at face value?

SAMUELS: You would have if the shit hadn't hit the fan.

HOAG: And if somebody hadn't tipped me off. Sent me to Farmington.

SAMUELS: No shit? Who did that?

HOAG: The same person who's been trying to get me off of this project from the beginning. I wish I knew who it was, and how it fits in with him killing Skitsy and Charlie.

SAMUELS: I don't know anything about that, Hoag.

HOAG: You wouldn't be scamming me now, would you, amigo?

SAMUELS: I'm not, I swear. Listen, Cam's publisher called me first thing this morning, salivating. They want to get the book into print fast. Are you in?

HOAG: Only if you give me the whole story—his real background, how you made him up and marketed him. I can put it together with the tapes I already have, and with Charlie's illustrations. It should make for interesting reading.

SAMUELS: *Interesting?* Shit, we'll nuke the best-seller list! You want the real story, crank up your recorder. I'll give it to you. No point in hiding it now. It's all going to come out at his trial—assuming he's caught, and he will be.

HOAG: Good point. And this way you get fifteen percent of the action, right?

SAMUELS: You're wrong about me. I'm his friend. Always have been. . . . Ferris Rush is poor white trash. Grew up an only child in a run-down shack on the outskirts of Port Arthur, Texas. His dad, Ferris senior, is an itinerant oil rigger, sign painter, carpenter, drunk, and full-time douchebag. Killed a guy once in a bar fight. Spent some time in jail for it when Ferris was a baby. Grandpa Rush did some time, too, for robbery. That bowie knife was his. Probably stole it off some rich guy. . . . His mom is a beautician. She and his dad got married when they were sixteen, for the usual reason.

HOAG: That would be Ina Duke Rush?

SAMUELS: Yeah. He sort of likes his mom. Stayed in touch

with her after he ran away from home. Not anymore, I don't think. But for a while there she remained his legal guardian. He ran away when he was twelve. Headed north with cowshit between his toes and an accent you could cut with a knife—sorry, poor choice of words. He ran because his father beat him. He ran because all he could see down the road was him ending up no different. His dad's brother, Jack, had been in the Navy a long time, working on submarines at the Groton sub base. When he got out, he took a job repairing pleasure boats at an Essex boatyard. Jack wasn't much more of a bargain than his brother—he drank, too, and didn't have any money. But he could put Ferris in touch with people who did. So Ferris moved in with him and set about finding his future. That's something he's never had much trouble doing. Even when he was barely into his teens he was six feet tall and well built, with the wavy blond hair and blue eyes. Older women have always taken a hands-on interest in him. Two, in particular, have had a major impact on his life. The second, Skitsy, you already know about. The first was a woman named Maude Champion. Thanks to Uncle Jack, who had contacts around the Essex Yacht Club, Ferris landed himself a summer job crewing on a sixty-footer owned by a wealthy Farmington banker named Harrison Champion. Champion was in his early sixties. His second wife, Maude, was forty and a very proper Yankee lady—the kind who think their shit tastes like Häagen-Dazs. Former deb with lots of free time and no children of her own. The model for Jane Abbott Knott. She immediately took a quasi-maternal interest in Ferris, who was so bright and handsome and eager to improve himself. She tutored him. Helped him lose his accent. Taught him how to dress and act like a young gentleman.

HOAG: So that explains it—that self-conscious, mannered way he has. His gestures, his speech.

SAMUELS: Right. It's all acquired, from Maude. She taught

him everything. Gave him spending money. Bought him clothes. And on or around his thirteenth birthday, she also started fucking him. . . . Now, less than a year after Ferris moved in with him, his Uncle Jack died. Liver failure. The last thing Ferris wanted was to go back to Texas. That was the last thing Maude wanted, too. She had some family money of her own that her husband didn't know about. She used it to send Ferris to Deerfield for a proper education.

HOAG: Which is where you met him.

SAMUELS: Yes. He was the only member of the freshman class who was already a professional gigolo. (*laughs*) Actually, Ferris was a truly amazing guy to me at age fourteen. I mean, I had some wild instincts, but I still came from a conventional suburban environment. Not Ferris. He lived strictly by his own wits and his own standards. He was like some kind of modern-day adventurer. Not that he ever bragged about it. I was his best friend. I knew he was fucking Maude, and that she, not his parents, was putting him through school. But none of the other guys knew.

HOAG: Where did he tell them he was from?

SAMUELS: He didn't.

HOAG: How much of what he told me about your Deerfield days together was true?

SAMUELS: Aside from his background, almost all of it. Him getting kicked off the football team . . .

HOAG: The suicidal binge? Did he hit that busload of kids?

SAMUELS: Yes, he did. But it was no profound suicidal binge. He was just loaded, that's all.

HOAG: You talked him out of turning himself in?

SAMUELS: It never came up. Ferris didn't even consider it. Guilt wasn't something he knew much about then. He's acquired that along the way. Now what he did eats away at him—though I guess he has some fresh sins on his mind these days. Summers he stayed in the guest room over the garage of the Champions' historic home in Farmington—

the house he described to you as his own. Most of his time
was spent in Essex taking care of the yacht and Maude
while her husband was busy working in Hartford.

HOAG: He mentioned a Dana Hall girl named Kirsten who
he fell for one summer. He said her mother broke it up.

SAMUELS: Half true. He met Kirsten the summer before our
senior year. Her parents sailed from the Essex Yacht Club.
I think it was the first and only time he's been seriously in
love. Anyway, he got permission from Maude to stay overnight alone on the yacht instead of at the house. And as
soon as he did, he started slipping it to Kirsten. You can't
keep secrets around a small-town yacht club—everybody
knew Maude was fucking Ferris behind her husband's
back, and before long everybody also knew Ferris was
fucking Kirsten behind Maude's. She got wind of it soon
enough. Freaked out. Total jealous rage. Told him he was
low-class trash. Told him he and Kirsten were through or
else. He refused. She said fine, then I'm pulling the plug on
you—no place to live and no Deerfield . . . Poor little
Kirsten never knew what hit her . . . Ferris was never the
same after that. He was very bitter. Despised Maude for
what she'd made him do. And made him realize about himself. Still, he let her keep him. She paid his way into Columbia. It wasn't until he was making enough modeling to
support himself that he finally, once and for all, told her to
fuck off. But I think he's always had this need for a mother
figure, because it wasn't long before he'd found himself
another Maude in Skitsy. . . . He did well at modeling.
Made righteous bucks at it. Could have become a superstar
if he'd wanted. Gone into acting even. The ladies loved
him. But he didn't like it. Kept saying he felt like some kind
of show dog. To keep himself sane he started keeping a
journal of all the weird, strange shit we came in contact
with freshman year instead of going to class—the clubs,
the models, the coke. He made me read them. Asked me if
they were any good. I honestly didn't know. I was no liter-

ary scholar. I'm still not. I told him he ought to show them to Professor Tanner Marsh—if someone like Tanner Marsh says you have talent, then you have talent. I mean, literature is not like the hundred-yard dash. There's no stopwatch. There's only the master opinion-shapers like Tanner. If he says you're a genius, then you are one. I swear if you got him to call a book of completely blank pages a "major redefinition of abstract minimalism in modern American literature," you could sell fifty thousand copies at $17.95. It's all bullshit—I'm the first to admit it. But you need people like Tanner if you want to get a book off the ground. That and the right image. Like with Cam Noyes and *Bang*. I wanted people to think reading it was synonymous with a hip, dangerous good time. And they did, not so much because of its content but because of the public life Cam Noyes leads—the people he hangs out with, the women he fucks, the clothes he wears, what he eats, drinks, smokes. I wasn't selling literature. I was selling *attitude*.

HOAG: In other words, you promoted it like a bottle of cologne with him as its spokesman: The Man from *Bang*.

SAMUELS: Go ahead and laugh. Until we came along, a publisher's idea of publicity was to take out an ad in the *Times*. I put Cam Noyes in jeans commercials. I put a wine cooler in his hand. I put him on MTV. And why not? He's not just an author. He's a spokesman for an entire generation. I know the old fucks in tweeds think that it isn't dignified, that it cheapens literature. To me it's bringing publishing into the modern age. It's bringing new readers to your product. I'm doing it with Delilah now. Starting next week she's national TV spokeswoman for a new feminine hygiene spray—sassy but tasteful. There's nothing undignified about it at all. It's good, sound business.

HOAG: And the way you got Ferris out of his contract with Skitsy—was that good, sound business, too?

SAMUELS: I don't apologize for that. I needed a loophole so

I manufactured one. And hey, there were no hard feelings between Skitsy and me. She took her hat off to me for outsmarting her. That's why I let her have Delilah. That was me taking my hat off to her. Her company's going to make millions off of Delilah. You just watch that chick take off.

HOAG: We were watching Ferris Rush take off.

SAMUELS: Right. Where was I? Oh, yeah, so he took some of his stories to Tanner Marsh.

HOAG: Using which name?

SAMUELS: Cameron Sheffield Noyes, because it sounded so dignified. Tanner turned him down cold, but that didn't stop him. He kept at it. Wrote his novel. And this time Tanner went apeshit. Why, I'll never know. Personally I didn't see that much difference between the diary sketches and the novel. But Tanner did, and more power to him.

HOAG: How much did he know about Ferris's real name and background?

SAMUELS: He knew only what Ferris told him, which was zero. Since the lead character in *Bang* was privileged, Tanner assumed he was, too. I told Ferris—encourage the guy. Drop some names like Farmington and Deerfield and the Essex Yacht Club.

HOAG: Why? What was the point?

SAMUELS: *Image.* Tanner had to like the book even more if he thought he had a real live blue blood on his hands, an author with rich friends and relatives. People like Tanner, with their little nonprofit snob magazines, they suck up to money like nobody's business.

HOAG: He did eventually find out the truth though, didn't he?

SAMUELS: Oh, sure, from Skitsy. Ferris couldn't keep anything from her. When she told Tanner, he got a little pissed at us for misrepresenting Ferris's background, but hey, by then Cam Noyes was a household name, and *Bang* a national best-seller. How pissed could he be?

HOAG: Ferris told me he hit something of a snag with Tanner because of what happened with Skitsy in his cabin at Stony Creek. Or should I say didn't happen.

SAMUELS: What do you mean?

HOAG: He said he blew Skitsy off, and that as a result Tanner blew him off. He said you had to set him straight.

SAMUELS: Never happened. Forget that wide-eyed innocent bit. It's total fiction. Ferris Rush had been kept since he was thirteen. He didn't need me to tell him the score. He fucked her that very night in his cabin at Stony Creek. Fucked her without hesitation because he knew she could do him a lot of good. Then, the next morning he was so overcome with self-loathing he ran off and hid. I think he must have realized he was embarking on another Maude-type relationship, and he didn't like himself for it. Didn't like seeing himself for what he is—a hustler. See, that's always been his problem. He's always wanted to be somebody dignified and classy. He's always wanted to be Cameron Sheffield Noyes, the poor wigged-out bastard.

(end tape)

(Tape #1 w/Tanner Marsh recorded May 17 in his office at Columbia University. Wears rumpled corduroy suit, smokes pipe. Books, papers, are heaped everywhere. Room hasn't been tidied or aired out since the Truman administration)

MARSH: They said you were there just after it happened, Stewart. That you saw my Skitsy.

HOAG: I did.

MARSH: Tell me, did she know what was happening to her? Did she suffer.

HOAG: It was over very fast.

MARSH: I feel so much better now that she is in the ground. These past few days and nights all I have been able to think of is, where is she? Is she in a plastic body bag somewhere?

In some refrigerator? Now I know where she is. . . . We divorced, of course. But I-I never stopped loving my Skitsy.

HOAG: I'm sorry, Tanner.

MARSH: Thank you, Stewart.

HOAG: Make it Hoagy. The only person who calls me Stewart is my mother.

MARSH: Skitsy was not perfect, Stewart. She had her insecurities. She was capable of ruthlessness, cruelty. But she knew talent and how to handle it. She was the best. *He* was the best. Young Noyes. What a tragedy . . . She felt so strongly for him. Not like the others. And there were others. She collected them, just like she collected her antique dolls. My writers are just like my dolls, she said to me once —childlike and rare and extremely breakable. . . . Skitsy wasn't shy. If she saw someone she wanted, she took him. But none of them meant a damn to her—until he came along, that cold-blooded, murdering bastard. Tell me, Stewart, how does it feel to be collaborating with a man who has killed two women? Two women who loved him?

HOAG: I can't say it's the most fun I've ever had.

MARSH: Why do you do this crap, Stewart?

HOAG: Everybody ought to be good at something.

MARSH: I suppose I was awfully hard on your last novel. It was only because *Our Family Enterprise* led me to expect so terribly much. You're the most gifted of them all, Stewart. You do know that, do you not?

HOAG: Careful. My ego swells easily. How did you feel when Skitsy eventually revealed his real background to you?

MARSH: *(pause)* I felt, I suppose, a bit used. Duped. Angry . . . I imagine I felt just like you are feeling right now yourself, Stewart.

HOAG: Possibly. Would it have mattered to you if you'd known it from the start?

MARSH: Let us put it this way . . . There is a great deal to be said for Texas authors—provided they write about

Texas. Actually, my first impression of him was that he did not seem the writer type at all. By that I mean he was so robust and handsome and charming. Looked me right in the eye. Smiled. I found myself wondering what on earth this beautiful boy would be writing about. I suppose that was why I agreed to look at his stories, even though I do not generally accept freshman submissions.

HOAG: And?

MARSH: They were crude and juvenile, aswim in run-on sentences, wild mood swings, shifts in tense, voice. I did not understand half of his references. More significantly, I did not want to. I told him so. I was not particularly tactful.

HOAG: How did he respond?

MARSH: He did not get defensive or huffy, which is what they generally do. He simply thanked me for my time, shook my hand, and told me with utter conviction that he would be back in the fall with new and better material. I expected never to see him again, or if I did, to receive more of the same. . . . Undaunted, he did return a few months later, now clutching the manuscript for a novel. Inasmuch as he had shown no talent before, my inclination was to refuse to read it. But again, I was intrigued. Who was this boy? What drove him to work so hard? I glanced at his manuscript that evening. It was . . . It was nothing like what he had shown me before. He had grown so tremendously, both as a talent and as a man. He had his own voice now, a voice filled at once with self-assurance and with self-doubt, with strength and with hurt, with cynicism and with idealism. There was a sense of wholeness and purpose, a *vision*. Rereading the first page of *Bang* never fails to give me goose bumps, Stewart. . . . I sat here in my chamber until well past midnight until I finished. And when I did, I put down my pipe and wept. I wept because only once in a lifetime—and only then if he is very lucky— does someone in my position have the privilege to discover such a great talent in its very infancy. To be allowed to refine it, shepherd it. The manuscript was not perfect, mind you. There were numerous spots where his pacing faltered, the quality of his observations diminished. The ending was not nearly momentous enough. But all of this was minor. All that truly mattered was this robust young sophomore, this magazine cover boy, was a genius.

HOAG: He told me that the ending was your idea.

MARSH: At best, I pointed our conversations in a certain direction. Toward a fuller, more dramatic climax. It was he who came around to the suicide idea. . . . Working with him was a most interesting experience. The boy simply did not *get* what he had done. I had heard of writers like him—totally instinctive—but I had never worked with one before. If I were to ask him about a particular sentence or observation, what it meant, he would simply reply, "It means what it says." Not disagreeably, mind you. He simply did not know how to talk about his work. . . . I arranged a fellowship and residency at Stony Creek for him so he could complete his revisions at once without distraction.

HOAG: And you introduced him to Skitsy.

MARSH: Yes. I had called her in a daze that first night upon reading the manuscript. Told her I had come upon a brilliant young pupil who I felt certain would shortly have a manuscript she would agree was more than worthy of publication. She was, naturally, anxious to meet him.

HOAG: I'm a little vague about what happened up there between them.

MARSH: I do not trade in bedsheet gossip.

HOAG: Nor do I. I'm simply trying to understand their relationship. I have to, considering what has happened.

MARSH: Very well. . . . I knew the instant she set eyes on the boy that she wanted him. She acted nervous and girlish the entire ride up there, chattered incessantly. I left them up there that evening fully aware that by dawn they would become lovers. And they did. They made passionate love for the entire night in his cabin. Ferris is an inexhaustible and violent lover, she advised me.

HOAG: Did she always fill you in on the details of her conquests?

MARSH: Yes, she did.

HOAG: Didn't that bother you?

MARSH: Far from it. I insisted upon it.

HOAG: I see.

MARSH: Then at dawn, without warning, he suddenly became abusive and cruel toward her. Called her the vilest names. Yanked her from his bed by her hair and pushed her out the door into the woods, naked. He would not let her back in, or even give her her clothing. She had to return naked to the main house in the semidarkness, debased and humiliated. After she had bathed and dressed, she returned to his cabin, determined to have words with him. Only he was gone. Packed up and left the place without a trace. Disappeared for weeks. To this day, I do not know where he went. Skitsy told me all of this as soon as she returned to New York. She also told me that if I ever so much as uttered the name Cameron Sheffield Noyes in her presence, she would have me disemboweled. When he resurfaced with his finished manuscript, I let him have it. I told him that I had gone to an extraordinary amount of trouble to introduce him to the finest editor in New York, and that the stupidest thing a boy in his position could do was make an enemy of her. I told him that to make an enemy of her was to make one of me. I told him to get out of my office and to take his manuscript with him. He left with his tail between his legs. . . . Their romance resumed almost at once. I used that word advisedly, Stewart. For it was a romance. Stormy. Emotional. It was love.

HOAG: That's not exactly how he described it.

MARSH: I am not surprised. For him to be so attached to a woman twice his age does not fit with his public image. The rest of the story you know. The book was published nine months later to excellent notices.

HOAG: You yourself wrote the most important one, the one in the *Times*.

MARSH: I did.

HOAG: Didn't you regard that as a conflict of interest on your part?

MARSH: Absolutely not. I regarded it as my due. I had discovered him. I was entitled to present him to the publishing community. Besides, it is not as if the boy *needed* my help. He has a unique gift for drawing attention to himself. People *wanted* to read him, and to read about him. Meet him at parties. Be seen with him. Look like him. Talk like him. From the outset he has been, quite simply, a star. It is his gift and, I believe, his curse. Nothing about his celebrity has helped him as a writer. I have always believed the writer is a marathon runner. His eyes must remain focused on the long distance, and shielded from the easy diversions —the movie deals, the cocktail parties, the women. Boyd Samuels, alas, does not happen to share my belief. He proceeded to turn him from a budding literary talent into a marketable commodity. I wanted nothing but the best for Ferris. I had the highest of literary ideals. Samuels wanted bucks. Such a waste. Think of his potential, Stewart. Given time and nurturing, he could have been among the giants of this century. Instead, he is a drugged-out, burnt-out, angry young mess. A murderer. I hope he rots in jail for a long, long time. After all Skitsy did for him.

HOAG: She did a lot for herself, too, according to Ferris.

MARSH: *(pause)* Meaning what?

HOAG: Her little kickback scheme. He told me she did mighty well by it. He didn't slight you, in case you're wondering. He told me all about how you skim off the profits from your writers' conferences. I never got a chance to ask Skitsy for her response. I'd like to ask you for yours.

MARSH: *(silence)* She warned me he might try to rattle the cage.

HOAG: And how do you respond?

MARSH: Allow me to assure you his charges are utterly false and groundless. I do not know the source of his information, but—

HOAG: Skitsy. He got it all from her—pillow talk.

MARSH: I must say I find it vile and reprehensible to discuss this matter for the purposes of a book that Skitsy's own murderer intends to profit from. I will not. And if I have to take legal action against your publisher to prevent you from doing so, I shall. Do I make myself clear?

HOAG: Your power must mean a lot to you. After all, you're the ayatollah of American lit. It would be awfully tough on you to get taken down, wouldn't it?

MARSH: What are you—?

HOAG: Ferris's charges stand to raise a few eyebrows. People just might look at you a bit differently. Certainly the IRS will. The *Quarterly*, the Conference, will suffer. Maybe even die. It's pretty understandable that someone in your position might take some pretty drastic steps to hold on to what he has.

MARSH: I do not know what you are—

HOAG: Delilah Moscowitz's pub party. Perhaps you recall it. We were aboard the *Gotham Princess?* It was a rather warm evening . . . ?

MARSH: I recall it, as you well know.

HOAG: You said in front of a number of adoring listeners that I should no longer be allowed to own a typewriter.

MARSH: A figure of speech. What of it?

HOAG: Are you sure you didn't back it up—with a sledge-hammer? Are you sure you haven't been trying to get me off of this project ever since you got wind of what we were up to? That you didn't send me those threats? Try to blind my ex-wife?

MARSH: This is preposterous. I did none of it.

HOAG: You didn't send me to Farmington to expose him— this boy who humiliated you in front of all those famous people? Who you tried to shoot at Elaine's?

MARSH: *(silence)* I-I was in a state of shock. Traumatized. I did not mean to. Kill him, I mean. I meant to defend myself. He had left me so . . . so defenseless, you see. I lost control. A momentary thing. I regretted it at once. I would not . . . could not willingly hurt him, or anyone.

HOAG: Possibly you "lost control" again the evening that I was to visit Skitsy. Possibly the two of you disagreed over how much, if anything, to reveal to me.

MARSH: This is outrageous! I will *not* sit here and listen to these groundless accusations! The police are quite certain who killed Skitsy. Just as they are quite certain who killed Charleston. You have no right to interrogate me like this. None. This interview is terminated. Turn off your recorder. Shut your notebook.

HOAG: I get the feeling you want me to leave.

MARSH: At once! *(sound of rustling)* No, wait. Not yet, Stewart. Before you go, there is one thing . . .

HOAG: Yes, Tanner?

MARSH: I am a fair man.

HOAG: I've always said so.

MARSH: I know you are doing this out of loyalty to Ferris. Out of friendship. I understand that. I want you to write another novel, Stewart. A grand, glorious novel. I hope with your gifts you will. And when you do, Stewart . . .

HOAG: Yes?

MARSH: I will be anxiously waiting to review it.

HOAG: Wonderful.

(end tape)

Chapter Fifteen

The day of Charlie's memorial service was the first hot, muggy one of spring. The air was so moist and rank it felt as if someone were holding a plastic bag over the city's head.

The service was held at Rat's Nest. Not many people showed up for it. A couple of grand pooh-bahs from the Whitney and MOMA. Some gallery owners, critics, and fellow artists. Vic Early, who wore a navy-blue suit and sat stiffly with his hands folded in his lap like a good, huge boy. Me. Boyd Samuels wasn't there. Charlie wasn't there, either, in spirit or body. Her only relative, an older sister in San Francisco, had requested the body be shipped out there for burial. I had made the arrangements.

My police tail waited discreetly outside after following me there from my apartment, just as I'd been followed the previous two days wherever I went. Very was taking no chances. I was on a leash, all right, for as long as my celebrity was on the loose. That morning's papers had reported no new leads in the manhunt, other than a story in the *Post* that a witness claimed he had seen Cameron Noyes enjoying lunch at a Pizza Hut in Clinton, Iowa. The claim had been discounted when the witness turned out to be someone who'd previously spotted Elvis having coffee there. Reporters were calling me constantly now for quotes and tips. I was hanging up on them. It gets easy after the first dozen times you do it.

It was a short service. A couple of people got up and said some words about how important an artist Charlie could have become, and how her death was such a terrible waste. I didn't pay close attention. I was getting sick of hearing about waste.

Afterward, I headed uptown to my apartment with Vic and my tail to pack up Charlie's things for her sister. There really wasn't much, and I was fully capable of boxing it myself, but the big guy insisted. When he does that, you give in. We worked in silence. Neither of us felt particularly chatty.

Lulu watched us from under the bed, trembling. Packing upsets her. Some trauma buried deep in her early puppyhood. What, I don't know. But I do know I'm not putting her in therapy.

We didn't pack up Charlie's personal papers. Very had said he might want to look through those. We also left the portraits, photos, and sketches she'd done for the book. Those belonged to the publisher.

When we were done, I helped Vic carry the boxes downstairs. Then we put them, and him, in a cab bound for United Parcel.

"I wish I could give you a reason to stick around, Vic," I said to him through the open cab window. "But I'm afraid I can't. So if you want to be heading back to L.A., you may as well. Your end of this job is history."

Vic sat there in the backseat, rubbing his forehead. "I don't feel like I did much good, Hoag."

"I don't feel like I did either."

In the front seat, the cabbie, who wore a turban, began drumming his fingers impatiently on the steering wheel. He stopped as soon as he saw Vic glowering at him in the rear-view mirror.

"I'll be sticking around his place until they catch him," Vic informed me. "I'd like to be here. I'd like to ask him why he did that to that nice little girl. You don't mind, do you, Hoag?"

I patted his heavy shoulder. "Not even a little."

Lulu was still cowering under the bed, her eyes glowing in the darkness. I was trying to coax her out with promises of bouillabaisse and coquilles St. Jacques when the phone rang. It was Very.

"How's the belly, Lieutenant?" I asked him as he popped his gum in my ear.

"Sour, dude. Just got a sweet break, though—his wheels turned up."

"The Loveboat? Where?"

"Trenton. Low-income housing project. Cruiser spotted it there early this morning. Bunch of homeboys were breaking into it. Plates and registration still on it. Suitcase full of clothes in the trunk. He wear real preppy shit? There's a Ralph Lauren suit, white. Bunch of Brooks Brothers shirts and boxer shorts . . ."

"That sounds like him."

"Nobody saw him—at least nobody says they saw him. It's not one of your more cooperative neighborhoods. FBI is in on it now, which is about egos and territorial bullshit and stomach acid that I can live without. They began canvasing the people on the street. All anybody will tell 'em is they think the car was left there sometime last night. Any idea what he'd be doing around Trenton?"

"None."

"He have any family or friends there?"

"Not that I know of."

"Okay if I try a theory on you, dude?"

"Go right ahead, Lieutenant."

"What it is," he began, giving his gum a workout, "I was eyeballing this book of his, *Bang*, and his character in that, when things get real crazed for him psychologically—when he starts to, like, crack up—he runs to Atlantic City for a blowout. You think Noyes could be headed there like in his book? Or is that too wigged-out?"

"I can't tell you if he's headed there or not, Lieutenant," I replied. "I can tell you that with Cam Noyes the line between fact and fiction is extremely fuzzy. I'd say it's worth pursuing."

"Me, too. Trenton's a little off course between here and A.C., but not much. I figure he's taking an indirect route in case we're watching the Garden State Parkway and Route Nine. We're checking the buses in case he took one there from Trenton. Also limo services, taxis, car rentals. You got any addresses for him down there?"

"No, but if your theory holds true, he's probably heading for the hotel were the movie was made. That's where I'd try."

"Good thinking. I gotta run now. Dude?"

"I know, I know, Lieutenant—stay with you."

"Not what I was gonna say."

"Oh. What were you going to—?"

"Dude?"

I sighed. "Yes, Lieutenant?"

"We're gonna nail his ass."

"Yes, I believe you will."

Then he said, "Stay with me," and burped and hung up.

I immediately got my Il Bisonte overnight bag out of the closet, stuffed some clothes and shaving gear and mackerel cans in it, and told Lulu we were leaving. She still wouldn't budge from under the bed. I had to grab her by the front paws and slide her out, shaking, covered with dust balls. Then the two of us headed out.

A cab dropped us at the garage on West Sixty-seventh where Merilee keeps the Jaguar, my police tail hovering a careful half-block behind in an unmarked navy-blue sedan. I gassed it up, put the top down, and headed out. I didn't have time right now to ask Merilee for permission. I worked my way down Broadway, making no effort to beat the sluggish flow. My tail stayed his same half-block behind. There was the usual bottleneck at Columbus Circle before Broadway became all one-way and the flow opened up. I cruised through what was left of the theater district and then the trashy splendor of Forty-second Street before I made a right at Thirty-ninth and headed west toward the Lincoln Tunnel, which is how you go under the Hudson into New Jersey, especially if you're heading south to Atlantic City. My tail stayed with me.

The tunnel traffic choked up just before it reached Ninth Avenue. Truckers, cabbies, delivery-van drivers, were stuck there honking and cursing at each other hotly. I casually inched ahead of a cab and then not so casually cut him off as I swung left onto Ninth and tore downtown. The Jag is a phenomenal darter—it's almost as swift and elusive in traffic as Merilee is in the shoe stores of Milan's Montenapoleone. By Thirty-seventh, I was losing sight of my tail in my rearview mirror. I made a right there on two wheels and shot through the crosstown traffic to Eleventh, where I made a left and then sped down to Thirty-fourth, no tail in sight. I took Thirty-fourth back across town toward the East Side. Certain I was alone now, I got on the FDR Drive and made my way up the East River toward the New England Thruway. And Connecticut.

Ferris Rush was many things. Brilliant. Disturbed. Tragic. One thing he wasn't was stupid. If he was headed for Atlantic City, there was no way he'd abandon the

Loveboat there in Trenton for everyone to find. That was to throw the police off. He knew Very would draw precisely the conclusion Very had drawn. He knew they would spend days combing the hotels and casinos for him.

They would find nothing. Ferris Rush had gone in the direction I was going now—the opposite direction. He was making a run for his shack on Crescent Moon Pond, just as he had run for it after that night with Skitsy in his cabin at Stony Creek. Every man, Smilin' Jack told him, needs his secret place. The shack was his. He was headed for the pond. And so was I. To have it out with him.

The shack was dark.

No light came from its busted windows as I rowed around the bend in the dusk, Lulu seated stiffly before me in her life preserver, nostrils aquiver. What had been sticky haze in the city was cool dampness here. The pond gave off a fetid, yeasty smell. It was very quiet. No sound except for the soft plop the oars made as they broke the glassy surface. It was completely dark by the time I reached the shack, dark like it doesn't get in the city. I couldn't even see Lulu in the other end of the boat. I needed my flashlight to guide me to the remains of the mooring. No other boat was tied up there. The kid at the boatyard said no one besides me had rented one in days. Was I wrong? I couldn't be. He was here. Had to be here.

Lulu remembered where we were. She guided me up the shack's rickety steps to the open front door. The oil lantern was sitting there on the rough table as before, only it had oil in it now, and a box of kitchen matches next to it. I lit it, bathing the room in golden light.

The wood stove had been used in the past day—the heavy cast iron was still warm to the touch. Fresh firewood was piled before it. Cans of chili and soup were piled up over with the kitchen things. A tin of crackers. A crumpled pack of Marlboros. His brand. A half-empty bottle of tequila. His drink.

I carried the lantern into the tiny bedroom. Lying there on the stained mattress was the copy of *The Great Gatsby* I'd given him a couple of weeks before. I know it was the same one because it was my own cherished copy, the autographed first edition I'd found hidden among the old Dartmouth yearbooks in grandfather's attic one hot summer day long ago.

I went back out onto the front porch and called out his name as loud as I could, in every direction. I waited. After a moment, I heard footsteps off in the brush. Coming toward the shack. Closer. Closer still. I shone the flashlight—it was a raccoon. Lulu growled at it but didn't budge from the porch. Raccoons fight back.

It had gotten cold out. I made a fire in the stove and sampled the tequila. Out back I pumped some water into a pail from the well. I put a bowl of it down for Lulu along with a can of her mackerel. I opened one of the cans of chili and heated it in a pan on the stove. When it was hot, I ate it with some crackers and washed it down with tequila and well water. Then I stretched out on the mattress with the lantern and F. Scott Fitzgerald and waited for Ferris Rush to come home.

I waited for a long time. I waited the whole night, sleeping fitfully with my old leather jacket and Lulu over me for warmth. I waited through the long next day, a day I spent skipping stones on the pond and sitting on the porch in the sun thinking about Ferris Rush and his story, the story I was about to write. It was a story of genius, ambition, and greed. Of sex, drugs, fame, fraud, and murder. A lot of your basics. It was not a pretty story, and there was no happy ending to it—at least I sure couldn't see one coming. One question still nagged at me. Was Ferris Rush the villain of this story or the victim? Was he responsible for what had happened or were those around him responsible—Boyd Samuels, Tanner Marsh, Skitsy Held, and all of their machinery of literary celebrity? I still didn't know the answer to that question. I would have to face him to know it.

Toward late afternoon I put Lulu back in her life preserver and rowed us across to the Jag. I left the boat there and drove to the general store a few miles up the road from the boatyard. No one there remembered selling any canned goods to a blond guy in the past few days. I bought some ham sandwiches and a six-pack of Guinness and used the pay phone out front to call Merilee.

"Why, it's Mr. Hoagy," she exclaimed warmly.

"Just wanted to let you know I borrowed the Jag from the garage," I told her. "It was an emergency, and I didn't have time to ask if you—"

"Quite all right, darling," she said mildly. "I still think of it as half yours anyway. Hoagy?"

"Yes, Merilee?"

"Hello."

"Hello yourself," I said, pleased she was being such a good sport about my stealing her car. "Listen, there's one other thing. If Very happens to call, don't tell—"

"If a very *what* happens to call you what?" she broke in, confused.

"Romaine Very. He's a short, muscular cop with an earring and a bad stomach. If he calls you in the next day or so, and he will, tell him I've been writing in seclusion and that I cannot be disturbed by anyone for any reason. Tell him I'm always this way when I write. Tell him I'm weird. Tell him anything. Just don't tell him where I am, okay?"

"Okay," she agreed. "And where are you?"

"You don't want to know."

"Horseradish."

I tugged at my ear. "I'm in Connecticut. I've found him. At least I think I have."

"But half of the police in the Northeast are looking for him in—"

"The wrong place."

"Hoagy, may I remind you that this man has already killed two people?"

"I'm well aware of that fact."

"What's to stop him from killing you, too, if you get in his way?"

"I have my methods." I glanced down at my protector, who lay curled at my feet, daintily licking her soft white underbelly. "Besides, all I want to do is talk to him. As a friend. I care about what happens to him. Face it, there aren't a lot of people around now who do."

"That's because he's murdered the others. Hoagy, Hoagy, Hoagy. You loyal fool."

"You got that half right. Merilee, will you tell Very what I said?"

"Of course, darling. You can always count on me."

"Thanks. And thanks for being so understanding about the car."

"It's true, I am being terribly understanding. It must be because you let me see Sweetness on Sundays. She'll come stay with me in the country sometimes, won't she? She loves the outdoors so."

"Of course. But you have to remember that deep down inside she's still a city dog. She likes the hubbub, the ballet, breakfast in bed . . ."

"She's not the only one."

"I remember. Champagne and fresh-squeezed orange juice for starters. A slice of muskmelon, followed by a caviar-and-sour-cream omelet, followed by—"

"*Mister* Hoagy. There are laws against discussing *that* on interstate phone lines."

"No law against remembering though, is there?"

She was silent a moment. "No. None," she admitted softly. "Hoagy?"

"Yes, Merilee?"

"Be careful. Lulu is much too young and innocent to lose you. And so is her mommy."

I took the long way back to Crescent Moon Pond. Up the winding country road into Hadlyme, then onto a narrower one that twisted its way through a forest before it dead-ended at a small farm set behind old stone walls encrusted with lichen. I stopped there and turned off the engine. The house was set way back behind fields of wildflowers and green grass and fruit trees and a pond, where I could hear the ducks quacking. It was a snug old house, creamy yellow in the late-day sun, with white shutters and trim. The carriage barn was red. It was a lovely place, a safe haven, a refuge. She was right—it was home.

I sat there gazing at it, wondering if it would ever be *my* home. It would never have lasted with Charlie. It would have turned up Merilee again. She and I were destined for each other. Or doomed, depending on how you want to look at it. And maybe it *was* time for this. Time to surrender what was left of New York to the Yushies. I didn't belong there anymore. Maybe I never had, but when you're the center of attention, you tend not to notice. Was this the ending for novel number three? Hoagy the country squire—scribbling in his chapel in the morning, shoveling manure in the afternoon? I sat there gazing at it and thinking it didn't sound too terrible. Of course it didn't. Daydreams seldom do.

Ferris Rush wasn't the only one whose line between fact and fiction was awful damned fuzzy.

I started up the Jag and floored it out of there, cursing myself.

. . .

I ate the ham sandwiches and drank the Guinness and spent another night on that sour-smelling bare mattress. And another day on the porch, where I reread *The Great Gatsby*, and enjoyed it more than I ever had. And still one more night. And with the dawn came the reality—he wasn't coming back to his secret place. I had gotten close, closer than anyone else had. But I'd missed him. He was gone, and this time I didn't know where.

I had no choice now. It was time to go back to the city and get out my mukluks.

Chapter Sixteen

r. Adelman had nearly wept when I'd shown up at his shop on Amsterdam with my hammered, ruined Olympia. It was he who had sold it to me and lovingly maintained it through the years. I'd begged him to save it. He'd said he was a typewriter man, not a magician.

He *was* a magician. It shone like new there now on his counter, straining for action. He shone, too, a proud craftsman of the old, old school. Before he would let me take it home, he made me swear I'd never run over it again with a Jeep, or whatever I had done to it—he didn't want to know. I made him swear he'd never let Benetton or The Gap push him out on the street. We shook on that.

When I got home with it, I made a pot of coffee and arranged the transcripts of my interviews in piles on Ferris Rush's writing table. I had mixed feelings about his table now. Part of me wanted to saw it in half and throw it in the street. For now, I intended to keep it. I'd earned it.

I got my mukluks out of the closet and put them on. I wore them when I wrote the first novel. I've worn them every single time I've sat down in front of my typewriter since. They're starting to get a little ragged, but so am I. After I poured myself a cup of coffee I sat down at the table and got started. Lulu stretched out under me with her head on my foot, swallowed contentedly, and dropped off.

I am not who you think I am. I am not Cameron Sheffield Noyes. My name is Ferris Rush, and I am a murderer.

I took it from there. My opening approach was to weigh the privileged, made-up Farmington upbringing of Cam Noyes against the gritty, real Port Arthur childhood of Ferris Rush. I gave him a sardonic, slightly weary voice, the voice of his *Bang* storyteller. His voice. Quickly, I realized that this would be my hardest memoir to get down on paper. Unlike the other celebrities I'd written for, this one happened to be an acclaimed novelist. His prose, his observations, would have to have some kind of literary merit. The words couldn't just come tumbling out onto the page any old way. In fact, they soon wouldn't come tumbling at all. I got stuck in deep mud after three pages, my wheels spinning, and I couldn't get out.

Something was wrong.

It wasn't writer's block. That's a void, a fear. The stomach muscles tighten. The hairs on the back of the neck stand up. No, this was the nagging itch I get when a scene I've written doesn't work. Oh, it seems fine on the surface. But deep down inside I just know something is wrong with it. Only I don't know what it is. It's an itch I can't get to. Not until I've analyzed the scene from every possible angle, taken it apart piece by piece, turned it inside out. Eventually, if I keep at it long enough, I find the flaw. But I can never rest until I do. Because my itch is never, ever wrong.

I didn't have the whole story. I thought I did but I didn't. I was wrong. That's why I was stuck. I was still missing something. Something crucial. But what?

I got up and paced from one end of the living room to the other. It's not very far. I paced, the floor of the old brownstone creaking under me. Lulu watched me, her eyes darting back and forth, back and forth. I went over my approach. I went over everything that happened from the beginning, step by step. What was I missing? Was it something he'd said to me once, something that didn't fit? Something somebody else had said? What?

I took Lulu for a walk in Riverside Park, a man possessed now. I turned the soil over and over as I walked, my hands shoved in my pockets, lips moving. That's one big plus about living in New York. No one in the park paid me any attention—their lips were moving, too. I got nowhere. I stopped at a Greek coffee shop and ate a cheeseburger that tasted like flannel. I climbed back up to my apartment and made another pot of coffee and started working my way through the transcripts, line by line, searching for I didn't know what. I read all of them. It was nearly four in the morning when I was done. I found nothing. Nothing that took care of my itch.

Lulu was fast asleep now on the love seat. I opened a Bass ale and fell into my chair and drank it. I went over my Farmington trip notes. Nothing there either.

It was only out of utter desperation that I started looking through the carton full of Charlie's papers, the one Very had asked me to hold on to. He still hadn't had a chance to sift through it yet—the manhunt was keeping him busy. There were sales records in there for work she'd sold. Some pretty prominent collectors involved. . . . Letters. One from her sister in San Francisco, who was going through a difficult pregnancy and wondering whether the baby would save her marriage. Another from a man named Alan Berger, who lived on East Sixty-third and whom she'd evidently dumped for Ferris. I set this letter aside. . . . Clippings—rave reviews for her work from the *Times*, *Newsweek*, *Artnews*. . . . Tax returns for the past two years. Passport. Checkbook, bank statements, canceled checks. I leafed through her checkbook. She'd evidently taken care of their domestic life in Gramercy Park—New York Telephone, Con Edison, Allstate. Each entry was in her square, careful handwriting. I yanked the rubber band off the canceled checks and rifled through them. She was organized. In the lower left-hand corner of each check she'd detailed precisely what service had been rendered. Phone service, April. Home insurance, first quarter . . .

And then I saw it. One particular canceled check. And a bomb went off in my head. That odd fact. Here it was. And here was the key that unlocked the door. Maybe. I glanced at grandfather's Rolex. It was six-thirty now. What better time to catch someone in. I reached for the phone and dialed the party whose name was on that check. Someone who was rather surprised by my call, especially at this hour, but who was not at all uncooperative. We talked briefly. But plenty long enough to confirm my worst suspicions. I hung up shaking, my mouth dry.

It all made sense now. Horrible, ugly sense. Worse than I could have imagined, and I have a vivid imagination. Now I knew why I couldn't write Ferris Rush's story yet. I was wrong. About all of it. We were all wrong.

But I'd need Very's help if I was going to make it right.

He was waiting for me with his bike out in front of the building on Fortieth and Lex where Skitsy's company, Murray Hill Press, had their offices. The secretaries in their summer dresses and Reeboks were eyeballing him standing there in his tank top and spandex shorts as they went through the revolving door. He was ignoring them. He was too busy glowering at me.

"Yo, what's this all about, dude?" he demanded coldly, muscular arms crossed in front of his chest.

"A theory I want to test out, Lieutenant," I explained. "Can't do it without you."

"Seem you can do *plenty* without me," he said, jaw working his gum.

"I can?"

"You purposely slipped your tail outside of the Lincoln Tunnel, disappeared for two whole fucking days. I wanna know where."

"Didn't you speak to my ex-wife?"

"Sure, I spoke to her. Got my chain jerked about how sensitive an artist you are, how you require seclusion. . . ."

"You didn't believe her?"

"Show me some respect, huh!" he exploded. "I'm a person! You *talk* to a person! You don't jerk chains! I want to know where you were! Was it Atlantic City?"

"No, it wasn't."

He waited for me to tell him more. When I didn't, he started nodding to his own personal beat, the muscles of his neck and shoulders bunched tightly. "Okay. That's cool. You wanna fuck around, we'll fuck around—in a interrogation room. Let's go."

"Wait, Lieutenant. Hold on. All I'm asking of you is—"

"Too fucking much, dude. I'm trying to find a guy who blew away two ladies. The trail's cold. My stomach is in involuntary spasms. You're holding out on me. And *now* you expect me to play along blind with you. Uh-uh. No way. I'm coming down on you—suspicion of aiding and abetting. You are under arrest. You have the right to remain silent. Anything you say may be—"

"Okay, okay, Lieutenant. You win. What do you want to know?"

"Everything. Until I get it, you get nothing from me, except a cell."

"And if I tell you, you'll help me?"

He didn't answer me. Just stood there glaring at me and popping his gum.

So I told him. I told him all about Ferris Rush of Port Arthur, Texas, and how he'd slammed into a busload of kids and gotten away with it, and how Skitsy Held had owned him because of it. I told him about the shack on Crescent Moon Pond, and how I'd been there, and thought he had, too. I told him all of it, because it didn't matter anymore. All that mattered was that I get into Skitsy Held's files upstairs, and I couldn't do that without him.

When I finished, he closed his eyes a second and made a face and rubbed his stomach, mulling it over. "Okay . . . okay . . . and now you got some theory involving Murray Hill Press."

"Correct."

"What's this theory got to do with Rush?"

"Everything and nothing."

He frowned. "I don't follow."

"Do you trust me, Lieutenant?"

"No."

"Look, just do this one thing for me and I promise I'll make it up to you for having been so uncooperative."

"How?"

"I'll take you to Ferris Rush."

His eyes widened. "Wait, you know where he is?"

I started for the revolving door. "Stay with me, Lieutenant."

He stayed with me.

Chapter Seventeen

T*ape #2 w/Boyd Samuels recorded May 20 on the patio of Ferris Rush's Gramercy Park town house. Also present are Lt. Romaine Very, Vic Early, and Samuels's assistant, Todd Lesser)*

HOAG: Thanks for coming here like this in the middle of the workday. I know it was short notice.

SAMUELS: You said it was an emergency, amigo. Whatever we can do, we'll do. To tell you the truth, I'm not exactly thrilled about the police being in on this. . . .

HOAG: It has to be this way. I'm sorry.

SAMUELS: *(pause)* If you say so. Go ahead.

HOAG: I wanted to talk to you about one of your scams— your biggest scam, in fact. I really have to hand it to you. You're an artist.

SAMUELS: Thanks, but I'm not sure I know what the hell you're talking about.

HOAG: Your freshman year at Columbia, Boyd, when you and Ferris were hanging out a lot at the clubs, and he was modeling, and getting bored with it. He started writing stories about your scene, and he submitted them to Tanner Marsh under his modeling name, Cameron Sheffield Noyes. Tanner told me he was really knocked out by him. His looks, breeding, personality. The kid had star written all over him, except for one small problem—his writing.

SAMUELS: Yeah, Tanner didn't like the stories. So Ferris went back to work, and the novel was a whole different thing. Tanner loved the novel.

HOAG: Yes, he said it was nothing like what Ferris had shown him before. That he'd grown tremendously, blossomed. But that isn't what really happened, is it?

SAMUELS: *(silence)* Meaning what?

HOAG: Want to tell us how it happened, Boyd? *(no response)* Or perhaps Todd can fill us in.

LESSER: Me?

HOAG: You. You told me at Delilah's party that you left Columbia because of personal problems.

LESSER: Yes, I did.

HOAG: According to Ferris, your personal problem was that you were one of Boyd's biggest cocaine customers.

SAMUELS: Hey, no need to get into that, amigo, especially in front of—

VERY: Shut up, Samuels.

SAMUELS: Yessir.

LESSER: It's true. I-I had trouble being away from home for the first time. Fitting in with new people. Couldn't seem t-to talk to anybody. So I started spending more and more time alone in my room. And getting deeper and deeper into coke.

HOAG: How much did you owe him, Todd?

LESSER: J-Just under two thousand dollars. But I paid it back before I left school. I paid back all of it.

HOAG: I know you did. Want to tell us how? *(no response)* Come on, Todd. Tell us what were you doing there in your room with the door closed.

LESSER: I . . . I . . .

HOAG: You were writing a novel, weren't you? The story of one sensitive young man's breakdown. Your breakdown.

LESSER: Yes.

HOAG: You were desperate. No money to pay Boyd back. No money to get more coke. So when Boyd came to you with a small proposition, you listened. You had to listen. Isn't that right, Boyd?

SAMUELS: I'm thinking to myself, whoa, this Marsh guy smells class and money on Ferris. Can maybe turn him into a major celebrity. I'm thinking what a shame it is we don't have a book the fat slob can run with.

HOAG: So you bought yourself one. You erased Todd's debt and fed him some more coke, in exchange for which he gave you his manuscript. No big deal, was it, Todd? No different from getting paid to do a term paper for somebody. You were just a college kid, a strung-out, fucked-up college kid. All you cared about was getting Boyd off your back and your nose filled. How could you possibly have known what was going to happen? How could anyone?

VERY: Yo, you're saying *this* guy wrote *Bang*?

HOAG: I'm saying Ferris Rush has never published a word in his life. Or even read a word, for that matter. He's a front. A face. A personality. A scam. Tanner told me how strange he found him when they worked together on the manuscript. How Ferris seemed not to grasp what he had written. Of course he didn't—he hadn't written it. That's the real reason why he ran away from Stony Creek. He was afraid if he spent too much time around there with all of those real writers, somebody might get wise to him. So he hid out at his shack. You met him there, didn't you, Todd? The two of you went over Tanner's suggestions together.

Then you did the rewrites while Ferris fished. When you were done, he resurfaced with his finished manuscript. And sold it. You freaked out at this point, didn't you, realizing that your book was actually going to get published and that someone else was going to get the credit for it. Pretty tough to handle. You couldn't. You dropped out of school. Took off. Why did you let them get away with it, Todd? Why didn't you speak up?

LESSER: Because I had no real proof that I wrote it. No handwritten manuscript. No contract. It was just my word against theirs, and nobody would have believed me—Boyd assured me of that. He also assured me he'd go to any length to ruin me if I fucked this thing up for them.

SAMUELS: Toddy and I made a legitimate business deal. He *sold* me the manuscript. Besides, I've always taken care of him. I gave him a job, didn't I? I didn't have to do that.

HOAG: You've taken care of him, all right. Because of him Ferris Rush became a world-famous literary luminary and a millionaire. In exchange for that you let Todd get your coffee for you. You're a gent, Boyd. A real gent. . . . The secret of *Bang* has stayed a secret. No one has ever found out. Not Tanner. Not even Skitsy, did she?

SAMUELS: Correct.

HOAG: Naturally, Ferris couldn't deliver a second novel. He became more and more angry and self-destructive— partly because of the schoolbus business, but mostly because he's been a complete fraud. He's been able to fool other people, but not himself. You cooked up your bullshit memoir idea to keep the money flowing in. Charlie's art was a nice bonus. And you brought me in. Why? Why not just have Todd write it? Why take the chance your secret might get out?

SAMUELS: To succeed it had to be prestigious. People around town had to know a name writer was involved, even if uncredited. You were the ideal candidate.

VERY: Yo, if I could jump in here . . . ?

HOAG: Go ahead, Lieutenant.

VERY: It's not that I'm not finding this a stimulating literary discussion, but where is it taking us, y'know?

HOAG: Be patient, Lieutenant. We'll get there.

VERY: Yeah, but you told me you knew were Ferris Rush is.

HOAG: I do.

VERY: So where is he?

HOAG: We're sitting on him.

VERY: *(silence)* We're what?

HOAG: Ferris Rush is dead. Has been since the day Charlie
died. He was murdered by the same person who stabbed
her and pushed Skitsy. His body is hidden under this nice
new bluestone patio the contractor laid down. Except it
wasn't the contractor who laid it—was it, Todd?

LESSER: I-I don't know what you mean.

SAMUELS: *Toddy?*

EARLY: *You* killed that nice little girl? *You!*

HOAG: Sit down, Vic. Stay cool.

SAMUELS: Jeez . . . what's the matter with him? He looks
like he's going to—

HOAG: Vic, can you hear me? *Vic?*

EARLY: *(silence)* Yeah . . . Sorry, Hoag. I'm okay. Sorry.
Go ahead.

HOAG: I found something when I was going through Charlie's canceled checks, Todd. Something that clicked. You
told me that after you dropped out of Columbia you drifted
around upstate for a while. Worked odd jobs. Worked *construction.*

LESSER: I did. So?

VERY: Who was this canceled check to, dude?

HOAG: One Michael Mordarski of Sheepshead Bay, Brooklyn. He's the contractor who's been renovating this place. I
spoke to him first thing this morning. Asked him if anyone
had been around in the past few days to put in a little dry

wall here, a little patio there. He said no one had. He apologized, promised he'd finish up here as soon as he could. *(pause)* He's down there, isn't he, Todd?

LESSER: *(silence)* The sleazy bastard got what he deserved. He didn't deserve his success. He was a fraud, like you said. A fraud! His very existence demeaned the world of literature! He didn't deserve her, either. Charlie. She was so sweet, so lovely. And he used her. Cheated on her. Hurt her.

HOAG: Want to tell us about it, Todd? *(silence)* Okay, feel free to stop me if I miss anything. . . . You wanted me off of this project from the moment Ferris called Boyd and told him what our plan was—a plan for a book that might actually have some value. You didn't want that. You wanted him to keep sliding down, down, down, this pretender who had achieved the success that rightly belonged to you. So you came to my apartment that first night, by way of my roof, and you left me a threat. When I didn't quit, you played it a little tougher. Sledgehammered your way in. Destroyed my typewriter—only another writer could know how much that would hurt. Then you tried to blind Merilee with that little jack-in-the-box. Except I still didn't quit. Neither did you. You sent me to Farmington so that I'd find out the truth about who Cameron Sheffield Noyes really was. What were you hoping I'd do?

LESSER: Quit. Tell everyone in town. Embarrass him. Humiliate him.

HOAG: Skitsy's murder really threw me. I kept thinking she was killed so she couldn't talk to me. She wasn't. Her death had nothing to do with our book, or with her crooked business dealing or any of that. *(rustling noise)* It had to do with this, didn't it?

SAMUELS: What is that?

HOAG: A rejection letter. Lieutenant Very and I found it this morning in her files at Murray Hill Press. That's something else you mentioned to me at Delilah's party, Todd. You told me you'd just finished writing a novel.

SAMUELS: I didn't know you were writing another book, Toddy.

LESSER: I wouldn't let you get your filthy scheming hands on it! You'd steal it! Make me say Ferris wrote it!

HOAG: What's it about, Todd?

LESSER: A brilliant young writer. His rise to fame and fortune. His burnout. It's called *Boy Wonder*. I-I'm very proud of it. I submitted it on my own to Skitsy. She was the best in the business. She had made Ferris. Now it was my turn. Time for the success I deserved. That's all I wanted—what I deserved. What I had earned. It was only fair.

HOAG: And she turned you down.

LESSER: She dismissed it. Said it was . . .

HOAG: " 'A small, predictable story about small, predictable people. The writing is flat and undistinguished. Sorry I can't be more enthusiastic, Toddy. Maybe next time.' "

LESSER: " 'Maybe next time.' " *Maybe next time!* I'm the man who wrote *Bang*, damn it! They've compared me to F. Scott Fucking Fitzgerald! But she didn't smell money on me. I wasn't hot. So it was sorry, Toddy. Tough shit, Toddy. I-I couldn't accept that. I just couldn't. It wasn't fair. I deserved more. I called her and she agreed to see me for a few minutes at her apartment after work. I went up there at six. Boyd had already left the office for a drink date. One of the other kids covered for me. I said I was getting my teeth cleaned.

HOAG: How come no one saw you go in her building?

LESSER: No one ever sees me. I'm part of the wall. The doorman was busy flirting with somebody's maid out on the sidewalk. He ignored me. I just walked in. I didn't sneak in. I-I never went there intending to *kill* Skitsy. It's just that she made me so damned mad. She *patronized* me. Treated me like I was some kind of untalented amateur, some *loser.* Didn't even offer me a drink. So I-I told her the truth. I told her *I* wrote *Bang.* I told her that Cam Noyes was a fraud. That she'd been taken in. Know what she did? She laughed at me. She was so damned sure of herself, and of her right to dictate who gets into the charmed inner circle and who doesn't. I just couldn't stand it, her laughing at me like that. So I pushed her. It was an impulse. Blind rage. And then . . . then I realized if I got out of there fast, if no one saw me, it would look just like a suicide. I ran into her bathroom and grabbed the clothes in her hamper. A yellow dress, some other things, detergent. I took the stairs down two flights in case anybody was coming up in the elevator. Then I caught the elevator down to the laundry room in the basement. I did a load of wash while the shit was hitting the fan. No one looked for me down there. When I left, there was still a lot of confusion out front and no one noticed me. By now, I'd been away from the office an hour. I was in a hurry to get back. I had the wet laundry with me in a shopping bag. It wouldn't have been smart to leave it there. And I didn't have time to drop it off at my apartment—I live way the hell out in Park Slope. It's all I can afford. So I dumped it a couple of blocks away in a trash can. I guess that was a mistake.

VERY: It was.

HOAG: Still, you managed to turn it to your own advantage, didn't you, Todd? Everyone assumed Ferris killed Skitsy. You certainly made it look like he killed Charlie. . . . You loved Charlie. More than you could stand. It was incredibly painful for you to see them together, her and Ferris—the man with the career, the woman, the *life*, that should have been yours. You were elated when she left him. You thought this was your chance. Only it wasn't, was it? She left a note for me at my apartment Saturday morning saying she'd meet me for lunch if I got back from Connecticut in time. A somewhat romantic note. You saw it when you let yourself into my apartment that morning by way of my easy-opening front door.

LESSER: I-I wanted to see if the two of you were . . . if she was . . .

HOAG: You freaked. Decided if you couldn't have her, no one could. You'd already killed one person. You decided to kill two more, especially because it all fit together so very neatly—at least it did if you moved quickly and carefully, and you did. You're very good with plots, Todd.

LESSER: Thank you.

HOAG: You hightailed it right over here and waited for your opportunity. You got it when Ferris and Vic went out for a nice long run. The second they left you slipped inside the house. Spare key?

LESSER: Boyd had one made for me in case I ever needed to drop anything off to be signed or whatever.

HOAG: You went upstairs and stole the bowie knife. You knew there were photos of Ferris with the knife, that it would be traced to him. Then you laid your groundwork for later on by doing some dry-wall work in the kitchen. What with New York contractors being so notoriously unreliable, you knew no one would question it, and that it would draw attention away from your main intention. You slipped out before Ferris and Vic got back. Went to Rat's Nest with the knife and waited across the street for the clerk to leave on her break. You knew Charlie would be alone in there waiting for me. You knew the setup there—you'd picked her up there a few times when Ferris was running late, or forgot her. You also knew you had to work fast. You buzzed the second the clerk left. Charlie let you in.

LESSER: She died in my arms. No more pain. I was the one who could make her happy, you know. I was the only one. But she wouldn't have me. She was blind. All she knew was the pain. So I freed her from it. It was an act of mercy, don't you see? It was beautiful. I put her back up on her canvas when she was gone. She deserved to be up there. She was a great artist and *Blue Monday* was her greatest statement. Her last statement. I gave it to her. It was from me to her. Something we'll always have. Together. No one can take it away from us. No one.

HOAG: You ducked out before the clerk got back, before I arrived. You came directly here and let yourself in. Ferris was asleep upstairs. Vic was out guarding Merilee. That was a stroke of luck for you—he left Ferris here all alone. Tell me, what would you have done if he hadn't?

LESSER: That's easy—I'd have killed him, too.

EARLY: Kill me? Just exactly how, pal?

LESSER: Mind if I take off my raincoat, Lieutenant?

VERY: Whatever.

LESSER: With *this*.

HOAG: *(silence)* What is that you're pointing at me, Todd?

VERY: It's a Mossberg pistol-grip pump-action .22-caliber shotgun, dude. Current weapon of choice among drug enforcers. Can be concealed along the leg and whipped out like a pistol. But it packs the punch of a longarm. Nice toy. Where'd you get it, Lesser?

LESSER: Bought it from a drug dealer I know.

HOAG: Is it loaded, Todd?

LESSER: Yes, it is.

HOAG: Just checking. Shall I go on? *(no response)* I'll go on. You went upstairs and murdered Ferris in his sleep. Did you use that?

LESSER: No, too messy. I wanted no traces to be found. I strangled him. It was so much more . . . *personal*. Intimate. I felt so powerful, so *right* as I held that sleaze there in my hands, knowing I was not only choking the life out of him but *ruining* him, too. His reputation, I mean. No one would ever think of him as a great writer now. He'd just be a murderer. A common murderer. I dragged him down here in the sheet and dug a hole and buried him. Then I smoothed it over and laid the patio. Then I went back upstairs and remade the bed and packed up some of his clothes, cigarettes, the book he was reading, anything that he might take with him if he were on the run. I stuffed it in the trunk of the Olds and drove off. I couldn't disappear for a long time—I knew Boyd would start calling me as soon as he heard about Charlie—but I wanted to get the car past the tollbooths before the police put out the word on it. I stashed it in a twenty-four-hour garage in Hoboken. Then I took the train home.

HOAG: And so began the manhunt. That was a nice touch, telling Boyd that Ferris had just called from a gas station in Mount Vernon. Boyd believed you. I believed you.

LESSER: People tend to. It's because I'm so nonthreatening. They think only winners know how to lie. After work I went back out to Hoboken, got the car, and drove it to Trenton, where I left it. I wanted the police to think he was heading for Atlantic City.

VERY: Score one for you.

LESSER: From Trenton I caught a bus to New Haven. I hitchhiked the rest of the way to Crescent Moon Pond. I assumed the police would eventually find out about the shack after they struck out in Atlantic City.

HOAG: And you wanted it to look like he'd been hiding there. Another nice touch. Convincing. I waited two whole days there for him to come back. How did you get out to the shack without a boat?

LESSER: There's a trail through the woods behind it that runs into a road after a couple of miles. I backpacked in and out. I had a flashlight. When I got there, I made a fire and lit the lantern and unpacked the stuff I'd brought with me—the package of Marlboros, copy of *Gatsby*, food, half-empty bottle of tequila . . .

SAMUELS: That sounds like an excellent idea. *(sound of chair scraping)*

LESSER: Where do you think you're going, Boyd?

SAMUELS: Nowhere. Just raiding the liquor cupboard.

LESSER: Sit down. Now!

SAMUELS: Okay, Toddy. If that's what you want.

LESSER: And don't call me Toddy! I hate that name. It's a name for an ineffectual wimp.

HOAG: Which you are not.

LESSER: You've always used me, Boyd. Treated me like a nothing. Maybe you've changed your opinion of me now.

HOAG: I think we all have, Todd. You're no wimp. You're the boss—whatever happens now is up to you.

LESSER: Nice to see that you know it. I guess this is what it takes. I guess you have to point a gun at people to get their respect.

VERY: You got it, Lesser. But what are you gonna do about it? Kill all four of us? You're gonna have to, because if even one of us survives this—and I don't think you can take out more than two of us before the other two jump you—you're smoked. We got your whole confession right here on tape. Don't make it any worse for yourself, Lesser. Just hand over the gun.

LESSER: What have I got to gain? My life is over no matter what I do.

HOAG: Maybe not, Todd. Everyone's going to know the truth about you now, about how you wrote *Bang*. You're going to be famous, and there's going to be a great deal of interest in your new manuscript. Don't you think so, Boyd?

SAMUELS: Give me ten minutes on the phone and I'll get you seven figures. Guaranteed.

HOAG: You've *made* it, Todd. Ferris is gone. It's *your* time now. You wanted to be a great author, not a mass murderer. Don't blow it.

LESSER: *(silence)* Maybe you're on to something . . .

HOAG: Sure I am. Hand over the gun, Todd. Just hand it over. That's the spirit. No, don't, Todd! Not that! No! *(sound of explosion, indistinguishable curses)*

(end tape)

Chapter Eighteen

They had to wait awhile before they could dig up the patio. The photographs had to be taken. The body had to be bagged and carted away, the blood and brains hosed off. It wasn't a neat job. You don't get a neat corpse when you blow your own head off with a shotgun.

Two of them moved the patio furniture aside and started in on the bluestone with picks and shovels while Very talked to the FBI on the phone inside. I watched them work. Boyd Samuels sat in a garden chair next to me gulping a large whiskey. He was trembling and quite pale.

It was a warm day, and heavy work. The diggers offered no resistance when Vic returned from the basement with a sledgehammer and joined them. Soon they were standing back, watching in awe as the big guy ferociously attacked the stones and mortar. The ground shook from each thundering blow. His chest heaved. The sweat flew from him. He had failed Ferris. Now he was atoning.

"Thought you had him there for a second, dude." Very was standing next to me now, popping his gum.

"Had him?"

"Talked him out of pulling the trigger. He seemed to be wavering there for a second, y'know?"

I shook my head. "Never. He had to do it."

"How come?"

"His hero had."

The stones and mortar were broken up now. Vic and the diggers began to shovel it aside.

"Felt kinda sorry for him, actually," Very said, eyeing Boyd Samuels, who was staring morosely into his glass. "He did get pretty royally screwed. That didn't give him the right to take out three people. No way. But still . . ."

I tugged at my ear. "Yeah. I think I know what you mean."

"Lieutenant!"

They'd found the shallow grave. A corner of white sheet stuck out of the bare, dark earth now.

Very nodded to them. They started digging.

"What will you do with him, Lieutenant?" I asked.

"Take his remains over to the coroner," he replied. "See that he's given a proper burial."

"Couldn't you just leave him here? He's dead and buried. Why disturb him? We know what happened."

Very narrowed his eyes at me. "Procedure, dude. Gotta be followed. Besides, this is a private residence. A body can't be buried here."

"He belongs here."

"In his backyard?"

"In Gramercy Park, with all of the other major figures in American literature. In his own weird way, he was one of them."

They lifted the body out by the sheet and laid it on a stretcher. Then they unwrapped it. It was him, all right.

They carried him through the house to the ambulance out front.

Boyd Samuels followed them, barking at them to be careful. "That's my friend there," he cried. "My best friend."

Very's jaw worked on his gum as he stared at the empty grave. "Gotta admit I doubted you there for a while, dude. Thought you were jerking me around, and you *were*. But I see where you were coming from now." He stuck out his hand and burped. "Take care of yourself, dude."

I shook his hand. "Likewise, Lieutenant. And take care of that stomach."

"What I gotta do is find a less stressful line of work," he said, nodding. "But hey, what else is there that's so much fucking fun, huh? Sometime we gotta get together. Like I told ya, I gotta million stories to—"

"Now wouldn't be a good time."

"Whatever," he said easily as he left.

Vic was sitting in the shade, mopping his face with a towel. I sat down next to him. Neither of us spoke for a while.

"There was nothing you could have done, Vic," I finally said. "If you *had* been here to protect him, Todd would just have killed you, too."

"I could have tried," he said softly.

"He had a shotgun."

"I could have tried," he repeated. "It's what I'm paid to do."

"No, you're not. You're not paid to die."

He shrugged that off, hung his head.

I went inside and found two beers in the refrigerator and came back out with them. He took one from me and drank some of it.

"Listen, Vic. Merilee is going to need a live-in caretaker at her new farm. Someone handy and reliable and self-sufficient. Might be a good situation for you. Nice area. Fishing's good."

"Don't know, Hoag. I was thinking about heading back out to L.A. It's where my friends are."

"You have friends here."

He ran a big hand over the lower half of his face. "To tell you the God's honest truth, I hate L.A. Always have."

I patted his meaty shoulder. "Good deal. I'll tell her you're interested."

"Thanks, Hoag. And you don't have to worry. I wouldn't make a pass at her or anything."

"I know you wouldn't."

"When are you two gonna get back together again, anyhow?"

"Hey, mind your own business."

He chuckled. It wasn't a pretty sound, but it beat silence.

It took me twenty minutes to find Lulu. She was upstairs cowering under the bed in the master bedroom. Gunfire is not one of her favorite things. Skitsy's red lipstick came sliding back out from under there with her. I picked it up and looked at it.

This time it was my turn to throw it against the wall.

I spent most of my time after that in my mukluks. The writing went smoothly now. I had the whole story. And another bestseller. Surefire.

In my free time I thought a lot about Ferris Rush, and how he'd scammed me and how I just couldn't seem to make myself hate him for it—no matter how hard I tried. I thought about Todd Lesser, whose hunger for respect twisted and ultimately devoured him. I thought about Charlie Chu, who was done in by both men through no fault of her own, and about what might have been. I thought about all three of them, and Skitsy Held, too, and felt no anger. Just sadness.

I don't ever want a kid brother again.

Boyd Samuels phoned me one evening while I was working, sounding immensely pleased with himself. "I did a beautiful thing today, amigo."

"Quit the business?"

He laughed. "Sold Toddy's book, *Boy Wonder.* It's brilliant, and it's going to be a major success. Maybe even bigger than *Bang.*"

"Too bad he won't be around to enjoy it."

"I'm not keeping my commission though. Tanner's helping me set up a scholarship fund at Columbia with it in Toddy's name."

"You're all heart."

"Can't just keep taking, you know? Sometimes you have to give a little something back. That's what's wrong with this world—not enough people do." He shifted gears —into grave. "Hear about Delilah?"

"What about her?"

"Bitch tried to kill herself. Slit her wrists just before she was gonna appear on a local talk show in Seattle. They had to rush her to the hospital. They said she'll be okay. Why would she do something crazy like that?"

"She loved him. Or the man she thought was him. Sorry to hear about it."

"Not as sorry as I am, amigo. It means her tour is off, and so are her sales. Fuck it, that's the business for you— win one, lose one. So listen, what are your plans after you finish up?"

"Why?"

"Got an anorexic prima ballerina I'm dying to put you together with. Seven-figure advance."

"I don't think so."

"How about the college basketball coach of the year?

It'll sell two hundred thousand copies hardcover in the Southern states alone.''

"Not interested.''

"Okay, I hear you. We'll talk again after you've had a chance to chill out. I want us to cook up some more scams together. You're family now, understand?''

"You could do me one favor, amigo,'' I said. "It's not a big one.''

"Anything. Name it.''

"Disown me.''

After I hung up, I called the hospital out in Seattle. Miss Moscowitz wasn't taking any calls. I left my name and number. I never heard from her.

Merilee wore a bare-shouldered black silk chiffon dress to the Tony Awards with her pearls and a heavy white silk shawl that had belonged to her great-grandmother. Her face was made up and her golden hair was up in a bun. She looked utterly gorgeous as I let her into the limo that was to whisk us off to the Minskoff Theatre for the show— gorgeous and nervous. She was nibbling on her lower lip, and she started wringing her hands the second she settled into the backseat, Lulu whooping and snuffling hello.

As our driver pulled away from the curb, I noticed Merilee staring at me with her big green eyes.

"Something wrong?'' I asked.

"Nothing, darling,'' she said, reddening. "I just never get tired of looking at you in a tux.''

"I never get tired of looking at you, period.''

"Bless you, darling,'' she said, wringing her hands some more. "Oh, God,'' she groaned. "Why are we doing this? I hate these things.''

"Nonsense. It'll be fun.''

"That, mister, is easy for you to say.''

I stirred the iced pitcher of martinis I'd brought, filled two glasses, and held one out to her.

She shook her head. "I'd better not—I'll forget my acceptance speech." Then she lunged for the glass. "Oh, what the hay, I'm not going to win anyway."

"That's the spirit." I held up my glass. "To the woman of everyone's dreams, particularly my own."

Her eyes got all soft for a second. She took my hand and squeezed it. Then we drank, and she stole my olive. She's always claimed mine tastes better than hers. I wouldn't know. She's never let me near hers.

"Ask me what I did today," I commanded.

"Okay—what did you do today?"

"Resigned from the Racquet Club."

"Really?" She tilted her head at me. "How come?"

"Dinosaurs belong there. I don't."

"Good for you, darling," she said approvingly. "That place always struck me as some kind of eerie throwback to the days of Chester Arthur and cigars and port. I've always hated it."

"I never knew that."

"Sometimes it's best to keep one's opinions to oneself." She sipped her martini. "And now what? Is there another novel?"

"I think so."

"Good," she said, pleased.

"Yes, there's nothing quite like a good strong dose of reality to send you running, screaming, back to the comforting world of fiction." I refilled our glasses. "Vic will be ready to take over for you out there tomorrow, if you like."

"I like. He seems so sweet and loyal, almost like a big St. Bernard."

"Just don't let anyone ever get him mad."

"Why, what happens?"

"You don't want to know."

Limos were backed up all the way down the block from the theater. We had to wait our turn for our grand arrival, which was fine by me. Gave us enough time to finish our pitcher of martinis. When we finally did inch up to the front of the theater, blinding TV lights and plenty of commotion were waiting there for us. Cameras were rolling. Flashbulbs were popping. Hundreds of onlookers were shouting and crowding the police barricades.

Our chauffeur hopped out and opened the door. Merilee groaned and squeezed my hand again. Then she took a deep breath, gathered her shawl and her star presence around her, and stepped out onto the curb, smiling radiantly at the crowd, which gasped and applauded at the sight of her. I took her arm and we strode inside, blinking from the lights, Lulu waddling along behind us.

The theater had been converted into a television studio for the night. A giant teleprompter was set up in front of the stage. Cameras and monitors were everywhere. Most of the seats down front were already filled with nominees and producers and angels. We said hello to Meryl Streep and Don Gummer as we passed by them. David Mamet and Lindsay Crouse. Joe Papp.

We were just about to take our seats when Merilee suddenly stopped and grabbed me by the shoulders. "Say yes, Hoagy."

"Say yes to what?"

"Just say it," she commanded urgently.

I shrugged. "Okay . . . yes."

"Good."

With that she took my hand, turned, and dragged me back up the crowded aisle, politely elbowing people aside to make way for us.

"Merilee, where are we going?" I called after her.

We were going out the front doors to the street again, and back to our limo, which was double-parked halfway down the block.

"Merilee, where are we—?"

"To JFK, please," she told our driver as she jumped in, heaving a huge sigh of relief.

Lulu and I got in after her.

"What did I just say yes to?" I asked her, mystified, as we pulled away from the theater.

She threw her arms around me and kissed me. It was some kiss. We were halfway to Queens before she pulled away, gasping, reached inside her evening bag and produced our passports. "The question, mister, was will you run away to Paris with me."

"Is that what we're doing?"

"Uh-huh. No luggage. No reservations. No mackerel. No nothing. We're just hopping on the Concorde and going. What's to stop us?"

"Only sanity, and we've never let that stand in our way before. But what about the Tonys?"

"*Fuck* the Tonys."

"Merilee Gilbert Nash!"

"I've asked you never to use my middle—"

"I'm going to tell your mother you invoked the F-word!"

"She'd never believe you," she huffed.

"You're right, she wouldn't." I stroked her face, got lost in her green eyes for a moment. "Maybe we'll be able to find that same little hotel in the seventeenth arrondissement, the one with the bed that sloped in toward the middle."

"Where, I seem to recall, we spent most of our time," she added, giving me her up-from-under look.

"Merilee, you really are getting awfully frisky."

"You mind, darling?"

"Nope. I just hope I can keep up with you, so to speak."

"I'll make sure you do," she whispered, her lips brushing mine.

"And what happens afterward?"

"Usually you fall asleep with your mouth open."

"I meant—"

"We're not going to think about afterward," she declared. "Afterward is the sort of thing that middle-aged people worry about, not people like us. Now shut up and kiss me."

I took her in my arms and did just that.

Lulu wriggled around between us, tail thumping. She'd always wanted to go to France. The tricky part would be finding a beret that fit her.